PENGUIN BOOKS

SLOUCHING TOWARDS KALAMAZOO

Peter De Vries was born in Chicago of Dutch immigrant parents and was educated in Dutch Reformed Calvinist schools. He was graduated from Calvin College in 1931 and for a short time held the post of editor of a community newspaper in Chicago. He then supported himself with a number of different jobs, including those of vending-machine operator, toffee-apple salesman, radio actor, furniture mover, lecturer to women's clubs, and associate editor of *Poetry*. In 1943 he managed to lure James Thurber to Chicago to give a benefit lecture for *Poetry*, and Thurber suggested that De Vries write for *The New Yorker*. He did. Before long he was given a part-time editorial position on that magazine, dropped his other activities, and moved to New York City. He has remained on the editorial staff of *The New Yorker* ever since. In 1982 he was elected to the American Academy and Institute of Arts and Letters. Peter De Vries is the author of more than twenty novels. Penguin Books also publishes his *Sauce for the Goose*; *Blood of the Lamb*; *Consenting Adults, or The Duchess Will Be Furious*; *Forever Panting*; *Madder Music*; and *The Tunnel of Love*. Mr. De Vries lives in Westport, Connecticut, with his wife, Katinka Loeser.

Books by Peter De Vries

Slouching Towards Kalamazoo

by

Peter De Vries

PENGUIN BOOKS

Penguin Books Ltd, Harmondsworth,
Middlesex, England
Penguin Books, 40 West 23rd Street,
New York, New York 10010, U.S.A.
Penguin Books Australia Ltd, Ringwood,
Victoria, Australia
Penguin Books Canada Limited, 2801 John Street,
Markham, Ontario, Canada L3R 1B4
Penguin Books (N.Z.) Ltd, 182–190 Wairau Road,
Auckland 10, New Zealand

First published in the United States of America by
Little, Brown and Company, Inc., 1983
First published in Canada by
Little, Brown and Company (Canada) Limited 1983
Published in Penguin Books by arrangement with
Little, Brown and Company, Inc., 1984

LIBRARY OF CONGRESS CATALOGING IN PUBLICATION DATA
De Vries, Peter.
  Slouching towards Kalamazoo.
  I. Title.
PS3507.E8673S6 1984   813'.52   83-25764
ISBN 0 14 00.7070 2

Printed in the United States of America by
R. R. Donnelley & Sons Company, Harrisonburg, Virginia
Set in Electra

Lines from "The Second Coming" from *Collected Poems* by William
Butler Yeats, copyright 1924 by Macmillan Publishing Co., Inc., copyright renewed 1952 by Bertha Georgie Yeats. Reprinted with the permission of Macmillan Publishing Co., Inc.; Macmillan London, Limited; and
Michael and Anne Yeats.

1

The Scarlet Letter

1

My old eighth-grade teacher, Miss Maggie Doubloon, said she was half Spanish, half French, and half Irish, a plethora of halves not entirely unnoticed by some of the brighter pupils. Joke though it was, it well expressed her superabundance of spirits, the verve and fire — sheer spitfire, fire-in-the-belly fire — that made her in the end decide that that golden oldie, *The Scarlet Letter*, had long been due for an overhaul; must, in fact, be dragged forcibly out of the gray, chill, toxic riverbottom fog of Puritan morality and up into the sunlight of sexually liberated twentieth-century America. To be sure, such stormy petrel stuff was only an intensification of the author's own implied disapproval of the colonial austerity he was depicting, but Hawthorne's "liberalization" left ninety-five percent of the way still to go. A man for whom the Boston Unitarianism of *his* day was a little far out isn't going to waltz you into the twentieth century. The modernization Miss Doubloon effected wasn't something she wrote — she *lived* it. That naturally involved committing Hester Prynne's sin, in a North Dakota city of which the mayor, a precursor of today's Moral Majority, said on hearing she had assigned *The Scarlet Letter* to us eighth-graders, "We're gonna tighten our Bible Belt! We're gonna show 'em we're the buckle of that belt!" Perhaps you share my secret taste for old-fashioned windbags. In any case I got the message. I must absent me from felicity awhile, and in this harsh world draw my breath in pain, to tell Maggie Doubloon's story. So here goes.

In the beginning was the word. Once terms like identity doubts and midlife crisis become current, the reported cases of them increase by leaps and bounds, affecting people unaware there is anything wrong with them until they have got a load of the coinages. You too may have an acquaintance or even relative with a block about paperhanging or dog grooming, a highflown form of stagnation trickled down from writers and artists. Once my poor dear mother confided to me in a hollow whisper, "I have an identity crisis." I says, "How do you mean?" and she says, "I no longer understand your father." Now we have burnout, and having heard tell of it on television or read about it in a magazine, your plumber doubts he can any longer hack it as a pipefitter, while a glossary adopted by his wife has turned him overnight into a sexist, to say nothing of a male chauvinist pig, something she would never have suspected before she encountered the terminology. The word was made flesh.

Rapid-fire means of communication have brought psychic dilapidation within the reach of the most provincial backwaters, so that large metropolitan centers and educated circles need no longer consider it their exclusive property, nor preen themselves on their special malaises. The assumption that nobody twitches in Cedar

Rapids may not bear close scrutiny, nor that Oklahoma dogcatchers are free of existential dread. Far from it. A close neighbor of ours in my North Dakota home town, which I will call Ulalume, considered a good night's sleep one from which he did not awaken with his feet on the pillow, and our mayor, not the nonesuch I've quoted about tightening the Bible Belt, but his predecessor, thought an administration well begun one in which he rose to deliver his inaugural address free of the delusion that he was wearing a tam-o'-shanter. My poor dear mother later went through a midlife crisis she might successfully have skirted had she not got wind of the expression, and, in consequence, the fashion. And by that time we in Ulalume, in the boonies there, had, of course, our share of star underachievers.

I was one. I had come by the distinction early, three or four classes before our eighth-grade Miss Doubloon decided to single me out for special attention. Previous teachers had liked me, but she was the only one ever to give me an apple, to my recollection. Rather than eat it for my lunch, I took it home and cut it into slices which I slathered with peanut butter, a favorite delicacy, munching the combination while immersed in erotic fantasies featuring Miss Doubloon naked as a jaybird, or as a figure in a Cranach print I had slipped into my civics book.

Notice of a strongly sensual nature is, I think, early given. Signs of a Dionysian temperament emerged in my case as far back as high-chair days, when I took pleasure in squishing a peeled banana in my fist and watching the pulp extruded through the crevices between my fingers, which might then be licked off my hand or flung at one or another of the cautionary mottoes hung about the

5

walls of our house. Most of these posed religious sent-
ments, having been passed down from my clergyman
grandfather to my father, also a minister of the Protestant
faith. There was a kitchen calendar with a leaflet for each
day, an inspirational homily to be digested a moment
after being torn off and before being thrown away. It
became a favorite target of the fruit pulp, breakfast
porridge, and mashed potatoes pitched at the walls from
my throne, in bare handfuls at first, and later, when
manual and motor skills began to develop, catapulted
from a spoon or fork. There was an embossed representa-
tion of Jesus gaudily colored and sprackled with gilt,
shown descending on clouds of glory to earth, where he
would "judge the quick and the dead." With the onset
of speech comprehension, I took this to mean that nobody was fast enough to give Him the slip; that evildoers
expecting to show Him a clean pair of heels instead of a
pure heart would be hopelessly outclassed, inevitably
collared, and given what-for. Later when my father read
The Hound of Heaven aloud to us, with pitiless expression, the Thompsonian image of a sprinting savior was
but the natural alteration, realized with nice fluidity, of
my own conception of Christ as a fleet-footed human
gazelle, padding easily along in the wake of puffing
shortcomers and transgressors. Only the fugitive was now
on the lam from mercy and forgiveness, rather than
retribution, as the motivation imperceptibly shifted gears
between the flying principals.

It was snowing in Ulalume as I gazed out the window
from my eighth-grade seat, waiting that Friday afternoon
after school, with Miss Doubloon, for my parents to
arrive for a scheduled conference vis-à-vis my under-

6

attainments. The school was on the south end of town, near a lake which I will string along with myself by calling the dank tarn of Auber. Assorted abominations from a paint factory had brought us well abreast of the national pollution level, and perhaps a nose ahead.

"You might be studying the chief products of Venezuela in your geography book," Miss Doubloon called over from her desk, where she was scribbling comments on English themes turned in that day. Her handwriting was like driven sleet, blown in steely diagonals off the edge of the page. The note to my parents suggesting this conference, which I had trudged home with a few days before, had advanced such familiarity with her penmanship as I had gained from remarks scrawled on the margins of my own papers. A curious thing, she had two handwritings — and two signatures — markedly dissimilar. There was one in which the characters were unconnected, and one "cursive" script in which they flowed together, though both were composed of straight and angular lines scarcely relieved by a curve. I supposed the difference was "significant," though God knew of what. Split personality? It was too early to tell. A script pitched so sharply to the right as hers, at an angle as horizontal as it is vertical, is considered by handwriting analysts to be a sign of extroversion. But hold it. Miss Doubloon is left-handed.

"Your parents were very nice about this. Some are quite angry when you criticize their jewels about anything. If they're falling behind in anything, it must be the teacher's fault blah blah blah. He's not being motivated to blah blah blah. I suggested a conference like this to some other parents last week and all hell broke loose."

"That's from *Paradise Lost*."

"What?"

I called more loudly from my seat near the back of the room, "That expression, 'all hell broke loose,' it's from *Paradise Lost*. Few people know that."

"So that's how you've been neglecting your homework," Miss Doubloon said with a smile — a smile like three dollars' worth of popcorn. "Reading John Milton."

"My father reads things to us. He's a great one for that family tradition, reading aloud. He takes all the parts and makes the welkin ring."

"The what?"

"Welkin. The vault of heaven."

"He chews gum while he says 'welkin.' I suppose since it's 'after school' I can't ask you to dispose of it," she said, again with the explosive smile, the lips bursting like a crimson pod discharging its white seeds. "A jurisdictional technicality. But it's curious why some people are always chewing gum. You know it's been called oral masturbation. I think we're both mature enough to talk this way. You know I'm not a Victorian schoolmarm, and my, oh, 'psychological' analyses aren't necessarily digs."

"As Spinoza said, 'Neither to weep nor to laugh, but to understand.' "

"What *are* we to do with you?"

There was a silence broken only by the faint scratch of her pencil on the theme papers. Then she observed:

"Your father's a very imposing man. He has the look of an actor. With that chiselled profile and that wavy iron-gray hair. In a sense he is an actor. I go to hear him preach now and again, though I'm not formally religious."

"Neither am I."

"*What?*"

"He's a great mimic. He does a marvelous God. And

8

his Satan! Why don't you come some Christmas Eve and share the *Christmas Carol* with us," I said, true to my habit of slipping in a little lubricant whenever I could. Any device to help me through a graduation thrown in doubt by my lack of classroom performance. I had been kept back a year in the seventh grade thanks to time spent reading Joyce and Proust that should have gone into homework, and so here I was in the eighth still, at age fifteen.

We lapsed into the silence that had preceded this exchange, one now broken by the faint slobbering of radiators that set up a train of associations further darkening my line of thought. If I didn't get into high school soon, when, if ever, would I get into college? Lights blooming at dusk along the Quad. Girls with convertibles. The glee club singing "Brown October Ale." Swallowed oysters retracted on the end of a string by potential fraternity brothers. Limburger set by wits on dormitory radiators. None of this would be mine if I didn't haul up my socks and get with it.

Miss Doubloon rose and walked to the window, where she stood nursing her elbows as she gazed outward into the lightly falling snow. She seemed to give a faint shudder before coming out with one of those suddenly assertive, even savage, remarks of which she was capable. They were often out of left field, but this one was sequential, albeit after a gap allowing for private rumination of an apparently acrimonious nature.

"Christmas today. The very thought of it makes me want to lie down on the ground and howl like a dog."

"Me too," I responded. This was wholly untrue; you can't make Christmas too commercial for a growing boy, if that was the objection correctly divined. But I must curry favor with a vengeance these days, and besides, I figured it probably the part of sophistication to be either blasé or negative about the holidays. I sucked my teeth as though this were Larchmont and crossed my legs insouciantly into the aisle. "Will you go home or spend it in Ulalume?"

She turned her head. "Where?"

I laughed apologetically at the slip, riffling the pages of my geography, which I had opened without exactly poring over it. "It's what I call this burg. Think of it as. This section right here is the misty mid-region of Weir."

Miss Doubloon snorted concurrence while I appreciated her flanks, which remained in profile during this crucial exchange. "I couldn't agree with you more. Here come your parents now. Yes, cuts a fine figure of the, well, classic kind, your father. And they say a small woman can be pretty but not beautiful, but your mother belies that. In that Chesterfield and Homburg your father should be one of the ten best-dressed men."

"He was even spiffier when he was young. I'll show you some snapshots if you'd like."

"That won't be necessary."

"Did you know that Mahatma Gandhi was a fop in his youth?" I called over.

Miss Doubloon here turned her head again, less in the spirit of inquiry than with a frown of impatience at all this ill-timed and burdensome erudition. She also seemed to emit a sigh, but with the sibilance of the radiators overlaying it, it was hard to tell.

"Where do you get all this information when you should be studying the chief products of Venezuela?"

"Around. I keep my ear to the ground. Few people

know that — about Gandhi, I mean. The figure we know and revere as a holy man in a loincloth once went around London in a frock coat and top hat, twiddling a walking stick, the works. Can you imagine? Nevertheless, I kid you not."

"A headful of amassed facts — probably picked up from *Reader's Digest* fillers in your dentist's office — does not an education make. Information is not knowledge, nor is knowledge wisdom, me bucko. You can keep your nose buried in the encyclopedia and still not be able to sniff the east wind."

"Yes'm."

Perhaps sensing that she had been overly harsh with a scholar doing his best to impress teacher, or just to keep the conversational ball rolling, Miss Doubloon came over and, pausing beside me in the aisle, ran her fingertips along the back of my neck. She tickled the skin under the pointed tip of a curl at its base. "You need a haircut — my beamish boy."

I raised my head, smiling upward at her. "You hate your — hate it here, don't you?"

"In Ulalume? I didn't say that."

"You've inferred it."

"Implied it," she said, glad to recover the offensive. "I imply something, you infer it. Just as you flaunt your wealth, but flout convention. Two sets of words people constantly confuse. Not that I did — imply any such thing." She poked a stiff finger at the geography. "What have you learned about South America?"

"That they have a lot of horses there, and probably eat them, as they do in this country too, if the truth were known. Even the statistics we have show that five percent of all Americans partake of horse hamburger. Not in the Southwest, of course, where they ride them. One ought not, you know, eat a means of transportation."

"He chews gum while he makes aphorisms." Despair was her portion.

She wandered over to a window closer by and stood gazing out of that. She heaved her shoulders upward and dropped them in a long sigh.

"This steeping yourself in complicated other interests while neglecting your homework, doesn't that give you anxieties about your future? You're a contradictory creature, Anthony Thrasher. Doesn't that ever give you pause?"

"*Au contraire.* I find it exciting to discover and explore divergent and even warring elements within myself, and exhilarating to pursue the adventure of synthesizing them into a coherent and viable whole, what I believe Eliot has called a balance of contrarieties."

"Jesus Christ," I thought she said under her breath, but couldn't be sure. She sighed again and, looking over her shoulder, indicated the book before me with a jerk of her head. "The chief products of Venezuela, *s'il vous plaît.*"

I bent resolutely over the text. "Venezuela has valuable deposits of petroleum, gold, iron ore, manganese, copper, coal, asphalt, diamonds, and salt," I read. "More than six hundred kinds of trees cover a rugged countryside, yielding rare woods, wild rubber, chicle for chewing gum, and balata, a gum used for wire insulation . . ."

"Your absentee record is no doubt a contributing factor," said the Doubloon from the desk to which she had returned, and where she consulted an attendance record. "Your mother thinks you catch those colds because of your insistence on taking your shower in the morning instead of at night, and then running off to school with your pores open. You ought to take your nice hot bath at night, Anthony. Why don't you?"

"I like to fare forth fresh, if only for the alliteration."

"Here are your parents, thank God," she said, at the sound of footsteps drumming on the wooden inside stairs. "*Jesus*."

There was my dear small mother in the doorway shaking out her rabbit fur, and my father brushing from the velvet collar of his Chesterfield equal parts snow and dandruff. They squeezed into the two seats directly in front of the teacher's desk, I moving down to join them there at a wave from Miss Doubloon, who plunged in straightaway.

"The potential is there, and he can write. Some of his exercises in earlier grades are still remembered. His third-grade essay, 'Why I Would Hate To Be a Basement,' survives as a classic of Cooper Elementary. Part of our lore."

"Town lore, in fact," my father said, twitching, or pursing, his lips forward in a kind of unsmiling smile that two billion years' ascent from the intertidal slime has given a place in the incredibly delicate repertory of human nuance. She was reading the still-preserved theme.

" 'They would put coal in me and old corsets and broken rocking chairs that somebody will throw out anyway when somebody else dies. And crocks of sauerkraut that might ferment like the Germans next door. Yech!' " My father twitchy-smiled again, as though he might be going to lean forward in an excess of emotion and pucker up for Miss Doubloon right then and there, while at the same time nodding and closing his eyes at the memory. The smile she herself directed at my father was for all its amiability like a dart aimed at a pub target. "Did you help him with it?"

"This one?" He wagged a thumb in my direction. "Huh!" As though by denying collaboration he might glory the more in the end-product, the work of someone who had sprung from his loins. Miss Doubloon quoted some more of the theme.

" 'And once a year the drains would gurgle back from the spring thaws, leaving a thin film of muck all over me more disgusting than the sauerkraut fermenting in the crocks of the Bronckhorsts. Yech!' " Miss Doubloon looked up. " 'Yech!' has found its way into common currency now, but then I rather think it was trailblazing."

"In the throes of coinage," my father agreed.

They all turned to regard me, my mother smiling sweetly in her way, my father shifting the Homburg, which was propped on one knee, his legs crossed into the aisle. Miss Doubloon popped erect, folding her hands on her desk.

"Well. *C'est une question* of getting him to stick to his assigned work. That's the problem. He would rather read novels in which the characters toy with a little Brie while waiting for their friends to turn up along the boulevard. If we can't get Anthony to concentrate, and hard, on the War of 1812 and obtuse triangles —"

"Like the dumb postmaster and his wife and that boarder they say is fooling around with her," I shot in. "Speaking of obtuse triangles?" Miss Doubloon stiffened even further in her chair and said, "We'll just ignore that," while my dear mother looked blankly about, not understanding what we were ignoring, and my father, who did, reached across the aisle and slapped me amiably across the arm with the back of his hand. "Enough," he said. "Do go on, Miss Doubloon."

"Well, he's just proved an additional point I was about to make. Playing the clown in class. Injecting some humor into the discussion he calls this disrupting influence. I'm here to give all the help I can to such as need it, I'll stay after school any day to give it, but there's a limit to what good even that will do. The fact is I think Anthony could do with some special tutoring. A good tutor is hard to come by in a town like Ul—, like this, and my time is limited . . ."

"We'd pay you well," my father said. "Truly. If you could see your way to a few hours in the evenings, or weekends, we'd be deeply grateful. We help him at home, naturally, which consists often as not of digging the spurs into him. He needs another stimulus. You need only name your figure, which would be an hourly rate of course."

"I might swing a few evenings in the next week or two — if the threatened heavy weather doesn't descend on us. Our Canadian neighbors are expected to send down some arctic temperatures and a few blizzards, pretty bad even for North Dakota. I was caught in one once, and all I could think of was an uncle who actually froze to death in Montana. Fact. I'd prefer to talk about fees after we've tried this thing out. Proof of the pudding sort of thing. Friday evening is good for me, again old man winter permitting."

"Done and done," my father said, slapping his desk in a gesture of enthusiasm. "We really appreciate this, Miss Doubloon. And you're right about the heavy weather predicted. The Indians in town all say it's going to be a cold winter, and when asked how they know, they say, 'See white man chop wood.' Mmmmheh-heh."

"Well, we'll see what we'll see. About eight o'clock would be fine for me. I think you know I room at Mrs. Clicko's, on Tuttle Street. Now does anyone have any questions? Yes, Mrs. Thrasher?"

"Might we have 'Why I Would Hate To Be a Basement'? As a family keepsake?"

"Of course. This is a copy that's been banging around here all these years. I can't imagine what's happened to the original manuscript, if you don't have it. Pity it's disappeared. Here you are. Are there any more questions?" I raised my hand. "Yes, Anthony?"

"Don't you think the important thing when you're freezing to death is to keep your cool?"

2

*I*NSTRUCTION began on the very stairway up which Miss Doubloon led the way to her room in Mrs. Clicko's boardinghouse, a twisting, heavily carpeted flight of steps at the foot of which Mrs. Clicko herself disapprovingly stood, a hand resting on the dome of a newel post, like Aristotle's on the bust of Homer in the Rembrandt painting. "No gentleman visitors in the rooms," she reminded Miss Doubloon, who called back, "He's no gentleman." Then over her shoulder down to me, traipsing cap in hand in her wake, "You'll note I didn't bother to add 'He's just a boy.' That's ellipsis. You remember we were discussing the word in class the other day, in relation to both geometry and grammar — literary style. The omission of an element the implication of which is, however, necessary to the complete understanding of a sentence or a thought. What I said was elliptical, and the joke."

"Aha."

Some appreciation of Der Doubloon's calves and undercarriage, as we mounted steadily to her second-floor room, might have justified another construction of her rejoinder to Mrs. Clicko. No matter. No raving beauty, she did have luminous gray-green eyes and that full, sensuous mouth, with the smile already noted. Setting all this off was a cloud of hair neither red nor quite anything else — auburn, say — which she combed into a pompadour reminiscent of the Gibson girl. Asked why at twenty-nine she was still unmarried, she had replied, "Oh, I don't know. There always seemed more pressing things to do." A reasonable reply by any standard.

The constabulary note sounded by Mrs. Clicko was needless in the case of her two other lodgers. Mr. Haley was a retired postman who had never married, and Mrs. Dyer, widowed like Mrs. Clicko, taught knitting at the local department store. She was so tiny that on all fours she would have made a nice trivet. Since the one was at choir practice and the other in the parlor knitting while she chewed the rag with Mrs. Clicko, there was nobody upstairs but us chickens. A backup rule of Mrs. Clicko's, in case the one against gentleman callers was honored in the breach, was that the lady's door remain open when she was entertaining one, but Miss Doubloon closed hers behind us with a sense of gently steely independence. "You can't have enough privacy," she said.

The room smelled so strongly of incense that a clump of ashes in a cloisonné dish identified themselves on reflex as those of a joss stick burned earlier in the evening. There was a batik spread thrown across the bed. "I had a friend who was into things Eastern," she said, hanging my coat in the closet. "He's in Nepal now," she added, as though to allay fears that he too might slip past Mrs. Clicko and wander in, swathed in a turban and mumbling a mantra. She was trying to liquidate reminders of him by using them up as fast as possible, simply throwing them out being too callous for her. A window had been raised to clear the air, and after closing it against the November chill she struck a pose behind the lace curtain that had billowed momentarily into the room, drawing an end of it humorously against her face. "Do I look the Oriental type? Would you like a veil dance?" She writhed a little parody at which I dutifully laughed, as one does at the boss's jokes, wondering as I did so whether she had been at the sherry bottle standing on top of a bookcase. As she emerged from behind the curtain, brushing to rights a tuft of hair disheveled by the caper, she said, "Why, Mrs. Clicko and Madame Defarge down there, they both have strong Puritanical upbringings, and so they sit there chatting away but secretly listening for the creak of bedsprings. I'm going to oblige them." And she plumped herself on the bed with a bounce that must have served the purpose. "You don't mind if I park my weary carcass here while we work, do you? Sit you down. That's the most comfortable chair." She hiked herself over on the side, twitching her skirt to rights, and lay facing me with her head propped on a hand. "What was grammatically wrong with what I just said?"

I looked around, puzzled for a moment, then understood. "There are only two chairs, so it should be 'more comfortable,' being the comparative case."

"Well, not case — degree. But you're right. And did you get the allusion to Madame Defarge?"

"*Tale of Two Cities*. The woman knitting by the guillotine."

"Then how come you flunked the test on that book? I could give you a C minus in English, disgraceful enough for a boy of your intelligence, but I gave you an F just to stick a pin in you. You goldbricker. Well, you're fair in English, it's your history and biology that need work, so let's concentrate on them. Throw me my biology textbook, would you, it's right there on the table. God, what a busman's holiday you're giving me, Master Anthony William Thrasher, generally called Tony, and sometimes known as Biff."

Given the book, she settled herself upright against the headboard, on two pillows pulled from under the batik spread, and opened it to a chapter that seemed most in need of review, "Cell Structure."

I listened in my armchair as she read semifamiliar material, pausing after each paragraph and asking me to repeat what I'd heard, finally quizzing me on the entire chapter. Here my ankles began to itch, as they often had of late, and she noticed me furtively scratching them, drawing up a leg at a time, then, as they worsened, bending to do them both simultaneously. At last she spread-eagled the book on her lap and said, "What in God's name is the matter, Anthony?"

I explained that I suffered from a pruritus seemingly inherited from my mother, or possibly a psychosomatic tendency to it, using as many big words as I could to impress her. "Mom's going to take me to her dermatologist, Doctor Mallard, though she's been going to him for years and he hasn't been able to do anything for her. My father calls him the Curator of the Integument."

"The idea that dermatologists' patients never die and never get better. That's rather clever. I like that. The Curator of the Integument. I must remember that when I see old Doc Oakley back home in Kalamazoo. Your father's a bright man. But my God, look at you." She swung around on the bed, having caught a glimpse of the red streaks on my legs above my lowered socks. "Like a cat at a scratching post. You could get an infection."

"When you start clawing you can't stop. The scratching makes worse what you've got to scratch all the harder to relieve. A vicious circle that has to run its course. I often wake up scratching. I suppose it has something to do with my poor scholastic performance," I said pitiably.

Kneeling, she drew the legs of my pants up and pushed my socks down still farther, for a closer look. "They *are* infected, this leg anyway. Those little blisters you've broken open with your nails. Here, let me get an antibiotic salve I have around here somewhere. These things can get chronic, and then there's hell to pay."

"I suppose I'm worried about my schoolwork, and not graduating," I pressed on as she rummaged in a dresser drawer.

"Or itching to get out of Ulalume. Like some others I know. Now you've got me doing it."

"Itching?"

"No, calling it Ulalume."

"We're a pair."

This time she hauled my pants legs clear up above my knees when again she knelt to spread the cream on my skin. She squeezed it onto her fingertips and tenderly ran them along the oozing welts. "Let's take your shoes and socks off," she said at length, and we did. There were streaks on my insteps too, from previous bouts. She medicated these as well, continuing her ministrations with gentle, then caressive strokes which were no longer soothing, but exciting, as her hand travelled upward on my legs again. The scent of her perfume reached me, and under the hanging neck of her blouse I caught a glimpse

21

of her breasts, the white upper cusps bulging above the pressure of her brassière. Waves of the most delicious sensation lapped me from head to foot, and my throat tightened, causing me to gargle the words as, feeling somebody ought to say something, I remarked, "You're, gugh, nice. For someone so sarcastic. Well, not sarcastic . . ."

"That's all right."

"You're also, gugh, sensual."

"Oh, I hope not. You mean sensuous. *You're* sensual. It's a common mistake."

"What book are you going to assign next?" I asked, trusting some shoptalk might stem a sexual arousal of which Miss Doubloon could take full note if she so much as glanced upward.

"*The Scarlet Letter*, I think. Probably get some flak from the moral element who'll tell you that might keep till high school — but they complain about it there too. Half their daughters have probably had sex. Isn't that true?" she asked, and I fancied her eyes did now pause halfway in their upward glance, taking in my obvious condition.

"Oh sure. Everybody objects to it more for the girls than the boys, even though it takes two to tango. I suppose that's the double standard."

"Never to be eradicated, because it's instinctive with the race, however unfair we might intellectually think it. The woman is regarded as the treasure, the object of desire," she continued, after pausing long enough to squeeze some more antibiotic cream from the tube, and then to switch legs, "and therefore rates the term 'fallen,' which you would never apply to a man. Of course at my age it makes no difference any more." She laughed and changed the subject. "You're a very complicated boy, but not, I think, tied up in knots in the way that calls for a psychiatrist, so don't go running off to jabber about your earliest recollection and all that. It's considered significant because memory isn't just memory but a selective principle, offering a key to the personality. What is your earliest recollection?"

"I forget."

"Don't want to lower your guard, eh? I shouldn't have put you on the qui vive."

As she gently massaged my shin, propping my foot up by cupping the heel in her palm, I mentally revolved some infantile remembrances, wondering whether one could be singled out as a true first and thus pivotally self-betraying — and looking for any diversion in a scene that was getting a little steamy, if my secret sensations were any gauge.

Among the wall mottoes at which I had flung my oatmeal and banana pulp in high-chair days had been a large red-and-white one reading: "We're all like the cleaning woman. We come to dust." I had pitched foodstuffs at it quite in ignorance of its meaning, of course, being unable to read to begin with, but perhaps inadvertently giving the mot the treatment it deserved. Still to be evoked on demand was the tactile pleasure of squishing gruel and fruit and vegetable mushes like Gerber's in my fist, prior to the possibly even more depraved rapture of flinging them about, a sensation vividly echoed now in this wish to reach down and knead Miss Doubloon's creamy white breasts in much the same manner, along with whatever parts of her might prove obtainable. Then my thoughts swerved in another direction altogether, as though banishing the old Adam, about which — or whom — my father had preached the Sunday before, for the new. I thought of the corny wall aphorism quite sentimentally on Miss Doubloon's own behalf, with one of those piercing stabs of compassion children sometimes experience toward grown-ups. Here she was taking the steep and dreaded turn to thirty, and I seemed to sense in her a burning wish to Live, certainly to enjoy a life far richer than she was now, a self-realization for which getting the hell out of Ulalume would be only the beginning. I hoped she had it to the hilt, before she came to dust. I tried in this way to spiritualize my thoughts, imagining when Miss Doubloon set my foot down to raise a hand to her cheek that she was brushing a tear away, when she was clearly only smoothing up an errant strand of hair out of her eye. Then my hand of its own volition reached down and stroked it into place, my fingers remaining there, bathing in the auburn wealth, disheveling what I had meant to help tidy. She looked up and smiled, lifting an arm to press my hand in her own, and suddenly climbed to her feet, holding the soiled hand away. "In her lectures to the high-school girls, Miss Walcombe tells them that when they go out on dates they shouldn't start what they know they mustn't finish. I'm sorry you got into this state — beamish boy."

"This has been really nice of you. I appreciate it. You're a very . . ."

She pulled several sheets of Kleenex from a bedside box to wipe her palm with, but the tissues weren't heavy-duty enough, so she went across the hall to the bathroom, making a father and mother of a racket with banging doors and running water and what not, evidently having decided to reassure the bluenose listeners below rather than tease them. She came back drying her hands with a towel, which she laughingly threw at me as she again closed the door behind her. There was some sport about the way I looked, barefoot and with my pants rolled up, like someone about to go in wading. I flicked the towel playfully at her, and she caught the end and tried to jerk it away, and with both of us holding tight as we tugged as hard as we could, we collided in the middle of the room, dropping the towel. The embrace was antic enough at first, but even before the roughhousing itself had died away we were two different people, and presently, arms encircling one another's waist, we half walked, half stumbled toward the bed, like uncertain dancers learning a new step.

3

As November passed into December and winter fastened its iron grip on Ulalume and the Plains States in general, and we took our customary interest in hearing how Bismarck reported twenty below and Embarrass, Minnesota, thirty-three, the tutoring continued. The class read *The Scarlet Letter*, provoking the expected disapproval from parents, some writing letters to the local paper about "exposing children to adultery," which Miss Doubloon answered by tartly challenging protesters to point out a single page in the book on which anything remotely resembling sex occurred. "So you see. It's not about adultery at all—it's about hard-core chastity and the cruelty of vindictive Puritanism." I thought I would stop after school and congratulate her on her reply, but as I loitered behind the exiting scholars it was clear from a flagging motion that she wanted to see *me*.

"It still doesn't look as though I'm going to graduate?" I said, shuffling up to the desk where she sat frowning.

"That's not what I wanted to talk to you about. Look,

did you enjoy yourself the other night?" She laughed apologetically and said, "I'm afraid it's something we always wonder and often ask, isn't it? Men too, of course. What marks the other would give us."

"I'd give you an A plus," I said. Adding after a pause, and with a gingerly grin, "Hester."

"Thank you. I shouldn't have let myself be carried away like that, despite what many of us feel about the self-justifying beauty of life's greatest pleasure. Sovereign cure for the woes of man, the pagan dignity of mating and all that. At my age you too will have learned to gather all the rosebuds you can, and while you may. The question of whether in doing so you 'corrupt' someone younger is a problem for hairsplitting casuists. Casuistry is —"

"I know what it means."

"I'm off that hook if . . ." She lowered her eyes to her desk. "I hope I wasn't your first."

"Not at all," I lied, to make her feel better and to spare myself an embarrassing admission. I felt honesty, and even honor, to have been satisfied by a moderate history of what is known, in the horrid little phrase of the sex sociologists, as "petting to climax." "Look, I just wanted to compliment you on that letter in the *Bugle*. I took genuine pride in delivering my papers yesterday. You're right of course. The story begins after the misdeed, and frankly for a good read I'll still take *Lady Cha* —"

"That's still not what I wanted to talk to you about. I'm afraid we have more than enough proof of your —"

My what? She appeared to choke on whatever word she had meant to utter, and breaking off with a sudden grimace, sat looking silently out the window. She seemed so distraught that to cheer her up I rattled off the chief

27

products of Guatemala, as remembered from a recent cramming session, and adduced as proof of her ability to snatch one soul back from the jaws of *flunkenkeit*.

"Forests of mahogany grow wild in the lowlands, as do rubber trees, bamboo, coco palms, and sapodilla trees, from which chicle is obtained. Next to Mexico, Guatemala is the greatest source of chicle, which is used in the manufacture of chewing gum. Guatemala has few mineral deposits. Sulfur is obtained from volcanic eruptions, whose deposits also account for the deep black soil. Some lead, copper, and chromite are produced, but mining generally has not been greatly developed."

"I think we are three."

I looked around for another loitering classmate, but saw none.

"I don't know what you mean."

"I mean it seems I may be pregnant."

The interval between hearing and comprehension was about like that between seeing and hearing when, seated in the far bleachers, we first get the swung bat and then the crack of the ball against it. I stood open-mouthed for about that duration, really a spectator myself, for the moment listening to something that concerned somebody else. Then, "My God, Miss Doubloon, what'll you do?"

She sat as often we had seen her do while gathering her patience with a dull scholar, elbow on desk and brow bent to the heel of her hand, the fingers curling loosely around the upward sweep of the pompadour. "You mean what will *we* do, don't you, Anthony?" It was the tone to take with underachievers. "Why, what we'll do is, you'll run along to Patterson's drugstore and get me a dozen ergot capsules. You'll bring them back here, and then I'll take them. That is, begin to take them. That's what we'll do, Anthony."

It was to the mind's instinctive alacrity in screening out the unendurable that must be laid my persisting view of this as all happening to someone else, say the recently shed suitor who gave incense and batik spreads, and who had been sent packing to Nepal with his walking papers and his mantra, to say nothing of his belief that he would return as something else, like a water ouzel or a dung beetle. She corrected that impression in no uncertain terms.

"Because, you see, you're the father."

I shot a wildly irrelevant look at the clock, simply, I suppose, to focus on something bland, like time. Eleven minutes after three. My voice when I spoke again was remarkably like it had been when I had been choked with passion.

"Why, gugh, should you want me to hotfoot it over for pills *you* have to take, Miss Doubloon?"

"Because that way Mr. Patterson won't know who's in a delicate condition, as he would put it in keeping with the quaint morality we have seen to be prevalent here, and that would make a girl doubly hesitant to face him with that on her shopping list. He'll just assume you're asking for somebody else."

"Somebody *I've* got in a delicate condition. Where does that leave me?"

"He chews gum while he discusses this. No wonder chicle keeps popping up in his recitations. If Mr. Patterson asks you, and it's not his business to, you can say it's for a chum who's got *his* girl in trouble, and whose parents it would kill if they found it out, one of whom is a mother who wouldn't have far to go as she is wasting away with an incurable disease. Say anything. You're inventive enough when it comes to rewriting American history or shuffling the chief products of South American countries like a deck of cards. Where were we? Yes. You have this chum who's got this girl in trouble. That way everyone remains comfortably anonymous." She took in my dubious expression with one of her own appropriate to continuing, again as with a dull scholar draining one's last drop of patience, "You can certainly see that I can't afford to risk my reputation in this town by — that it would be infinitely worse for me."

"Yes, but why can't you say the same thing? That you're asking for a friend of *yours*."

"I'm not even to be linked by association with any such breath of scandal. I have a position to be scrupulously safeguarded."

"I'm a minister's son."

"I've taken that into consideration. It's why I suggested Patterson's away at the other end of town, instead of that drugstore near the parsonage. You've got to do this for me, Anthony. It's little enough to ask, to get us out of this jam." She paused to regard me in a contemplative, more stocktaking way, her head cocked to one side. "People's nicknames are often a key to their personalities. I know we've discussed this before, without any conclusion, but I wonder if yours doesn't offer a clue as to how you might possibly have gotten yourself into such a muddle. Listening at the window to the shouts and cries of children in the schoolyard, as a teacher does, a wringingly nostalgic sound, I notice how they sometimes call you Biff. 'Hi, Biff.' 'Hey, there's Biff, let's ask him. Good old Biff.' "

"It won't last. It's a thoroughly adscititious soubriquet."

"I shan't give you the satisfaction of asking you what adscititious means."

"Irrelevant."

"I wonder. Your soubriquet may suggest an, oh, wade-in, devil-may-care attitude, or nature. One quite germane to this contretemps."

"I'll sometimes give a guy a chummy sock in the gut. Or swipe him across the arm. 'Hiya, fella, when did they let you out of jail?' But getting back to these pills. Will they help?"

She sighed worriedly. "I hope so. I know of one college mate they got out of a jam and one they didn't." She dug in her bag and drew out a ten-dollar bill. "I'm sure this will cover it. Now remember. A dozen ergot tablets. Or capsules, or however they come. Can you remember that? E-r-g-o-t. God, it sounds like a school pep-rally cheer."

"I know. A derivative of a fungus parasitically affecting the seed of rye."

"How on earth did you know that?"

The fact was that I could remember looking the word up in the dictionary without being able to recall why.

"All right, off you go. We've not a moment to lose. I'll work here till probably five or so, plenty of time for you to hustle back in. And may God have mercy on our souls."

As I steamed along to Patterson's drugstore, I wondered if any kid had ever been kept after school for this before — for getting the teacher in trouble. Could be, considering the things you read in the paper illustrative of a human scene my father frequently called a mell of a hess. A youth of nineteen recently marrying a seventy-two-year-old woman who remarked to the press that he was "wise for his years." A sister and brother looking for a preacher to join them in holy matrimony in Sausalito, California. A man in rural Nebraska who raised parrots to cook them up into potpies. If I had to marry Miss Doubloon, would I be allowed to whisper and chew gum in the house? Or be required to take out the garbage if I did? Would home, in other words, be something like class? Would we have regular fire drills and recite the pledge of allegiance every morning? Would my comic books be confiscated? And until what age? I was too young to get married, as one is too young to die, I thought with a sinking sensation in the pit of my stomach that was like feeling as though some kind of sawdust with which I was stuffed, as it turned out, was running out of me. If I looked back over my shoulder I might see a thin trail of it in my wake. What would the other guys — my contemporaries, as they were now called — think if they got wind of this? I would be mercilessly ribbed, the subject of graffiti everywhere. "Biff Thrasher gets promoted to fatherhood." "Teachers pet — and that's not all they do." Of course I would have to bloody a few noses to show that chivalry was not dead, defend a woman's honor. Still, I felt Miss Doubloon had got me in trouble as much as I her; being older, and presumably more sensible, she must take the bulk of the responsibility for this particular "mell of a hess." On the other hand, I must do the right thing, no matter how much more it meant than hightailing it to the other end of town for the ergot.

Suddenly I remembered where I'd heard the word before and why I had looked it up. Of course. It was the chief ingredient in cafergot, the pill my mother took for felling migraines, which seemed as elusive of cure, finally, as the skin inflammations against which the Curator of the Epidermis was powerless. She would lie prostrate for days, while my father brought her cups of bouillon, like a ship's steward, or read to her, long passages from Homer and Milton, which rarely stilled and sometimes intensified the hammering headaches and the nausea that accompanied them, a complication that Doc Turley said was classic to migraine. That baffled me. How could the *Iliad* and stomach sickness both be classic? "Please," my mother would say, staying my father with a hand weakly raised in mid-passage. His dramatic renditions were hard on all of us. I vowed that if I ever had any children of my own I would read to them without expression, if at all.

See Biff run. Where is Biff going? Biff is going to the drugstore with a ten-dollar bill. See Biff stuff the sawbuck in his pocket so he won't lose it. What will Biff buy? He will buy some ergot. What is that? It is medicine for his teacher. Is his teacher sick? Not as sick as Biff. Biff stops a minute, afraid he may throw up in the gutter. But the danger passes, and Biff starts running again, thinking that maybe when he gets home he may have to swipe some of his mother's cafergot, take it, and then lie down. He has always known there was something girls took when they got into trouble, and now he knows the name of it. They also went bowling and horseback-riding, and jumped off tables. He must remember to tell Miss Doubloon to jump off her desk. Mr. Merkle, the janitor, will pause in his floor-mopping to listen to the thuds overhead. . . .

Is Biff mature? Yes, it seems so, and getting more mature with every step he trots. See Biff get more mature with every step he trots. He didn't know he had it in him.

He shoots a look at another clock, the bank clock past which he jogs. Three-twenty-five. By suppertime he will be wise for his years.

Peering through the drugstore window, I saw that there were four customers inside. Two were at the candy counter, one browsing at a revolving paperback rack, the fourth a woman at the back clearly waiting for a prescription to be filled. Mr. Patterson, a bald man with a cherry nose, was busy with it on his dais. At least I assumed it was he, looking proprietorial as he did. Two customers emerged, but another went in. Mr. Patterson remained busy. What would he do when I asked for my preparation? Raise his eyebrows? Sniff suggestively? Clear his throat archly? Fix me with a skeptical gaze and think, "You?" As I stood there trying to pluck up my courage an inspiration struck me. I would feel him out by telephone. Glimpse of a booth half obscured in a rear corner gave me the idea. Any doubts about it dissolved at the sight of Mr. Patterson interrupting his alchemies to answer a ringing phone back there on his mezzanine. The public phone would obviously have another number, so I could conduct a conversation with one eye on the druggist himself. A sort of feeler to see how the land lay in matters like this.

I'll never know what makes the rain to fall, the grass so tall, the pages of telephone books to dog-ear themselves, slowly, inexorably, over the course of time. Half the pages of the frazzled directory hanging on a chain in the musty old booth into which I furtively sidled had turned their corners back on themselves. Such books are like frowzy old broads who have been handled by a thousand men. I found the store's number in a tattered column, dropped in a coin, and dialed. By that time Mr. Patterson had hung up. Now he picked up the phone again as, listening to it ring, I watched him through the glass door behind which I wedged myself. Since I had him in profile, just past a large apothecary jar standing on a corner of his domain, there was no danger of his seeing me.

"Mr. Patterson?" In a hollow tone.

"Yes?"

I disguised my voice, I don't know why, by raising it half an octave or so, as though it had never "changed."

"Why, I'm calling about this because I'm not well, not at all, and I have to send a friend to fetch it, and I just wanted to make sure you have it, so he wouldn't go, you know, make the trip for nothing."

"Where is he going?"

"To you! But, so, do you have, gugh, ergot?"

"Yes, I have it. Why?"

"I'm shut in at the moment, a shut-in as they say, not at all well, and I have to send a friend for it, and I just wanted to make sure you have it, so he wouldn't make the trip in vain? So it isn't for me, but I'll send the friend right over for it then. Well, swell. My friend's name is . . ." Here I muttered something intended to be unintelligible, while at the same time assuring him that there was no secrecy about the messenger's identity, in case he knew him by chance. "But I suppose that's unnecessary. Well, okeydoke then, swell. Good enough. He'll be over in, oh, I should judge about ten minutes. 'Preciate it." As I turned to hang up, I thought I caught Mr. Patterson calling something to stop me, but click, it was too late.

I sneaked out as I had in, by dint of more sidling and slithering among counters and racks, killed ten minutes by walking around the block a few times, and then, noting with relief that the store was empty, I darted in and hurried breathlessly up to the prescription counter.

"My friend just called about some ergot? He said you said I might pick it up for him. A dozen capsules, please? Ah, I need some toothpaste too. Glad this Crest happened to catch my eye."

Mr. Patterson dismounted his dais and held out his hand.

"The prescription?"

"What?"

"Where's the prescription for it? You need a prescription. It's an ethical drug."

"Ethical. Oh, I'm afraid he didn't know that. Realize it."

"Well, he does now."

"Hm. That is rather . . ." I hesitated, unglueing my gaze from Mr. Patterson's little exit bulb of a nose long enough to run my eye along some other merchandise. "Isn't it given out, you know, without prescription?"

"Regularly. But not by me. I don't sell anything under the counter." Fixing me with a pointed look, he added, "Tell your friend that."

"Right. I sure will. Okeydoke then. Bye."

I skipped the toothpaste and instead bought a lollipop to lick on the grim canter back, and so, the gray Azores behind me, brought the good news to Cooper Elementary. To wit, the rock-solid assurance that integrity was not dead but was to be found in the humblest apothecary, no, all was not venality and corruption — in fact rectitude might rear its ugly head around any corner we turned. Miss Doubloon did not take these tidings at all well. She shut a book over which she had been poring with a clap like a rifle shot, and then flung it down on the desk top with a second reverberation, and such force that it bounced to the floor. I bent to retrieve it, to show that gallantry also was alive and well, though breathing heavily, handing it over with a sort of quixotic implication that I realized she was leaning over for two and must be careful, forgetting for the moment that exactly the contrary policy was now in order. That there must be the most strenuous physical exertion such as horseback-riding, bicycling (occasionally falling off the vehicle being far from undesirable), bowling, yes a good deal of bowling. She must jump off the top of her chiffonier, if not her very classroom desk, causing Mr. Merkle, the janitor, to pause in his mop swishing to look upward and ask, "What was *that*?" Or I myself might just jump in the dank tarn of Auber, more commonly known as Moosefoot Lake, now so polluted by the paint factory that merely to picnic on its bank was to breathe toxic waste. Or maybe take the next bus out of Ulalume.

Watching Miss Doubloon pace the darkening schoolroom, back and forth past the blackboard on which was displayed with roughly chalked illustrations the difference between prone and supine (both of which the scholars consistently misused), standing there still clutching the ten-dollar bill, I wondered what was to be done now, particularly what was to happen to me. I was, after all, a minor. Why shouldn't I simply be sent to the principal's office for a stiff reprimand? I would stand a moment while Mr. Plowditch swung choppily from side to side in his swivel chair, my head hung in shame, and promise never to do it again. That had put an end to so many matters of misdemeanor in times past. I shifted uneasily from leg to leg, finally glancing at the clock, which now stood at a quarter after four. The winter dusk was rapidly closing in.

"I've got to get to my paper route," I said, taking a step forward and laying the money on her desk.

"That seems of secondary importance at a time like this, wouldn't you say?"

"I do have my customers to think of."

"And it's pronounced root, not rowt. Though maybe it's optional now, with all the dictionaries capitulating to bad usage. Soon ain't will be given the seal of approval."

"Yes'm."

"Things fall apart, the center cannot hold. And what rough beast, its hour come round at last, slouches towards Bethlehem to be born?"

"I don't know. I give up."

"It's the future. The horrible What-will-be. Some hideous apocalypse. Some think the antichrist. In any case it's William Butler Yeats. You'll read him later, if you get to high school, let alone college. I'm sorry, Biff. That's not the immediate problem. I shouldn't be jumping on you."

"No," and here I decided to make the advisory pitch while also striking a much-needed light note. "You should be jumping off the desk, or off your table at home. I hear that often helps. Clears things right up. But meanwhile, what will you do medicine-wise?"

"Medicine-wise — and how I loathe that 'wise' suffix — medicine-wise, what we'll do is, you'll go ask your doctor for a prescription. Then we'll be home and dry."

"Why can't you ask your doctor? You're in this just as much as me, you know. I couldn't have done it without you."

"In this town? I keep telling you I can't have any shadow of scandal cross my path. My doctor would know it was for me, even if I told him I was asking on behalf of a friend. No, you'll have to do it. It's just a question of whom you're dealing with. Some doctors will, some won't, just as some druggists will give them to you under the counter and some won't. The doctor may even just hand you the pills. No prescription necessary."

"And if he won't?"

She threw her hands up in a gesture characteristically histrionic, and at the same time again pedagogically reproachful, as though in the shadow of the blackboard she could not help meting out punishment to the wayward. "I'll jump off that bridge when I come to it. Or we will, together, hand-in-hand. Go."

This seemed a more hopeless mission than the gallop to Patterson's. In old Doc Turley we were up against an even more formidable slab of integrity than the druggist. Seated under a framed copy of the Hippocratic oath, he sat facing me in his swivel chair with his hands laced behind his head, his ample brown hair slicked with some sort of pomade in either direction from a middle part, so that his skull looked as though it was covered with a meticulously divided coat of peanut butter. It went well enough with what seemed a consciously stylized set of idiosyncrasies, which included wearing his necktie without a knot, simply folded over between the points of his collar, and the public use of a gold toothpick said to be hereditary, and a collectible. Also, as most people shove their reading glasses temporarily up onto their foreheads, he dropped his down to his chin, on whose jutting tip they rested securely, wagging when he talked.

"What is it this time, the sniffles again, Thrasher? Dress more warmly, take plenty of vitamin C, and put nickels into the collection plate, not take them out. Guilt can do anything, including make our nose run."

"I don't take nickels out of the collection plate, Doc."

"Liar, liar, pants on fire. I see you're looking at my family pictures."

That was not the case, or only ostensibly so. My shamed gaze was avoiding both his eyes and the Hippocratic oath, shifting, as it did so, to a wall photograph which he claimed had been taken by Mathew Brady in the 1860's, around the time he was doing Lincoln. It showed a cluster of forebears of generally repellent aspect, posing, together with some trusted employees, before the door of a log cabin in which his great-grandfather had first mixed a medicinal tonic once held in high esteem among American families not to be cozened by substitutes. The group reminded me of perhaps my favorite line from *The Ancient Mariner*: "We were a ghastly crew." They were typical of personnel photos still used in magazine advertisements or on bottle labels aimed at emphasizing the venerable qualities of some product or other — a patent medicine, bourbon whiskey, a soft drink. Products often concocted from a formula the secrecy of which the assembled lot will defend to the death, judging from the air of menace with which, clutching in some cases spades and axes, they seem to be blocking the doorway of the rude original factory (long since outgrown for snappier quarters with no compromise of standards). The men have on woolen stuffs that wear like iron, and indeed look like suits of armor, a vest here and there spanned by a watch-chain with which alone a rival bent on stealing the formula could be beaten into insensibility. They are generally bearded, and there is one cross-eyed party adding somehow to the general air of hulking readiness to murder anyone suspected of trying to steal the recipe.

Doc had swung about in his swivel chair and then risen to point some things out.

"This is Publius Turley, the great-grandfather who invented the tonic," he said, indicating the central figure in the front row. "This is Publius Junior, and this is Publius the Third, who inherited the business in succession until it came to an end in 1917. The rest are all cousins and trusted workmen. The original log cabin factory still stands, just outside Bozeman, Montana. There's always been a Publius in the family as far back as anyone can remember. Four generations that I know of, in the family tree in the old family Bible."

That was when I knew my goose was cooked. No family boasting an unbroken line of Publiuses for over a hundred years is going suddenly to spawn a member who will give you a prescription for ergot just like that, any more than if he were a druggist he would hand it to you without that prescription.

Doc pointed out some more photographs, my heart sinking deeper into my socks with each accompanying spiel. Some were daguerreotypes, some recent snapshots, some newspaper clippings laminated for preservation. There was a minister of a couple of generations back who had frozen to death in Saskatchewan when caught in a blizzard while making a pastoral call on horseback. There was a cousin who now taught high school in the East, who had been given Publius as a middle name to soften the blow. A Great-Aunt Sarah was pictured with a rolling pin, not because she had by wielding it slain a thousand Amalekites, but as three-time winner in the apple pie category of a county fair bakedown. So it went. Doc Turley himself was a stellar pillar of the community wholly worthy of membership in that redoubtable company. He headed the United Fund, handled a Scout troop, supported two aging parents, and often performed tonsillectomies and appendectomies free of charge for the poor, all this on half a stomach and one kidney, without being in the least cloying.

"Well, what seems to be the trouble?" he said, returning to his chair.

"I've got cold feet."

"Ah, your father's son all over again. Something we call Raynaud's complaint. Blood circulation doesn't quite make it to the extremities, the hands and feet. Spasms." He dropped his glasses to his chin again and shrugged. "What can I tell you, Tony? Take plenty of mittens and socks and call me in the morning. Keep out of the cold all you can. Wear two pairs of socks instead of one. They form a vacuum that helps keep the frostbite away. Fleece-lined boots. Doesn't your father wear spats in the house? Don't I hear tell?"

"Sometimes to bed."

"I can see him going around the place in spats spouting Shakespeare. Oh, that this too, too solid flesh should melt, something dissolve itself into something or other."

"Into a dew, Doc."

"You'll go far."

I blurted it out. "Can you give me some ergot?"

His brow contracted over narrowed eyes. "You got some girl in trouble?"

"Not exactly. I mean it's not for me, it's a friend of mine. Deserving chap, really. Hell of a swell egg. Salt of the earth."

Doc Turley heaved a sigh of relief. "I'm glad to hear that. I've known your family since your father became pastor of our church, and I'd hate to think . . . I mean I've known you from whooping-cough days. Sat up half one night with you getting the sludge out of your crankcase. Now here you are doing something on a chum's behalf. Tell him he must go to his own doctor. Or the girl must. You'll go far."

And start damn soon, I thought as I plucked my cap off my knee and rose to leave. Perhaps I had been born into a family not really suited to my needs. Or somehow had been given a wrong start in life. If I had been named Publius I probably wouldn't be in this mess now. Or I might be in worse shape still. Who was to say?

4

*T*HERE is nothing like a calamity to make us forget our troubles. An exploding oil boiler once drove completely out of our minds the threatened arrival of a crazy aunt whose shenanigans made increasingly urgent the worry about which of the relatives must nudge her into the funny farm toward which she was driving *us*, and whose eventual descent in turn made the freezing parsonage seem a trifling matter by comparison. Long family squabbles about how a deceased grandfather's estate would be divided vanished, and with them the corrosive feelings of guilt, when it fortunately turned out that the old fraud hadn't a plugged nickel to his name, and there was nothing to bicker about. A neighbor widow's fear of foreclosure, by a banker mustachioed like a skinflint of the olden time, together with a slipped disk and concurrent worries about a son being indicted for armed robbery in another state, were all suddenly eclipsed by the news that she must have all her teeth pulled. Similarly, anxieties about Miss Doubloon's condition vanished in a blizzard in which my mother and I perished — or were so certain of doing so as amounted to the same thing. "This is it," I figured as we foundered, and it must be to my credit that my dying thought was for the "seed" never now to be part of my "portion" on this earth, not entirely worthily mixed with relief at the eternal liquidation of that worry. Seed, portion. All part of the ambivalently borne Biblical heritage to be snuffed out with me in the howling North Dakota winds, sent down that December as promised by Miss Doubloon during that first fateful underachiever conference.

Whenever possible, Mother liked to distribute her Christmas cards herself, ringing the doorbells of neighbors and friends and forking them over in person, rather than mail them, which she considered a mechanically routine thing. Of course the post had to be resorted to in the case of people living out of town, but anyone within walking distance had them hand-delivered, often with a stick of cinnamon or a sprig of aromatic herb affixed. The warmhearted custom triumphed over inclement weather, winter colds, and even over deteriorated personal relationships, to be mended in this season if ever; as in the case of one old bat with whom Mom was on the outs, but whose doorbell she rang anyway, thrusting into her hand a card garnished with a leaf of rosemary, and saying, "Here."

My father would never have let us go out that afternoon into a storm already well under way had he not been in a euphoric glow over having caught the King James Version of the Bible in an error, or at least a preferential translation which a chauvinist for the Standard American Revised Version, like him, would jump on. Cruising about in the King James Genesis for a sermon text, he read, in a verse relating the first eviction by a landlord, "And he placed at the east of the garden of Eden Cherubims." "Hold on there, that's wrong," he'd been heard to exclaim. "Cherubim and seraphim are already plurals of the Hebrew cherub and seraph, old chaps. This won't do." The suspense must have been unbearable as he turned to the same passage in his beloved Standard American Revised, to find it blameless of any such booboo! "And he placed at the east of the garden of Eden the Cherubim." That was the ticket. One for the home team. And not just one. A concordance check on all references to cherubim and seraphim found the King James Version guilty of the double plural everywhere. Exodus, the Psalms, First and Second Kings both, and Ezekiel! My God, Ezekiel was a positive feast of them. It was in a trance of scholarly rapture then that he let Mother and me venture out into a storm to whose gathering dangers he might not have been so oblivious in a more normal mood. In his high, he called from the doorway into the whirling flakes a request that we pick him up some shampoo if by chance we found ourselves passing a drugstore.

"It's Sebulex, the medicated preparation, you know," he shouted through cupped hands. "Se-bu-lex! It's the only kind I can use! Don't let them give you any other brand!"

A tweed coat as the only thing to be done for dandruff was (besides being a counsel of despair) not a solution widely open to a clergyman expected to wear dark to the pulpit, or on sickbed — certainly deathbed — pastoral calls. Oh, he might wear herringbone or hound's-tooth to a tonsillectomy or a forty-eight-hour flu, or even an appendectomy without complications, but other than that any hints of levity in dress were to be avoided as echoes of the old Adam, which included salad days as a fop oddly enough paralleling Gandhi's dandiacal period as explained to Miss Doubloon that afternoon. The pearl-gray spats on his feet as he called out the shampoo instructions were a memento of those days as a spiffy gink, and there were those of us who suspected he was secretly grateful for the Raynaud's complaint that provided an excuse to sport them about town, at least in the winter months. The requirements of public restraint were relaxed with the bright shirts and yea-saying neckties he sported in the house; a blue foulard splashed with white dime-sized polka dots, nestled between the lapels of a maroon smoking jacket decorated with some heraldic emblem suggesting fragments of scrambled egg, gave a sense of plangency to the instructions about the shampoo shouted from the illuminated doorway. The porch light picked up winking glints from the buttons of the spats, as it did highlights from his thick gray hair, as though to dramatize that his chief afflictions lay at either end. Even on summer days he would seem to have come in out of a light flurry, so that you half expected him to stamp his feet as well as brush at his coat collar and shoulders with both hands. "I'm snowing," he would say, true to his principle that a little humor sees us through. Sometimes he would run the vacuum cleaner over his head, one of the nozzle attachments that come with the Electrolux tube model, in the perpetual struggle against epithelial debris, as he sometimes called it with oratorical effect. *He* was plangent.

Bundled and mittened and booted and scarved to a fare-thee-well, we set out merrily enough on what started out as another Yuletide lark, Mother clutching the shopping bag that held the two dozen or so cards systematically arranged for an itinerary that would take us on a meandering course through nearly the two-mile length of Ulalume. Using the family car wouldn't much have met the case, judging from the motorists soon seen skidding about the streets — for the blizzard suddenly intensified with unexpected force, catching the unwary. We quickened our pace

47

after dropping off our first five or six cards in the first four blocks, breaking into a trot, or as much a one as we could in the snow rapidly thickening underfoot. The flakes pasting our eyes shut seemed thick as tarts, soon coating our persons with a winter meringue that left us so blurred as to outline that we soon looked like snowmen, or victims of a tar-and-feathering party. A strangling wind blew a good deal of the white stuff down our throats whenever we opened our mouths long enough to joke about it. The few townfolk we passed were as unrecognizable as we ourselves were to them, although once I thought I saw Mrs. Clicko, Miss Doubloon's formidable landlady, hurrying by. We encountered an old man holding onto his muffler with both hands, as though thereby to keep himself from falling, but as a result only pulling himself the more precipitately to his knees. We helped him to his feet, and he slithered away merrily cackling, "All balled up. Merry Christmas." That again brought Miss Doubloon forcibly to mind, recalling the time I had explained the meaning of the term to her. "It comes from snow caking up on horses' hoofs, so they lose their footing." That began happening to Mother and me, as our boots found it increasingly hard going in what must now have become three inches or more of wet accumulation. Once, clinging to each other for support, we fell down in a heap together, laughing like fools. But now our mirth had a nervous hilarity about it, and I suggested we turn back, though our mission was only half completed. Jokes about the Royal Canadian Mounted Police blundering on our frozen bodies and Saint Bernards picking their way toward us through six-foot drifts soon wore thin. I remembered my wisecrack about keeping your cool when freezing to death, and it didn't seem very funny now. Mom's determination to finish the route and perhaps catch the bus back began to wane; she agreed we should turn around. But she did want to make one more call, on old Mrs. Pettigrew at the end of the block. The ten or twelve remaining cards could wait.

Bent double against the rising wind, and all but blinded by the plastering flakes, we crossed the street to Mrs. Pettigrew's cottage. Dusk had fallen by now, but that meant the street lights went on, so that the entire scene, hitherto all but invisible, suddenly sprang aglow in a kind of ghostly, muffled magic, one to which the few passing cars added their mottled golden beams. We became part of a charming Christmas card, though one better appreciated from one's own firelit parlor, musing on the sight between window curtains and with a mug of cocoa in hand. Mrs. Pettigrew's own cottage was dark except for a faint kitchen glow, away back. My mother and I made our way up the stairs, she clutching my arm. We stood like ghosts, revenants in an eerie tale of the supernatural, waiting to have our knock answered in order that we might accomplish our retributive return.

We stamped our feet and slipped off our mittens to wipe at least our faces clean. A minute passed. I rapped the brass knocker again. A voice was heard calling something unintelligible inside, as the parlor light went on. The door opened at last, and there in the hallway was Mrs. Pettigrew on all fours, or three of them, one hand being lowered from the doorknob to which it had been raised to turn it, grinning up at us. Her arthritis had been complicated by some fresh affliction, making it necessary to get about on hands and knees in the house to which of course she was confined. She had crawled from the kitchen to answer the door.

It must be in the memory of this scene — my poor dear

floury mother, deprived of outline by the storm through which she had come, reaching a Christmas card to the bony old claw upraised to receive it — in this tableau must be embedded my abiding sense of indomitable Womankind. I have suffered at its hands seduction, scandalmongering, chicanery, garrulity, silence, false witness, non sequitur, prune whip, and quotation out of context, but respect has endured and affection prospered. Who would not adore Mom and admire old Ma Pettigrew? There is one of each on your street, the younger mayhap heading for the tribulations already unmurmuringly borne by the older. Enduring without complaint an ordeal that finally had her locked in arthritic knots, Ma Pettigrew fended for herself in a stubbornly executed solitude unrelieved save for one surviving child, a strapping state trooper named Oswald who "did" for her with faithful daily calls. I couldn't remember not knowing of this parched old entity, smelling like the gingersnaps she munched in quantity, the bones under her bombazine like a bundle of kindling. Time was when the vicissitudes ordained for her by the President of the Immortals had been relatively slight, when Pop might make his pastoral calls on her in a plaid jacket, or even, in summertime, the beige Italian silk with random nubs. But his clothes steadily darkened as her illness worsened, settling at last on the Oxford gray adumbrating irreversible cases (but from the pockets of which multicolored mints might be always prestidigitated at bedside, a thumbnail prising from the packet of Life Savers the lozenge next in line for consumption, a kind of gay Presbyterian host at a sickroom communion). But however garbed, Pop always came away with a spring in his step, testimonial to the example of courage Ma Pettigrew set, and a renewed resolve not to whine, or to let you and me get away with whining. Mark her well, complaining one, prize her example, self-indulgent child of the times, etc., etc.

"Aw, this is nice of you. Come in and have some coffee and pfeffernuesse that I made myself. The old woman is plucking the geese this day."

"That's just it, Ma. We must start back, or we'll . . ."

We'll what? Perish in that howling desolation? Could be. Ma peered through the open door and past us into the street. "Good heavens, it is coming down. You'll never make it back. Tell you, I'll phone the barracks and have Oswald drive you home in the cop car. Well, so. Come in, set you doon."

Ma Pettigrew was of a generation that "Fletcherized" its food, at least those who were disciples of Horace Fletcher, the American nutritionist who in the early years of the century urged the thorough mastication of small bites as the road to physical felicity. "The teensier the better, and chew everything thirty times," Ma told me over our coffee and pfeffernuesse, an injunction fatal to the visit, as I could only sit in my parlor chair helplessly mesmerized by the spectacle of Ma in hers, a Morris chair onto which she had climbed like a forest creature out of its hole, Fletcherizing a pfeffernuss dipped into her cup. "One, two, three, eight, nine, twenty-five, twenty-six," I counted compulsively, "twenty-nine, thirty, *and* swallow." Her teeth were like pearls — both of them. At least that seemed the total count in her upper jaw, with which a suitable occlusion was somehow maintained with whatever survived below.

Oswald hadn't been at the state police barracks when Ma phoned from the extension beside her Morris chair, and when a half hour or so later he hadn't called back, we decided we must get going or Ma would have overnight guests. Mother stuffed the remaining handful of cards into her coat pocket, leaving the now thoroughly soaked shopping bag behind for disposal, and in a spate of exchanged "Merry Christmases" off we went on the return walk.

It was the longest mile and a quarter I've ever undertaken. Later weather reports were to speak of the twenty-three inches of snow "dumped" on North Dakota. Half of that seemed already underfoot, and down the meringue tarts continued to come, collectively pasting us in the face on a scale with the custard pies thrown at silent comedians. Or another fancy with which Dearest, as like little Lord Fauntleroy I sometimes called my mother, tried to keep our spirits up: they were "like doilies I'd like to take home." But under all this puffing banter was the genuine fear of really joining the marooned Alpinists about which we had joked on the way out. There were now no fools abroad on foot; all we saw was motorists foundered or still slithering and skidding about on the street, banging into each other like miniature cars in the amusement park Bumpmobile ride. This would be like the Blizzard of '88, no consolation if we didn't survive it.

"When we get home," Dearest panted as we slogged along, "we'll have a nice hot dinner. You know that nice pot of lentil soup, with the kielbasa I cut up in it?"

"That Mrs. Cherwinski gave us? Do I!"

"Then after dinner, puff puff, we'll have a nice cup of hot chocolate."

"Yes."

"With a nice marshmallow on top. In the kitchen," she continued, determinedly sketching the winter idyll toward which she preferred to think we were heading. "Warming our tootsies on the oven door."

"Yes."

"While your father reads *Snow-Bound* aloud to us."

I think that was when I gave up. Sank gratefully to my knees, then over onto my side, yielding at last to that famous drowsiness in which mountaineers freezing to death are said to lie down in the enfolding drifts with an almost voluptuous surrender, deliciously welcoming the oblivion in which alone deliverance is to be found: a sort of rescue in itself. I have heard people lament the passing of the tradition of being read aloud to by the paterfamilias, around the old hearth. These are the same nostalgists who professedly hanker back to the time when family members gave each other for Christmas things that they had made themselves. Such hymnists for the bygone have never had to listen to my father read John Greenleaf Whittier with a maximum of interpretation, after having found under the tree a tie-rack made by a brother in shop class, or eaten a plum pudding cooked by a sister in Home Ec. My touting all this to Miss Doubloon had been disingenuous, seemingly O.K. as a channel of communication at the moment, but not felt from the heart.

"Do you think he would?" I murmured.

"Made for him. Oh, you want to rest a moment? Just for a second then."

It was like falling asleep in a feather bed, to a fantasy merging blissfully into a dream. I was the youth who bore 'mid snow and ice the banner with the strange device, "Excelsior," but calling it quits midway the climb, not even tempted by the village maiden to lay my weary head upon her breast. I had already laid my head on one breast too

53

many, and excelsior was just something I'd rather curl up in than snow, though glad to put it all behind me in either case. . . .

Dearest was shaking me by the shoulder. "Look!" she said, pointing to the street.

There was a behemoth itself mountainous, all but invisible within the golden glow it emitted on every side, but vaguely discernible as yellow within a halo of whirling motes as it ground slowly among the stranded cars, giving off a rasping roar that eventually identified it as a snow plow.

"We can walk behind it," Mother said as I pulled her to her feet.

Not even that was necessary to salvation. Immediately behind it was another, smaller beast, its chains clanking, a rotating beam of its own rhythmically slashing the wildly whirling snow. It had enormous teeth, white as the snow itself, which turned out to be Oswald Pettigrew grinning behind the wheel of a state police car. He had returned his mother's call, got her message, and come to rescue us.

Dad greeted us at the open door, still fondling his beloved Standard American Revised.

"I've been worried sick," he said. "Did you get my shampoo?"

5

*S*now-Bound is subtitled *A Winter Idyl.* Our own was to be disrupted by a scene two of us at least had known for some time was inevitable, indeed long overdue.

I put on a show of anticipation for the reading, no doubt out of guilt over my death wish of a few hours before, when there had seemed no point in battling the elements only to stagger exhausted across the threshold to find your father waiting to read John Greenleaf Whittier aloud. That had apparently snuffed out for me the last remaining spark of will to live. But what I had been rescued only to face I faced with the best will in the world, as on countless evenings before I had faced declamations of the *Inferno, Paradise Lost, The Ordeal of Richard Feverel* — ordeal enough, God knows, when you can read it to yourself and skip to your heart's content. I bustled about the kitchen making preparations for the customary cocoa break, setting out the tin of Droste's, the cups and saucers, the plate of fig newtons, even the marshmallows that would top our frothing mugs (later learned to be a touch deplored by true chocolate connoisseurs). "Don't forget the poonykins," Dearest said, using her taxing variant for spoons. She too put on a good face, though inwardly steeling herself for the crisis she knew she alone must precipitate by asking Father please to just *read*, and knock off the histrionics that were grinding his auditors to pulp. She settled herself in her rocker near the kitchen stove, with her wicker basket of knitting gear and the green scarf already too long for anybody imaginable, unless we managed to locate a relative eight feet tall. It seemed a mesmerizing source of comfort she couldn't seem to part with and so went on and on, like Ma Pettigrew's chewing.

Winters, we were driven into the kitchen as the only tolerable room in probably the most miserably insulated parsonage as well as the most chink-infested house in North Dakota. "If you can't stand the cold stay out of the parlor" might have been the builder's attitude as he hammered this edifice together, already visualizing my father's spatted feet propped on the open oven door — reminder of the Raynaud's complaint on which Doc Turley had touched, in turn bringing back in flood force the worries about Miss Doubloon. Father felt good, primed to act up a storm, as he wriggled into a comfortable position in his own armchair, the Whittier open in his lap. He had just vacuumed his head after a brisk shampoo with some leftover Sebulex, a fair guarantee that he himself would not "snow" for at least a day or two, after which, of course, the flurries of epithelial debris would resume.

"The sun that brief December day rose cheerless over hills of gray," came the familiar opening lines. Of course we were quite snowbound ourselves now, supposedly snug as figures in a glass paperweight such as fell from Citizen Kane's fingers at the last, and yet the howling of the gale outside seemed to have the same theatrical quality as Pop's rendition. There appeared to be something fake about it, as though a technical crew sent up by M-G-M had arrived armed with wind machines and were blowing God's dandruff around the house like crazy, plastering the windows and whistling down the chimney.

An hour, another inch of scarf, later, I stole a glance at Dearest, to find it furtively returned. At last the clock struck nine, and a faint discreet stir from the two of us hinted that enough was enough, and it was time in all conscience to find a stopping point and pause for cocoa. Which Pop did, spread-eagling the book on the table. "Is Tony going to whip us up the nightly libation?"

The thought of what must be done had weighed heavily on Dearest all evening, and now she got it over with as quickly as possible.

"That was wonderful, and it's nice to hear it again, especially with the blizzard outside, and us nice and comfy inside. But . . ."

My father's bushy eyebrows went up in a look of inquiry. "But what?"

She blurted it out.

"If you just wouldn't read with expression."

Silence. Hills, fall on us. Mountains, cover us. Floor, yawn at our feet, swallowing us up forever. The guilt on Mother's face and mine fully betrayed our complicity, that we had been in treacherous cahoots on what must be said. The evening lay in fragments at our feet.

Yet perhaps not quite, not irrecoverably so. Leave it to Pop to reassemble the ruins and from them reconstruct a fresh dramatic edifice, with himself the martyred principal. While Dearest bit her tongue in remorse as, before the flung charge, she had bit her lip in preparation to hurl it, he rose and with great deliberation conjured from the icebox a platter on which reposed the cold remains of a previous dinner, and, wheeling about, held aloft a carving fork from a tine of which hung a thick fat slab of ham.

"This is what I am, then. That's what you're trying to say."

Cries of "No, no!" Denials that any such implication had been intended, or even remotely thought. It was just that he, well, like put too much of himself into it for simple cozy hearthside purposes. Yes, that was it. He would buckle under the strain of taking all the parts in a Dickensian effort that must leave him as emotionally wrung as it did us. On came the hypocritical apologies to which, savoring all the more his crucifixion at the hands of loved ones yet — "Drive in the nails, send the spear home after quenching my thirst with a sop of vinegar" — he listened in silence as he bit off a great mouthful of the ham, watching us as he chewed it. I slithered around him to get the tin of cocoa from the other side of the table, then scuttled past him to the stove, where I could stand over my pan of milk with my back to him. Yet in the glimpse I'd caught of him, a ham actor of the old school was exactly what he looked like, with his tall erect figure, wavy iron-gray hair, and handsome craggy profile, on some occasions and in certain lights uncannily reminiscent of John Barrymore. Years later among worldly theatrical friends I was to hear the term "chewing the scenery," and in retrospect it struck me as more than applicable to my father's readings, as it was to the histrionic delivery of his sermons also. Easter week was not to be missed as, pulling out all the stops, he reenacted the Passion drama from the triumphal entry into Jerusalem, in which transfixed parishioners could *see* the ass pantomimed between his legs, to the ascent to Golgotha, all this in a rich baritone many said I showed signs of having inherited. There was even some talk of my studying for the ministry in turn, though not by me, especially now with *l'affaire Doubloon* in the brewing. Would I fit into the archetypal legend of the clergyman's son as bad penny?

Even the sipping of cocoa offered plenty of "business" for the scene going forward, with Pop playing to the hilt the role of the Wronged, using pregnant pauses for broad brushwork and fine equally. I glanced covertly again at Dearest. Living for sixteen years with a man who read with expression had taken its toll of a fragilely pretty face, whose delicate skin left her prey enough to Time's slow, remorseless scrimshaw. When she first began lamenting the appearance of crow's-feet and other such tiny lines, the reassurance she got from Pop was, "Don't fret, my dear. Gray hairs will come to soften them." And come they had, with all the consolation they had to offer, along with a subtle increase in her resemblance to Billie Burke, at least as marked as his to Barrymore. His "This is what I am, then," as he held aloft the slab of ham like his own head on a pikestaff, must etch yet another tiny ineradicable crease to those gray hair was called upon to mute. The speech had been delivered with impeccable craft. "This is what I am" — pause — "then," enunciated with the faintest upward curl of interrogatory inflection, that had been a kind of posed question the implied affirmative reply to which would constitute the dagger thrust into his back by Conspirators One and Two. The comma after "am" could be *seen* by his crestfallen hearers, their averted gazes a form of visual shuffling. It was true art, while Metro-Goldwyn-Mayer's wind machines howled at the windows. I was to remember it all years later when reading Elizabeth Bowen's *The Death of the Heart*.

Anna is telling St. Quentin about coming on her niece's diary and reading the entry, "So I am with them, in London." "With a comma after the 'them'?" says St. Quentin, a novelist. "The comma is good; that's style." An old scar momentarily throbbed like the original wound. The comma after my father's "am," irremovably lodged in memory, like a bit of shrapnel.

Reading was resumed with a good deal of self-consciousness all around, though Father's restraint subtly took on a kind of punitive irony, as though he were again travestying the kind of "mumbling naturalism" he had already deplored as taking over a stage once graced by heroic declaimers in a tradition ranging from Sir Henry Irving to Maurice Evans, whose *Hamlet* album Mother had given him as a birthday present some years before. There was one passage in which Pop was unmistakably doing Whittier as Marlon Brando, swallowing his vowels and garbling the cadences, and then we even had some Cagney too, over which Dearest dropped her knitting long enough to clasp her hands in delight. But the dollop of bourbon that had helped send Pop off on the tangent soon had him his old self again, soaring to cornier heights than ever, much to the relief, it's hardly necessary to say, of the two Judas Iscariots sitting there listening. Years later I was to realize what a beautiful pastoral poem *Snow-Bound* is, reading it to myself without prejudice, but with echoes of that winter idyll of our own reverberating fondly through the text. That lay in the future, when as God is my judge my father was doing voice-overs for television commercials, our beginnings, indeed, not knowing our ends. For now, we had our nearly two feet of snow, and it wasn't until the next afternoon that, shovels in hand, and bundled to the jowls in woolen duds, we could go forth and take "with forehead bare the benediction of the air."

School reopened the next day, and there again was Miss Doubloon signing for me to stay after class.

"You flunked the botany test."

"You know what I've got on my mind."

"Come to my place tonight and we'll go over flora."

"How is Flora?" I sobbed, swivelling a fist in a tearful eye.

She reached a hand to mine. "You'd crack a joke to buck me up. Pagliaccio for both of us."

"It's as though you were carrying my buh — buh — baby brother."

My God, I was breaking up! It was my leave-taking of tears. "There, there, don't lose your courage. Be a real Punchinello. Fellow."

I dried my face with a handkerchief, and we laughed together, Miss Doubloon remarking that my eyes looked bluer that way, sparkling in merriment. "You know what Nietzsche said," I remarked. "That —"

"Yes, we all know what Nietzsche said, Biff. It's the oldest wheeze you could find as a filler in the oldest magazine in your doctor's waiting room." That sent a fresh tremor through both of us, as she had of course been briefed on the blank I had drawn with Doc Turley. "That man has invented laughter because he of all species needs it." Again settled back in her chair, she assessed me with her head inclined to one side. "You feel sorry for what you've done."

I stuffed the handkerchief back in my hind pocket with a closing snuffle and, pulling myself together, drew a distinction between regret and remorse. Troubled by the former — that is, simply that a mistake had taken place — rather than anguished by the true contrition that alone constitutes the latter, meant that I was failing to live up to potential in the moral sphere as well as the scholastic. "That is my titubation," I said.

"Your what?"

"Titubation."

"What on earth is that?"

"A halting, or stumbling in my progress toward what I should be. That's the point, isn't it? How all this got started?"

"I suppose. Go on."

As an underachiever, I next drew on Emerson's basic doubt of the value of compunction as such, moral philosopher though he was. He made a massive distinction, as I understood it, between sin and evil. The fact that one has committed a transgression does not necessarily link him with that eternal, monolithic something we call Evil. Thus I might in the spirit of frail human rationalization justify my stopping short of true remorse over an act we had engaged in together, because it was Such Fun, feeling only a lower-grade type regret over its results: to wit, the mell of a hess we now found ourselves in. "I hope this isn't all sophistry, or too much for you to follow."

"Whatever it is, it won't get us out of the jam. Where do you get all this stuff anyway, while seemingly unable to master the difference between a pistil and a stamen?"

"I don't know. Around. I keep a sharp lookout."

We both glanced at the clock over the door, she for an entirely different reason than I with my concern about my paper route.

"Well, that's neither here nor there for the moment. What I wanted to say was this. Walking by Patterson's drugstore this morning I noticed a sign in the window, 'Delivery Boy Wanted.' Now you hotfoot right down there and get that job."

"What for?"

"Good God, so you'll be on the premises, and can snitch the pills when no one's looking. It may take a day or two, getting back into the prescription section when Mr. Patterson is out to lunch or something, learning the ropes there and so on. It's our only chance."

"But I can't take another after-school job. I've got my paper route. I'll *never* graduate."

"You can do both, maybe combine them. I notice you've got a bicycle with one of those big boxlike things in front. You can carry newspapers and drug deliveries both in it, surely. Or if necessary turn your route over to a friend for a week or two. It shouldn't take any more than that. Once you spot where the stuff is it'll be no more than reaching your hand into a cookie jar. This is an emergency. So *go*. And for Pete's sake don't apply for a job with gum in your mouth."

See Biff run again, this time between already dirtying banks of snow. He has to make the trip on foot once more because his bike is at home. Otherwise he would pedal up to Patterson's. Padding along in fur-lined boots, I reviewed the distinctions I had just been making. Did they hold water? I also puzzled over Miss Doubloon's eagerness to assign *The Scarlet Letter*, no stranger to me since my father had spouted some of that at home too. Was she identifying herself with Hester Prynne? And if so, to "punish" herself, or as a protest against anticipated censure by local yokels? Biff couldn't be sure, but lately he was into things like ambivalence and dichotomy and stuff. Of course now he remembered learning on the night of their "sin" that she had planned even before *then* to assign the Hawthorne. All these things must be taken together as part and parcel of her character. . . .

My heart leaped at the sight of a figure hurrying toward me, jogging home from the high school my aspiration to which had been the original cause of these terrible entanglements. Spuds Wentworth had given me hope before. He had got into high school thinking the French and Indian War was a war between the French and the Indians. How could I, who at least knew it was the English pitted against the French and their Indian allies, fail to make the grade after all? Now as I spotted him chugging toward me I remembered he had recently worked at Patterson's himself, and might brief me about the pharmaceutical section in a way that could save me days or even weeks of skulking and snooping behind Mr. Patterson's back. His famous record of exploits with the girls, even rumored predicaments with one or two, might make him a valuable source here. So after buttonholing him I came to the point with a minimum of shilly-shallying.

"Gettin' much?" I panted, wincing under my first use, to my knowledge, of a standard greeting of his own.

"Par. You?"

"Enough. And everything is copacetic. But I have this friend who's got a chick in a jam, and I'm on my way to maybe get your old job at Patterson's, and you being familiar with the ethical drug stock —"

"The what?"

"Ethical."

"Hell kind is that?"

"The kind for which you need a prescription." So, like the Molière character who had been talking prose all his life without knowing it, Spuds had been tooling all over town with ethical drugs unaware that that was the case. "It's what they call it."

"Yeah, well, when Patterson gets ethical that'll be the day. He's never heard of child labor laws, which is why you can get the job to begin with, and as for the minimum wage law, forget it. You're lucky to get a buck an hour out of that turnip."

"I don't care too much about that since I can integrate the deliveries with my paper route, at least to some extent. But the thing is, do you know from maybe getting backstage there, or watching Patterson fill orders, where I could find the —" I glanced furtively around to make sure I wasn't overheard as I whispered the name.

Spuds grinned broadly back at me.

"Hell you been? Out to lunch? When you gonna get back from Muskegon? That's old hat now. There's a new pill called just that — *the* Pill. Everything else is unnecessary, including the old Akrons. Boys don't need no rubber garments, girls don't have to worry. The Pill, that's the name of the game now."

"Where does he keep those?" I asked in hollow tones, my pulse already hammering at all the skulduggery into which I was pitching full-tilt.

"That I know. The bottom shelf of a row along the back wall." He waved a hand in description. "You can't miss them. They come in packages of twenty-one or twenty-eight. Women have to take them practically every day. They're white and look a lot like aspirin. In fact there's a joke about a girl who got pregnant taking aspirin every day thinking they were her mother's pills. You ever hear that?"

"No, I can't say I have."

"Jeez, when are you going to get back from Muskegon?

This is the sixties we just got into, get with it. Patterson has a cow every time he has to fill a prescription because he thinks they contribute to fun without worry. Which he's hitting the nail on the head, the old bluenose bastard."

"You're sure these are the right ones you're talking about?"

"Absolutely. I use to snitch them for my main squeeze, so she's got practically a year's supply without going to the family doctor. But the black Marias you were talking about are a thing of the past now." He smiled again, studying me. "This for your main squeeze?"

This was further evidence that we were not exactly the boondocks here, but quite in the stream of things. It has supposedly only been in very recent years that the term for one's best girl, or major date, became at all current. Yet here it was in pioneer use — possibly even being coined for all I knew. *Somebody* has to give birth to any expression; it doesn't pop full-orbed into universal usage. Somebody first said "shacked up," or "took a powder," or referred to an acquaintance as "flakey." Who is to say Spuds Wentworth, wanting as he may have been in matters like American history, hadn't the ring of creative genius when it came to vernacular speech — wasn't the very first to call his girl his main squeeze, or, alternatively, basic bundle?

"Not mine, no," I answered evasively, and, thanking him, hurried on my way greatly buoyed in spirit.

As for inceptions, what apothecary long since turned to dust first took it into his head to enthrone his profession by setting it on a dais? There stood Mr. Patterson, so much monarch of all he surveyed as not to deign to descend to my level for the interview.

66

"Anthony Thrasher," he said when I introduced myself. "Haven't I seen you somewhere before? Weren't you in here for something the other day?" he asked, suddenly turning suspicious.

"No, Mr. Patterson. There's a kid around town who looks like me," I improvised. "People always get us confused." I had the feeling of standing before a tribunal. "Is the job after school and Saturdays?"

"Roughly, at a dollar an hour. I'm only too glad to pay it to get kids off the street, kids who can't get the work they'd like because of a lot of government interference."

"I couldn't agree with you more. The child labor amendment was all right in its time to correct abuses — children pulling carts through the mines from dawn to dusk or ruining their eyes doing piecework in ill-ventilated and otherwise unhealthy sweatshops, run by exploiters totally without conscience —" I paused to get a grip on my syntax, also wondering whether I wasn't making too strong a case against Scrooges of whom he was certainly one. "But its strict application has become an evil in itself. Sir."

"You're all right. Can you start now? All these orders to deliver." He indicated a stack of packaged merchandise on top of the upper counter at which he worked. He seemed to set great store by the six-inch elevation secured for him by generations of bygone predecessors. "Have you got a bike?"

"Yes, *sir*, shipshape and rarin' to go. I'll just trot home to get her and be back in two shakes." I thought it best not to say anything about the paper route the plying of which would somehow have to be doubled with his deliveries. Luckily I caught a bus that dropped me off practically in front of my house. I pedalled hell-for-leather to the office of the tri-weekly *Bugle* where my bundle of papers awaited me every Monday, Wednesday, and Friday, and then on back to Patterson's.

It was a mere two days later that, seizing my chance while Mr. Patterson was having coffee in the diner next door, I ducked back into his domain, instantly located what I was after thanks to Spuds Wentworth's directions, scooped out two packets of them, and was able to hightail it back to school with the prize. Miss Doubloon was still there correcting papers, luckily saving me a trip to Mrs. Clicko's boardinghouse, and it was with a great flourish of triumph that I dropped them on the desk before her.

"Now our troubles are over, thank God," I said. "We're home and dry."

She was a moment taking in my largesse. Then she slowly lowered her head onto arms folded across the spread of papers, where it remained so long I thought she might have fainted, no doubt for joy. Yes, that was it. The relief was so great it left her spent. I stood waiting, with the schoolboy's natural pleasure in an assignment well completed.

But why the delay? Was she silently crying for happiness? That would be understandable too. I fairly felt like it myself. And now that we were off the hook I was able to view her with an appreciation once more untinged by the anxiety temporarily clouding the response that had in part led to all this. I realized again how beautiful her not-quite-Titian hair was, how you wanted, especially with the winter lamplight setting it aglow, to reach out and touch it, bathe your fingers in it — and once had, alas! Her figure was more than just not bad, as the tightened sweep of her dress at the waist and hips, caused by the stretch in her position, emphasized, and I thought that a guy a little older could have done worse for a main squeeze.

At last she raised her head, as slowly as she had dropped it.

"This is *the* Pill. It's a preventive, not a cure. You take it to *avoid* getting pregnant, dum-dum." (Another new expression not entirely unknown to us in the sticks. [Who first said "sticks"?]) "I've *got* these. Only just. Obviously not in time to work. Oh, my God."

She rose and began to pace the room, shutting the door before making a return march, flinging her arms and rolling her eyes to the ceiling.

"Home and dry, he says. What we are is wet. Wet, wet, wet, especially behind the ears."

"Yes'm."

"I wish you wouldn't say 'Yes'm.' It makes me sound like a schoolteacher. Did you know it was a kind of obsession with schoolteachers, especially maiden ladies, not to want to look like what they are? To be recognized as such. Also librarians."

"I gathered it was a bête noire. It it's any comfort to you, you don't look like a schoolteacher."

"I won't by April, you can jolly well bank on that! Unless you get your hands on what I originally said. You'll just have to go back and try again."

To put the facts in a nutshell, I failed. Spuds Wentworth had no idea "in what cookie jar he keeps the black Marias," and even had he been able to tell me, there were no more chances to slip backstage. Mr. Patterson seemed to have grown suspicious, and never turned his back on me now. All I was ever able to snitch again were a box of chocolate-covered raisins and an Oh Henry or two. I got

Miss Doubloon a small bottle of Evening in Paris perfume, hardly much help in the circumstances.

"Have you done any jumping?" I asked, to remind her of the importance of strenuous exertions in these matters.

"Off everything you can imagine, including this chair. There's only one thing left that I can think of to jump off of. The Brooklyn Bridge."

To cheer her up I multiplied thirteen by twenty-two in my head, then reeled off the principal rivers of North America, to show her how much progress we were at least making me-wise, but she was in no mood for this kind of encouragement. Walking the floor with a peculiar long, jerking stride used by innumerable impressionists doing imitations of Bette Davis (and possibly recalling ambitions of her own to be an actress), she said: "If it's mathematics you're so much interested in, how much do you make a week on your paper *rout?*" Sardonically exaggerating the pronunciation associated in her mind with ineducable oafs.

"Nine dollars."

"How much is that times fifty-two?"

"Four hundred and sixty-eight."

"You make four hundred and sixty-eight dollars a year, irrespective of your shining performance at Mr. Patterson's. Do you think you can support a wife and family on that?"

"No'm."

"Nome is a principal port of Alaska," she said bitterly, as though only by evoking a hundred years of motheaten ten-o'clock-scholar jokes might she project some sense of the outrage of her position.

I tried again to buck her up, by cracking some at least a cut above that, and certainly of more recent vintage. There was the riddle about what the one strawberry said to the other. "If we hadn't been in that bed together, we wouldn't be in this jam." This line of approach met with little success. She said she was going east one weekend soon, after which I might not see her again. I told her not to do anything foolish, remembering her remark about the Brooklyn Bridge. But east from here might be Kalamazoo, as in fact it was to many Ulalumians. That was exactly what she meant. It was her home town, where she had gone to college and been fast friends with a classmate who had got herself into the same fix once and successfully extricated herself in the precise manner Miss Doubloon had been hoping to. The classmate had remained on in Kazoo to teach sociology at her alma mater, and Miss Doubloon thought she might still have access to the emancipated doctor who had helped her out back then.

It was while sweating out that weekend that I was again diverted from my troubles by problems on the home front, this time hell and high water of a kind I should certainly never have anticipated.

6

Dearest had suddenly become strangely amenable to the after-dinner readings, not even boggling at the scenery chewing. She sometimes hummed faintly under the worst of it. We were now deep into *The Scarlet Letter*, which, of course, offered scene after scene to be milked like a herd of cows by any ham worthy of the name. Father had got it down on learning that it had been assigned, in keeping with a policy of integrating hearthside reading with my schoolwork whenever possible. I could certainly have no objections to that. Pop gave special fervor to the passage in which the Reverend Dimmesdale, unable to sleep for the guilt secretly gnawing at his soul, mounts in the dead of night to the scaffold where Hester stood alone in the ignominy they should have borne together. He is trying it on for size. A dry run for the obligatory tableau to come. Carping about ham performances should really cease here; Pop was only matching the material in hand. And his dramatic interpretation exceeded in power anything he had ever done with the possible exception of his Sydney Carton, soliloquizing at the foot of the guillotine that it was a far,

far better thing he was doing than he had ever done, etc. All my boredom with the book gave way to the guilt I now personally felt as a fornicator in my own right, for which I might be punished with an equal vengeance. I shook in my shoes.

Mother by contrast continued serenely — I can't say attentive. She seemed on the contrary oblivious, immersed in some kind of secret daydream as the knitting needles flew in her fingers, the scarf-in-progress lengthening unheeded, till the question of finding a Gargantuan relative dissolved in the realization that it could now at any time be sliced in two to make a *pair* of mufflers, fringed at either end, for normal people. We might even wind up with three halves, like Miss Doubloon's heritage. Just past and above my father's head as he mounted the colonial pillory I could see one of the wall mottoes at which I had pitched foodstuffs in the old days. "A good man can always tell a lie — when he hears one." It gave me little amusement now, only a quivering apprehension that the time drew inevitably on when I might be caught in a lie myself — that and the famous nostalgia for high-chair days, and even those farther back, said by the explainers to define our personalities. I sat with my heels drawn up on the edge of my chair, my arms clasping my knees, a variant of the fetal position for which Dearest had once provided the accommodations, as Miss Doubloon now was for my baby brother, as I continued helplessly to see the matter. Oh, my God.

Now these many years later, when the problem of teenage pregnancy is on everyone's lips and occupying at some time or other most of the media, we hear the common observation: *They just can't imagine it happening to them.* I could testify to the validity of that. At that age, parenthood is as inconceivable as death. The illusion of invulnerabil-

73

ity is as strong as that of immortality. Nobody that young can think he will ever die, or even grow old, as you can remember for yourself, without having your memory jogged by the William Hazlitt essay you read in college. Something, some protective mechanism, screens off the unthinkable. Most times I didn't really believe what I knew perfectly well to be the case about Miss Doubloon's condition, except for certain flashes of realization such as that night of the reading. The next morning the sky was the same blue, the sun the same gold, friends with their own limitless futures before them exchanged the same hellos and goodbyes. I would try to jar myself with the truth and believe nothing, as one can jab a needle into an anesthetized arm and feel nothing.

I was equally stunned into disbelief by the news that Mother was having some kind of relationship other than the patient-physician one with the dermatologist, Doctor Mallard. Through my parents' closed bedroom door I overheard a heated dispute whose nature there could be no mistaking. There were no applied histrionics about my father's end of it, except maybe for an increase of the withering irony with which he referred to Doc Mallard by the old name.

"How far have you and the Curator of the Integument brought this thing?"

"It's not physical, Matt, you know I wouldn't do a thing like that. But we *are* more than friends, and I wouldn't lie about that."

"Just soul mates for intervals of varying duration in his office. Wringing one another's hands when not your own. We'll take an early vacation this year. There's an April seminar in Aspen we can both enjoy. The theme is marital relations, so maybe I can get the church to pay at least our fees, since counseling is a legitimate part of pastoral work. The Rockies will be glorious then."

That was the trouble. When Mother first began to develop the migraines which necessitated excusing her from the readings so she could go lie down, my father emphasized her need of a good vacation, and took her to a three-week self-fulfillment seminar in Boulder. The headaches persisted, and the next year he enrolled her in a Total Person Conference in Wisconsin, at which he himself was scheduled to lecture on the mind-body unity. There were classes six days a week, and on Saturday nights registrants were free to go into Bad Axe and live it up by strolling around with the local farmers. Mysteriously, the headaches not only continued but were now accompanied by skin rashes, inflammations that kept colonizing themselves up and down her arms and legs at a rate that had her going to the Curator two and three times a week. In my rapscallion case, the etymological Latin connection between pruritus and prurience might be obvious — but *Dearest?*

The next spring Pop took her to a Deeper Perspective Conference at Lake Tahoe, one of whose courses was a Grief Recovery workshop for people recently bereaved, and which she came close to having reason to enroll in when my father fell out of a dinghy the size of a washtub, in which he'd set out alone to do some thinking, and nearly drowned. I'd be the last one to knock group sessions per se, which are to be credited at least with giving people the euphoric *sense* of being helped, but they were no way to spend spring and summer for someone who'd spent the winter listening to *The Rise of Silas Lapham* read with the meat extracted from every paragraph. The peccadillo into which she'd been driven with the Curator soon had us all itching, her with guilt super-imposed on frustration, me

75

with the fear of a domestic breakup complicating worry over Miss Doubloon, and my father with the embarrassment of being two-timed by Doc Mallard, so that we were all furiously scratching away at ourselves and each other in a family unity hitherto not experienced. Ours were literary rashes in the sense that Father could cite as precedent the woman patient in *Tender Is the Night* who was hospitalized in the sanatarium where Dick Diver worked for a psychosomatic malady presumably something like shingles, emotionally induced by shame and "related to the blush," which finally scaled her entire body so that she died, carrying her secret with her. "I trust that won't happen to any of us," my father said solemnly, snapping the novel shut before returning it to its shelf.

Mother assured us that she would never cause us open scandal, and there was no question of her wanting a divorce in order to marry Mallard, because she could not live with an unbeliever, which he was. As an atheist in the old-fashioned Ingersoll-Darrow tradition, he was vocal not only in private but in the letters-to-the-editor page of the *Bugle,* which he enlivened with free-thinking outbursts of one kind and another. He was among those answering the "fossil moralists" forever demanding that this book or that be banned from the schools or the library, generally forerunners of the Moral Majority who today want Darwinism outlawed and Creationism taught. One could hardly imagine a book my father might want banned, but as our ranking churchman he did defend Creationism and regularly replied to Mallard's infidel screeds as such. So the two had been intellectual adversaries before becoming romantic ones, and now each animus fanned the other.

At the height of one such exchange of fire, it was suggested by the editor that the two men clash head-on in a knockdown, drag-out debate of the old school. The idea caught on like wildfire in a town by now deeply polarized by the two disputants in any case, and a format was quickly worked out for a Saturday-evening battle in late February, in the high-school auditorium. There would be no "resolved this or that" proposition. My father would simply be given fifteen minutes to state why he was a Christian, the Curator fifteen to say why he was not, and then there would be four alternating ten-minute periods for rebuttal. What it came down to was Father playing C. S. Lewis to Mallard's Bertrand Russell.

They were both windbags, and perfectly matched. People streamed into the auditorium by the hundreds, expecting a show, and they got one. Each had rooters hoping to see him mop up the floor with the other, which he did, with an outcome none could have foreseen. Father had a slight edge in the sly obliquities and ornately subtle ironies beyond Mallard, who, however, could drown them out in his hell-for-leather delivery. They were a physical contrast too, Father lank and sinewy, Mallard short and stocky, with a round face that in argument seemed to grow ruddier and ruddier, like a setting moon.

Mother and I sat in the fifth row, nervous as cats of course. I could sense in my very bones the divided loyalties tearing her asunder, though there was no question of Dearest's pulling for anyone but her husband. There were three judges, as in a traditional school debate. I cast sidelong glances in search of Miss Doubloon, without spotting her, though I was sure I'd seen her enter the building.

Rising to a round of applause after his introduction by the president of the school board, Pop led off with Anselm's famous ontological argument for the existence of a God, "in whom we must of course believe before we can believe somebody named Jesus was His son." Every college student is familiar with the classic syllogism, though generally in the form put by Descartes, who took it from Anselm. "You begin with the idea of something than which no greater can exist — an all-perfect being. But to perfection, or completeness, belong all attributes: power, goodness, knowledge, and also *existence*. Therefore God of necessity exists."

The Curator was no fool. At least adequately educated, he had studied his share of thinkers in Philosophy 203 and was acquainted with Anselm's argument — and its deflation by successors. It just seemed slightly unsportsmanlike of him to pounce on it straight off, thus using for rebuttal an opening statement that according to the rules was to be restricted to a basic declaration of his own beliefs. But off and running we now were!

"Yes, I'm familiar with Anselm's argument," he said, "but perhaps my worthy opponent isn't with the mincemeat Kant later made of it. My memory's a little hazy, but I believe it's in his 'Dialectic' that he exposes the fundamental fallacy on which it rests. Namely, that not everything that's 'conceived' is necessarily real. So our esteemed reverend can imagine all the gods he wants, with Anselm or anyone else, without thereby proving they exist. I can imagine Santa Claus without necessarily finding anything in my stocking on Christmas morning." Burst of laughter from his partisans, of which there were not a few in the house. Mallard built on that note. "That's what the myths the Christians believe are on a par with — Santa Claus! At best they put coal in our stockings and ask us to believe it's pie in the sky. I'll string along with Kant — God cannot be proved!"

He was "starting high" as they say in the theatre, but

the round of applause he got was laced with boos from Reverend Thrasher's devotees, who were quick to chide him for his infraction of the ground rules. He settled down to his prepared apologia for atheism, resorting to notes as my father had not.

Happily for the audience, abstruse metaphysics gave way to the practicalities of belief and disbelief. They locked horns energetically and sometimes savagely over such things as Darwin, the testimony of fossils, the pagan derivations of Christianity, the reliability of the Scriptures. They naturally both loosed barrages of quotations from sources supportive of their views. Mallard cited atheists by the dozen, including Nietzsche, Freud, Mencken, Tom Paine, while Father countered with his Chesterton, Eliot, Jung, and even Stravinsky. He finished with the ringing paean to Christianity that closes Toynbee's epic *History*. When it was over and the two shook hands while flashbulbs popped, the audience responded with a standing ovation in which one sensed all partisan prejudices merged in a roar of general approval, and some kind of pride in a hick town that could boast disputants of such eloquence.

Now the climax of the evening, sweating out the verdict.

An audience ballot had been wisely ruled out as too vulnerable to the risk of people's voting their prejudices. Three judges were decided on, their impartiality and also anonymity guaranteed by their being teachers imported from a nearby college, unknown to all except the members of the program committee, and of a calibre vouched for by them. Since it hadn't been an affirmative versus negative debate, votes were cast for either Thrasher or Mallard, unsigned, and that was to be that. The audience rubbernecked as a girl in a silver gown collected the ballots from judges scattered throughout the auditorium, and took them up to the stage with a great deal of comely churning. The mayor, who was to read the votes, naturally milked for all he could the opening of the envelopes in which they were delivered. It was like Oscar Night.

The audience giggled hysterically in suspense. The debaters crossed and uncrossed their legs. My father twisted the ends of a mustache he forgot he had shaved off, while Mallard fingered his bow tie as though he were going to pull it out and snap himself in the Adam's apple with it, like a drugstore card. Mother wrung my hand in both of hers till I thought she might snap some of my bones.

The mayor opened the first envelope and read the ballot inside it.

"The first vote is cast for Doctor Humphrey Mallard."

My heart burst in the breaking wave of approval from the freethinkers.

The mayor opened the second envelope, and with maddening deliberation unfolded that ballot.

"The second is for the Reverend Matthew Thrasher."

The rafters shook with acclaim. Mother and I applauded like mad. The mayor opened the third envelope and raised his eyes. The audience was dying with suspense.

"Our third judge declares the debate to be a draw."

Mother and I collapsed against one another with relief as the most thunderous and prolonged roars yet reverberated through the hall. The mayor turned around and shook hands with the antagonists simultaneously, grasping my father's right hand and the Curator's left. Their faces and those of most in the audience were wreathed in satisfaction at an outcome generally realized as a happy and fair one. It was an hour before people had finished crowding to the front to offer their congratulations, and gratitude, for a red-letter night the town would be a long time talking about, and never forget.

But the real testimony to the balanced eloquence of the disputants was still to come. In the days that followed, my father listened to personal and telephone congratulations of friends and strangers alike with a strained and preoccupied air. He was not himself — or more himself than ever with his air of dramatic self-absorption. He went for long solitary walks, sat staring at the wall or out the window, picked at his food, drank coffee by the gallon.

"It's the letdown, after all the preparation and tension," Mother said. "You gave a brilliant account of yourself, with a persuasive opponent."

"He persuaded me."

"What are you talking about?"

"He's right. There is no God. Or none justifying the religion I've been preaching. I've always had my doubts, as you know, every thinking and educated man does, but I don't anymore. Only certainty. Christianity *is* a hodgepodge of odds and ends of pagan religions amalgamated into a myth for which Western civilization was ripe. It's an opium for poor mankind unable to take reality neat. I've been feeding hungry bellies with promises of heavenly feasts."

"Matt darling, you're tired. You'll feel better in a few days."

"In a few days I'll see even more clearly what I've secretly suspected. Reason has had its foot in the door for years. Mallard, or at least the centuries of thinkers he marshalled, flung it wide."

"But the Bible —"

"The Bible is a goulash of hokum, contradictions, and

tribal superstitions." He kicked at a footstool. "My ministry is a joke. The only thing I can honorably do is resign."

"What on earth will you do?"

"Drink up eisel, a kind of vinegar so-called by the Elizabethans. You've heard me read the passage from *Hamlet*."

"There you go again, drinking up eisel and one thing and another at the first hint of trouble. Gall this and wormwood that. What will you *do?*"

"Teach. I did that before I was ordained, and I can do it again."

"What will you teach?"

"Comparative religion. You can teach beliefs without believing, so there'd be no question of hypocrisy there, as there would remaining in the ministry. Ed Collins teaches a course in communism and he owns five hundred shares of Union Carbide."

"Maybe you'll feel better after next Sunday. It's communion then."

This, together with reminders that Easter would soon be here with its promise of moot resurrection, only brought on a fresh spasm of infidelity.

"Eating God. Can you imagine anything more barbaric?"

"At least you've got all your teeth."

Non sequiturs like that seemed to increase Mother's resemblance to Billie Burke, though seeing them as at best rather enchantingly silly was only one way of looking at them. Another might be to regard them as elliptical circuits to what in the long run were fairly relevant solaces in a time of shambles. Things could be worse and tomorrow was another day. But its cryptic absurdity only made my father kick at another footstool. He went on:

" 'This is my body. This do in remembrance of me.' The

only Gospel author who relates any such injunction, and on whose word we therefore base the communion sacrament, wasn't even present at the meal in question. How do you like them apples?" Here he was carrying the argument to extremes not even Mallard had, rolling along on his own gathering momentum.

"Why, what do you mean, dear?"

"Luke, of course! He's our sole authority for all that, and he wasn't a disciple any more than Mark was. Only Matthew and John were, and John doesn't even mention any such supper, let alone supply any basis for future commemoration. Yet year after year I've been pumping gullible people full of this mumbo jumbo."

Mother's blue eyes widened. "You mean Mark and Luke weren't disciples?"

"Oh, my God! My wife doesn't know that. She thinks they — oh, what's the use? But getting back to this communion business, it's why Emerson quit the ministry. He couldn't swallow the last supper, and I guess I can say that again. It's suspect on other grounds, being also a feature of one of the pagan religions from which Christianity snitched like a shoplifter going through Macy's. The Church took over its chief rival, the Persian cult of Mithras, the way Du Pont will take over a competing corporation. Swallow it lock, stock, and barrel. Mithras — you'd better sit down for this, my dear — Mithras was the Sun God whose birth was witnessed by shepherds, and who was annually commemorated with a ceremonial meal."

"Oh, dear. Are you sure?"

"Positive. If it were not so I would have told you. We honor him every *Sun*day, and celebrate his birthday every December twenty-fifth. Now as for Easter, the celebration

83

of the rebirth of vegetation in terms of mythologized —
oh, lord, here comes the Curator. I trust he will wear his
victory well."

That was unnecessary. He came to admit my father had
done to him what he had done to my father — shown him
the error of his ways. Each had convinced the other of the
validity of his viewpoint: they had exchanged convictions.
That was the long and the short of the power of their
forensic abilities. My father was now an infidel and Mallard
was a psalm-singing stinker.

"Your whole apologia for Christianity was persuasive,
but your quotation from Toynbee capped it, for me. You've
made me see the light, Reverend Thrasher," Mallard said,
tears in his eyes as he advanced to wring a hand Pop as
impulsively jerked back. "Blessed assurance, Jesus is mine,"
he sang. "Oh, what a foretaste of glory divine."

"Nonsense. *You* were right, or all the intellectual cham-
pions you quoted. You must realize yourself your attitude
now is all wish-fulfillment. It caught you at a time of life
when, perhaps, you've been forcibly struck for the first time
by the fact of mortality. You *can't stand the thought of
your extinction*, and so fall back on that invention, heaven.
This is not a feat of reason, but a discharge of emotion,
man!"

"No! The scales fell from my eyes. Like they did from
Paul's. On the road to Damascus, you know."

"No, he was blinded then. The scales fell from his eyes
later. But you might note the curious fact that Paul himself
never mentions any such road to Damascus experience, and
he a man who talked about himself nineteen to the dozen.
Others record the tale, in the Acts of the Apostles, which
he didn't write. And all this for good reason. It's a myth,
like that last supper business."

84

Mallard shook his head, both to plead with my father and to deplore his own responsibility for what he was hearing. "Matthew, Matthew. Don't believe what you're saying. Will you kneel with me in prayer?"

"I rather think not."

"Will you, Reverend Thrasher, again accept the Lord Jesus Christ as your personal savior?"

"Not by a long chalk. Not by the hair of your chinny chin chin."

"I shall pray for you myself then, in the privacy of my own home. Every night. Until you're saved."

"That should guarantee you everlasting life," Father said, his lip curling in a sardonic smile.

The loss of his faith, so far from plunging my father into despair, or even into depression, somehow braced him. It stung him into new life. He found it exciting, an adventure at a time in his career when he had thought himself wholly sunk in a platitudinous rut. He came alive like a mountaineer negotiating a steep escarpment in freezing winds. His wits were refreshed, and, certainly, his irony sharpened. This was nowhere more in evidence than in his determination, often a source of pride to unbelievers, to be more "Christian" than "Christians." It was very swiftly shown in his attitude toward Miss Doubloon, when the time came, preordaining for me a fresh installment of disaster.

My sex education had taken an early but highly erratic course. Whether from unreliable contemporary curbstone informants or out of my own speculations, I had somehow got the idea into my head that a woman wasn't really pregnant until she showed it; until then, certain preliminaries were merely going on inside her that might or might not culminate in her getting into a delicate condition, and eventually giving birth. By these lights, which I wished were still burning, Miss Doubloon had not been certifiably with child all this time, and only would when and if her physical appearance left no doubt. That was not till the end of the Easter vacation, when I learned the news that she was expecting from none other than her landlady, Mrs. Clicko, and also who the father probably was.

At that time, I had other worries occupying the forefront of my mind. For one, the question whether, true to the stated impossibility of Mother's ever being able to live with an unbeliever, she would now really get a divorce and marry the Curator. Much is made of the damage wrought by divorce on the children, without many of us being able to cite in quantity "scars still there" left by broken homes. In addition to being vulnerable, kids are also adaptable. You can guess the factor making for resilience in my case. I could scarcely have dreaded the breakup of a home in which, in its intact state, I might have to go through hell vis-à-vis Miss Doubloon. If it were dismantled, I would have to face not a tribunal of two, but only a pair of adults each of whom was in a poor position to sit in judgment, given the shambles they had made of their own lives. This held more for my erring mother than for my self-absorbed father, but not much. In truth, I seized upon any imminent separation as a dramatic occasion for self-pity that smartly turned the tables and in a twinkling transformed me from wrongdoer to wronged. I might on second thought jolly well *be* damaged, carrying to my grave more scars left by my parents than by my Doubloon crisis: split down the middle like a broiler and burned to a traumatic crisp by familial conflict. Would my mother eventually marry the Curator, saddling me with a stepfather delivering the coup de grâce to my psychic remains? Could be. And that after having been cruelly required to act as witness in a divorce trial making lurid headlines for a community gluttonous for scandal. I imagined the scene clearly.

"The case of Thrasher vs. Thrasher. The wife suing. Grounds?"

"Reading with expression, your honor. We call to the stand the son, Anthony Thrasher. Did your father in fact read with expression?"

"Yes. Every night."

"What did he read?"

"*Paradise Lost*, the *Inferno*. Stuff like that."

"Divorce granted, and the mother to have custody."

The reverse romanticism bred by woeful self-regard had me running away from home, or homes, a lad not really wanted by either parent and thus an orphan with both still alive, or all three if you counted the Curator. In the classic destitution of the penny dreadfuls, I could be seen "trudging" through the falling snow on Christmas Eve, pausing to press my nose against the windows of shops glittering with toys not mine on the morrow, my clothes in shreds and patches, like those of the limerick young belle in old Natchez, partly from scratching through them to appease the itch on a skin my stepfather didn't understand any more than he did me. All this in a heartless big city to which I had come to seek my fortune. Kalamazoo. Kenosha. Fond du Lac. Muncie. Who knew?

I was practicing my "trudge," in preparation for when I would be a homeless waif in the falling snow, when I saw Mrs. Clicko coming toward me on Tuttle Street, looking fifteen or twenty pounds more formidable than when she had stood frowning in the vestibule as I mounted the boardinghouse stairs to my tutorials on that fateful night.

She had on a coat of many colors that Joseph himself might have found a trifle busy, and an Easter bonnet that could have made our risen Lord wonder why He had bothered to start the day by getting up at all. It was of straw that had been woven under prune juice, blue-black in color except for a nosegay of wire-and-cloth flowers characteristic of women representing moral integrity in towns with populations between five and twenty thousand. I smiled as I approached her while mentally bringing her down with a low tackle.

"Mrs. Clicko. You're gaudy as a jukebox."

"Thank you." But her expression gave notice that flattery would get me nowhere, and she would adhere to standards now brought into total play, and without compromise. Full penalty would be exacted. I would not go hence till I had paid the last farthing.

"I see Miss Doubloon is in the family way," she said.

"Oh?"

"That can't be completely unknown to you." She sighed, not as from the "bowels" as construed by the early Christians to mean compassion, the tenderer feelings, but in a censorious way. "I was always opposed to having male callers in the rooms, or female in the case of men. It was my rule. I should have enforced it more strongly."

A terrible racket interfered with our chat. Building construction was going forward across the street, with one of those cement mixers on a truck, called a Port-O-Mix, going full blast. Slinging Mrs. Clicko over my shoulder in the fireman's carry, I staggered up a ramp contrived of two planks set together between the street and the tailgate of the truck, and dumped her into the maw of the Port-O-Mix, where after a number of revolutions she finally dissolved into the slip-slopping sludge, for eventual disappearance in the floor and walls being poured by the workmen. "A concrete solution," I murmured, apparently aloud, because she said, "What?"

"Nothing," I said, and bidding her good day, continued on my way.

When it was noised about that Mrs. Clicko had asked Miss Doubloon to leave, and why, I for some reason thought it best that I be the first to tell my parents. Probably because that might shield me from any appearance of complicity. It had never entered Miss Doubloon's own head to implicate me, whatever developed. Never.

The news gave my father his first opportunity to out-Christian the still formally affiliated churchgoers. He played the Good Samaritan to the hilt, I must say, setting forth instantly to pay a call of sympathy and encouragement on Miss Doubloon at the motel into which she had been driven. The loss of faith, and the corollary determination to Live a Little in the here and now, had made him revert completely to the sartorial dash of his salad days. He fared forth in a crisp beige poplin suit, blue button-down shirt, and blue and red checked tie. Set jauntily on his head was a tweed hat with a small feather in the band, and (there being no God) the brim turned down all the way around.

"My son has told me everything," he said. "You'll, of course, come stay with us. Start packing your things."

7

I HAVE never, to the best of my knowledge, chuckled. Or maybe I just deny having done so because the word itself gravels me so, no doubt out of all proportion, like its sister irritant, chortle (though we know that to be a supposed amalgamation of chuckle and snort coined by Lewis Carroll, and on that ground entitled to some clearance, however grudging). The dignity of a Latin or even Germanic root is not accorded by any dictionary to chuckle, which is simply written off as a "frequentative of cluck," thereby gaining for it an additional nuisance value as one has now learned against his will another insipid word, and compulsively looks it up to find it means "expressing or denoting repeated action." Reiterating "frequentative of cluck" a few times makes one feel like an old fat scratching hen, like Mrs. Clicko, perhaps stiffening one's resolve never to chuckle again during one's tenure on this planet. The tendency to associate chuckling with bespectacled codgers and apple-peeling grandmothers (the spiraling strand of skin dangling unfractured over the cat) suggests it to be a malady of old age, or at least mature years, when a more reflective humor has replaced the robust merriment of childhood and early youth.

What brings all this on is a recent spell of wakefulness induced by a more adult backward look at Miss Doubloon's story, insomniac voids in which chuckle was one of the words, along with sprinkle, purport, quorum and, of course, trudge, which revolved ceaselessly in my mind until they became drained of meaning and so chimerical in their absurdity that each mentally babbled repetition made that much more elusive the slumber it had been intended mesmerically to coax, in a smoothly monotonous recurrence like that of counted sheep. Everyone has experienced the phenomenon. You say a word obsessively over and over — "purple, purple, purple" — until it becomes a gibberish threatening your sanity. "People" is a word particularly possessing this insidious power, because to the finally ludicrous sound is added the wrenching discrepancy between that and its spelling.

Planning never to chuckle, neither do I wish to be the cause of others' doing so. Yet in memory, now, tossing amid the twisted sheets, I seem to bear my share of responsibility for the chuckles and chortles, all of them naturally nervous and not a few hideously forced, that went around our dinner table the evening Miss Doubloon arrived — first fruits of the overcompensating saintly behavior that followed my father's renunciation of formal Christianity, with the concomitant affidavit that the last Christian had in any case died on the cross two thousand years ago.

Not having accompanied him on his courtly call, I didn't learn till later what his exact choice of words was and the literal interpretation Miss Doubloon put on his report that I had told him "everything." So I had no idea we were dining with a time bomb ticking unheard under the table. Or I should say a stick of dynamite to which the erratic course of our conversation was an unpredictable but definitely sputtering wick, of indeterminate length.

"The dauphin here," my father said with his familiar glossy irony, pointing a thumb at me as he passed the bread to Miss Doubloon, "gives us rather conflicting accounts of how his studies are going. In fine, what the expectations of his graduating in June are. Do you have any opinion?"

"I think he'll squeak through, if we can get his nose out of Joyce and Proust long enough. His essay on *The Scarlet Letter* was interesting. He says Hester was subconsciously being worshipped by the repressed Puritans. By putting her on a pillory they were setting her on a pedestal, a goddess their censorship of whom was lust turned inside out. Of course Hawthorne hints as much, though innocent of the word subconscious. Thank God! But Biff developed it really quite well."

"Doesn't Lawrence give some such interpretation?" my father said.

"Lawrence who?" I said, gazing around with feigned imbecility, thus causing the first chuckle.

"Maybe it's somebody else, or I say that because it's obviously what Lawrence would have thought. As do I," my father said, nodding briskly as he often did after a statement, as though hastening to agree with himself. "As do I."

The subject of Miss Doubloon's "condition" had been sedulously avoided since she moved in that afternoon, with a care that only emphasized it the more, but the relevance of the discussion could hardly go unnoticed, walk on eggs though we might. So Mother plunged right in, to try to clear the air of the static electricity uneasily collecting in the silence that fell.

"I suppose the same thing is true now. I mean in people's, well, disapproval."

"I see Mrs. Clicko right there at the foot of the scaffold, gazing with sexual frustration at the scarlet letter," my father said.

"I got a scarlet letter," Miss Doubloon said. "In the mail the other day."

Father dropped his fork, and Mother's was arrested halfway to her mouth.

"You mean somebody actually sent you that?" he said. "I mean, a cloth letter A —?"

"No, no. A letter on red stationery. Saying he or she — it was anonymous of course — expected this from a teacher who would assign such a book, and vice versa. It was signed 'Decent Citizen.' "

"Good God."

Mother changed the subject by asking Miss Doubloon about a pin in the lapel of her suit. It was gold, with a blue enameled cow.

"It's from a boyfriend I recently had, who's left for India," Miss Doubloon said, with a sidelong glance at me. "An Orientalist who left my room reeking of incense. Tony noticed it on his first visit. I seem to attract men with a Far East penchant. The one before that had a radical slant. Intelligent, and really quite nice, but he was a Maoist."

"That was the chink in his armor," I said.

"Our beamish boy," she said, rumpling my hair. Another frequentative of cluck.

"The dauphin is cracking tonight. And so is the cook," Father said. "Come have some more of this homemade bread. French bread declines by the minute, you know. The veal stew is terrific too, my dear. More, everyone." He

93

dipped the ladle into the tureen and reached for Miss Doubloon's plate. "Everybody's hungry but the dauphin. What's the matter?"

The dauphin hadn't much appetite either for the dinner or these the first fruits of secular sainthood. Why had Pop gone and invited her in? Supping with publicans and sinners was all very well, but might there be something secretly carnal in this spiritual embrace of a fallen woman, something not far removed from the lascivious relish of Hawthorne's onlookers?

"Little more wine, Maggie?" Maggie was it now! "Eat, drink, and be merry. No better time to make the best of things than when they're a hell of a mess."

That caused Dearest an involuntary start, for her reflexes were still geared to the pre-debate Matt, before he and the Curator mopped up the floor with each other. Then, he would have said "mell of a hess." No more call for such euphemisms. No one could tell he was a preacher now, anymore than they could Miss Doubloon was a teacher, with that prow on her.

And Mother, what was she thinking for herself? Was her mind even then secretly on Mallard, turning over the idea of divorce, or at least separation? No more need for the conventional façade in her case either, now that Father had tendered his resignation and was no longer a minister. As Father's star convert, on the other hand, Mallard was regularly seen at divine worship currently being conducted by a seminary graduate rushed in from Chicago, and was also active in Bible study groups, seeking to atone for his life as an atheist, and particularly his swansong as such in which he had successfully damned to perdition a man of the cloth. Would his newfound piety forbid his marrying a divorced woman? Hardly likely. Mother's inability to live with a highly verbalized, motor-racing infidel and her continuing need for a devout helpmeet would more probably decide the issue.

These thoughts raced through my mind in a silence now broken by Miss Doubloon as, frowning into her wineglass, she turned the stem slowly in her fingers.

"If I may say this sincerely, Reverend Thrasher — or I guess it's to be Mister Thrasher from now on — if I may say this from the bottom of my heart, you remain to me, and always will, an unreconstructed Christian gentleman."

Father threw out his hands and said something modestly dismissing like "Poosh." The satanic notion crossed my mind that he might even take her off my hands. To my credit, it sent a shudder through me.

And now *kaboom*.

"No, I mean it. Taking me into your house under the circumstances. With Anthony involved and all."

My parents looked at her with puzzled expressions, while my heart bounced. That was the instant I had the hideous intimation she had read more into my father's chivalrous invitation than it contained. And it was true. We had heard the first preliminary tremor of a quake only seconds away. Another metaphor might be the tentative strand from fiddles and woodwinds that foreshadows a major change of theme to be announced in full by a belch from the brasses and a blast from the tympani. To vary *that* one just a tad, I felt frantically for the right feet under the table, like an organist off on his pedal work. By the time I had kicked Miss Doubloon in the shins she was saying, "You mustn't be too hard on him."

"Mrs. Clicko!"

Yelping her name in my wild attempt to change the subject gave me a glimpse into why a criminal might be drawn back to the scene of the crime in his very effort to escape detection. The motivation may not be irresistible fascination or quenchless conscience at all, but a quest for reassurance — even a declaration of innocence. I wanted to prove that I had nothing to fear from that fatal quarter in the least, I could whistle past it any time. I was secure from exposure by the one witness to whose citywide nattering I might be vulnerable.

"What?"

"Mrs. Clicko. She interests me. Kicking you out. Who the devil does she think she is?" I sat upright in my chair, having slid down in it for the pedal work. "I suppose you've got to make allowances for her. I hear she's not widowed at all, but her husband ran away. Where is he now? Chicago? Omaha? Working in the stockyards? Are there stockyards there? Not in Chicago anymore, to the best of my knowledge. Yet there she is in church every Sunday morning, with an Easter bonnet made out of prune juice and sauerbraten. Yet she tries to be with it, poor thing. Latest expressions as well as clichés, which she garbles no end. She once made a reference to when she was 'just a mote in my father's eye.' Fact. Don't you just love that? 'A mote in my father's eye.' "

"What in the world is the matter with you, Tony?" said Dearest. "Matt, I don't think you should give him even a half glass of wine. The European tradition about drinking being a family thing is all very well . . ."

"Oh, he's just excited, having his teacher and all."

Miss Doubloon made another frequentative-of-cluck noise in her throat, a little constrainedly, and after a corrective cough said, "He's right about Mrs. Clicko and her expressions. She prides herself on learning a new word

96

every day, or is it week? I guess week. Her latest is 'abated.'
'They're all waiting with abated breath to learn who the
father is,' says she. Well, they'll not find out from me. It's
our secret, that I swear."

"Maaaaw," I bleated, like a stricken sheep. I was out of
this, clean out of it, going crazy, thank God.

"Mainly for Tony's sake, of course. None of this must
come nigh him, ever. You must know how sorry I am, and
what I wouldn't give to expunge it all from our past. It's
my fault. I take complete blame. What's done can't be
undone, but when I leave town, with my scarlet letter,
come June, you'll never see or hear from me again. How,
you ask, aghast, can such a thing happen? There is no how,
or why. It just does. Two people . . . touch . . . sparks . . ."

Aghast was good. The skies over Ulalume were suitably
ashen and sober that day, if memory serves, but not so
ashen and sober as my parents' faces. They sat pale and
open-mouthed for several seconds, staring ahead. Then,
simultaneously pointing at me, they simultaneously gasped,
"*Tony?*" They seemed both to ejaculate and swallow the
word. Then Miss Doubloon's face took on the same expression as theirs, as the corollary truth dawned on *her*.

"My God, you didn't know that. . . . But you said Tony
had told you 'everything.' I naturally thought it meant
exactly that. That — oh, my God!"

"Maybe the stockyards are in Kansas City," I jabbered,
I hardly know why even now. Maybe to imply that the
words that had passed since my interjections about Mrs.
Clicko's husband had not actually been spoken, and we
had not been catapulted into this little hellbrew, but were
still on safe ground, chatting of this and that. The look on
my mother's face belied that as she rose and staggered into

97

the parlor, where she sank onto the sofa and began beating her head on the arm, at least the upholstered part and not the wooden frame. My father got up and went over to her. Miss Doubloon sat like a ghost, her arms hanging at her sides.

"I had no idea . . ." she whispered hollowly. "I thought..."

"You had no idea." I fished about in my growing repertory of cynical truisms, coming up only with "No good deed in this world goes unpunished."

I, too, left the table and went into the parlor, where I stood beside the sofa on which my father was now seated next to my mother with an arm around her shoulder. I set a hand on it also, so that for a moment we looked like a family having a group portrait taken. I could glimpse my face in a wall glass, and saw that it was unanimous: we all looked like wet putty.

There is always something spectral about people with whom we share a shock. They become imbued with the unfamiliarity of the occasion itself. A fantasy is created. Everybody here was weird. I didn't recognize any of them, or the rooms in which they had turned strangers. Miss Doubloon, like a dead weight somehow pulling itself to its feet, rose at length and started up the stairs to the spare room, to fetch luggage that hadn't even yet been opened.

After several minutes of what I remember as a volcanic eruption of silence, my father got up and poured himself a stiff whiskey. He drank it off and set the glass down. He stood a moment in the middle of the parlor, flapping his arms, then again, looking like a goose that had forgotten how to fly, and could not therefore join his fellows in the soft South.

"Well, it fits," he said, at last. "It figures. All of it. His homework is neglected, his marks slide, he falls back a grade. Maybe two. Now he gets his eighth-grade teacher knocked up." He sighed voluminously. "Well, so be it, I guess. Once an underachiever, always an underachiever."

8

*T*HE worst part of any community is likely to be the better element, which, of course, was all there *was* to the Boston Hawthorne was writing about. Ours was nearly a match for it in its attitude toward Miss Doubloon, whom none of the other two or three boardinghouses would take in, and who returned to the motel for the remainder of the term. After getting over the initial jar, my parents tried to persuade her to come back to our place, and that being gratefully declined, successfully pressed on her the difference between the motel rate and what she'd been paying Mrs. Clicko. It wasn't much, but we were a family of honor. Mrs. Clicko's continuingly adamant attitude was tempered by the assurance that Miss Doubloon was ever in her prayers, just as, rice pudding being not dreadful enough in itself, we put raisins in it. There were raisins in Mrs. Clicko's disapproval of me too, or perhaps I should say a dollop of skim milk poured on the whole: the confirmation that her lips were sealed as to me, proof of my complicity not being positive.

But I was to be squarely enough identified with the

Reverend Mr. Dimmesdale, unsuspected father of the child born of an adulterous hour, who must go about among the goodfolk of Boston with his terrible secret festering in his heart, the more so as Miss Doubloon now kept referring to herself with a sardonic laugh as Hester Prynne. There should be a scaffold in the town square for me to mount, one midnight when slumber eluded me, whither conscience would irresistibly draw me, where I would stand alone, to strike a tableau of shame my soul must needs in anguish require. "Hither," I found, rereading the scene, "likewise would come the elders and deacons of Mr. Dimmesdale's church, and the young virgins who so idolized their minister, and had made a shrine for him in their white bosoms, which now, by the by, in their hurry and confusion they would scantly have given themselves time to cover with their kerchiefs. All people, in a word, would come stumbling over their thresholds, and turning up their amazed and horror-stricken visages around the scaffold. Whom would they discern there, with the red eastern light upon his brow? Whom but the Reverend Arthur Dimmesdale, half frozen to death, overwhelmed with shame, and standing where Hester Prynne had stood!"

Or Biff Thrasher. Or his father, who seemed now to undergo a revival of his solicitude for Miss Doubloon, even to be secretly enjoying the suspicions he roused by looking in on her at the motel, sometimes walking her there after school. An alternative explanation would be a deliberate campaign to deflect any possible suspicions cast on his son. Maybe it was a combination of both, the latter affording a sly, playfully perverse, yet inwardly lubricious realization of the former. Who can say? Who of us so complexly entangled in our common human blah blah

blah can plumb the innermost recesses of another's and so forth and so on. Mixed up in all this may have been the decision that he and Mother would divorce, she ultimately to marry the Curator. That left him free to play whatever quixotic little game he was up to.

What next? Having long ago given up tutoring me, Miss Doubloon now turned over the question of whether I would graduate to the principal, Mr. Plowditch. He called me into his office one afternoon after school. He sat with an essay of mine in his lap, recently written for an English assignment.

"I see you're quite a philosopher," he said.

"I've been moving toward a Manichaean dualism."

"That why you've been falling behind in your grades again?" He lowered his glasses from his forehead and began to read from the theme. " 'And so we learn at last the hard truth that comes to all men alike, regardless of race, creed, or collar-size. That there is no bluebird of happiness, only the robin of resigned acceptance of things as they are. The plain everyday starling of common, un-deluded reality.' " Plowditch raised his head from the paper and fixed me over the tops of his specs. "And then what next, Thrasher? The grackle of total disillusionment? That where we wind up if we have any brains?"

"Maybe."

"Do you know what this leads to?" He tapped the essay with a finger. "Do you know what this pessimistic in-tellectual outlook opens the door to?"

"What?"

"Existentialism. It's in the wind. Existential godless despair."

"As Eliot put it, and he a Christian, 'End of the end-less journey to no end.' I see what you mean."

"You're well on the road to that, Thrasher." He gave a nod, as if to say "Note that," at the same time making a taut pleat of his mouth. A warning expression. "Well down that road."

"Oh, I don't know. I may grope my way toward a kind of pragmatic meliorism. That's not so bad."

"Well on the way," Plowditch continued, ignoring me. "It's in the air, this new existentialism, infecting intellectuals everywhere." It must be remembered that this was on the hinge of the sixties, before the term had become quite the essentially bland everyday catchall it is now, and with Plowditch's thinking in arrears even of that. He had probably just read something about existentialism in a magazine. "I wouldn't want one of our pupils in the forefront of the movement, opening the floodgates to fashionable pessimism."

"No, sir."

He set the essay on his desk and the glasses on top of that.

"This is well worded and all, but your work in general is lopsided. Fine here, spotty there. You give us philosophy galore, but you don't know the chief products of anything. First it's Venezuela, now Nicaragua. Have you got something against chief products?"

"Not necessarily. I think chief products are important."

"A thing about them? And principal exports and the like?"

"Not to my knowledge. I guess hemp and chicle aren't my bag. I'll admit lately I've been goofing off. Eating lotus."

"You certainly look as though you could do with a square meal. Are you worried about something?"

"I could be."

"What? I know you have family problems, things up for grabs there — but that's not my business. Anything else bugging you, that keeps you from living up to potential?"

"What difference does it make? We all have things disturbing us. Miss Doubloon."

"Ah, well, we all feel for her. She's not the first young lady got herself into a scrape and won't be the last. She'll have to work that out for herself."

"She gave me an apple once." As I reported a simple, factual schoolroom occurrence, it suddenly struck me as having symbolic implications. The mythological angle on which I had accidentally hit seemed to have surfaced from some layer of awareness in which it had remained buried. Plowditch could not of course have had any intimation of that.

He smiled, even laughed gently. "She gave you an apple, out of her lunch. That's cute. The teacher reversing it." Then he sighed, sober again. "Because she likes you is why she's passing this graduation problem on to me. She knows I'm neutral, but at the same time hopes I'll give you a more favorable decision than she conscientiously can. My hunch is she doesn't feel she can graduate you because of your erratic performance, worry or no worry. And you can't honestly make me buy that your studies are suffering because of *her*. I can't graduate you on that tale of woe."

"Why not?" Here I laughed myself. "Aren't you my pal? Think of your principal as your pal — that's the rule she herself taught us for remembering the two spellings. The p-a-l one from the l-e one, as in rule."

"You expect me to graduate you on the strength of something like that? I can't. So there."

"You stuck your tongue out at me."

"I did no such thing. I was wetting my lips, and accidentally may have made a grimace, or moue."

"How would you like a thing like that to get around? A principal sticks his tongue out at a student."

"It would be my word against yours."

"People are always ready to believe the worst, especially in a pious community like this."

"You *are* a cynic. Far down that road, Thrasher." His mood softened, and he looked at the essay again, drumming it with his fingers. "Maybe we can compromise. Term has nearly a month to go. So you can buckle down, do well on your finals, and we can maybe squeak you through. This lotus you say you've been eating. Is that another one of these health foods we keep hearing about lately? My wife is into all that big. Spends half my income at that new organic market. Wish I owned the darned place. If it isn't bean sprouts it's blackstrap molasses and whole-wheat flour that the worms in it show it's alive. Is —"

His phone rang just then, sparing me the necessity of continuing that line of conversation. By the time he finished the call he had forgotten its thread. For a moment, he frowned into his interlaced fingers, as though debating with himself whether he should broach a subject on his mind.

At last he said, "I want you to give Miss Doubloon all the cooperation you can. Make it as easy for her as possible, do your level best for her. Because some of us are afraid she may be heading for a nervous —" Here he broke off, the very sound of his words indicating that he had gone too far. "Well, that's none of your concern. But get in there and pitch. I have a copy of your report card here, and the good marks show there's damn well no excuse for the bad ones. I'm not one of those who think grades are *everything*. Lots of other factors enter into a person's growth. Yes, and into his education. Grades aren't everything."

"The tigers of wrath are greater than the horses of instruction."

"Who said that?"

"William Blake, one of the chief products of Great Britain."

We parted on that note. I thanked Mr. Plowditch for his time and concern, promising both that I would finish the semester with a bang and, more ultimately, not in years to come betray his kindness and the school's good faith by helping open the sluice gates to existential nihilism.

Graduation exercises were held not in the elementary school itself but in the high school to which the eighth-grade students, happily including me by the skin of my teeth, were now to ascend. So here were the goodfolk of the town pouring into the same auditorium that had been the scene of my father's and Mallard's mutual triumph, where they had put one another away in fifteen rounds. It was indistinguishable from a thousand other commencements. The mayor delivered an address reaffirming values and reordering options. A girl named Clara gave the valedictory in a dress infested with bows, and Spuds Wentworth's brother, Jim, read a class prophecy in which a straight-back dining chair falling out of the sky betokened my future as a tycoon high in the international air freight game. Of more pith and moment was my encountering Miss Doubloon the next day as she came out of Felton's dry goods store.

"I was just getting some sewing materials," she said, opening a bag to offer a glimpse of some bright red fabrics and threads. She quickly closed it, and with a taut smile tucked the package into the large shoulder bag she always carried. "No more pencils, no more books for teacher either. I'm leaving for Kalamazoo and home in a few days."

"Look, thanks for getting me graduated. From the bottom of my heart. How are you?"

"Fine. Had a slight scare last week. I thought I might be losing the child, but everything seems O.K. now."

"You promised you'd keep in touch, if there was anything we could do. I could even marry you after July twelfth, when I'll be sixteen. Of course I'll need a note from my parents. Some states let you do that, until you're eighteen. Just to make it, you know, legitimate. We could get a divorce later. We've both got our lives ahead of us."

"You're sweet, but I'll be all right. I'm going to quit teaching and go into business with my grandfather. He's a man of some means."

"What kind of business?"

"I have an idea. Well, so long. Get yourself a nice girl, you hear?"

Whenever bicycling past the motel where she stayed, I naturally glanced instinctively in its direction. I did so the next day, and glimpsed a sight that made me wheel abruptly around and go back.

A cluster of fifteen or twenty people had gathered on

the parking lot and were gazing up at a figure standing on the deck running along the second of two stories of rooms. It was Miss Doubloon, dressed in a beige suit under the coat of which was a collarless shirt slightly lighter in color, decorated, if I shouldn't say emblazoned, with what from a distance I took to be some sort of heraldic emblem. A chill went up my spine when on closer sight I realized it was a scarlet letter A, sewn, or at least pinned, to the front of the shirt. She stood quite erect, statuesque even, shoulders back and chin up, arms spread with her hands resting on the iron rail running round the deck, gazing outward into the blue. I had scarcely taken note of this crazy tableau, and of the gawking collection of locals and tourists below, when I noticed something I had missed before, and that really set my hair on end.

The scarlet letter wasn't the whole of the insignia. Affixed to it on the left, on the onlookers' right, was a plus sign. A+. That was the sardonic joke with which she would leave town, hurling back censure with a saucy quip proclaiming the girl to be found satisfactory as an erotic partner, thank you. Or, in the flat-out parlance of the day, good in bed. What now further froze my blood was a sudden recollection that made me realize the symbol was, in fact, quoting me. It was I who had given her the "grade," in a talk following our dalliance in her little boardinghouse nest.

One of the onlookers put into his mouth a cigar he had been holding and clapped, beginning a round of applause accompanied by a few laughs and cheers as the crowd, some of them at least, began to dig the gag. A few faces remained frozen, mostly women's, but Miss Doubloon's broke into its radiant smile as she removed her hands from the rail and waved at the crowd from her mock scaffold.

A car with a Kansas license plate drew into a nearby parking slot and a middle-aged couple climbed out and strolled over. They took the scene in curiously a moment, then the husband asked me: "What's this all about?"

"Have you ever read *The Scarlet Letter*?" I said.

He shrugged. He didn't know. The wife said she'd heard of it, and seemed to know vaguely what it was all about.

"All right," I said. "The woman up there is standing surrogate for the heroine, avenger for all the Hesters who have suffered ignominy at the hands of a Puritan world, those who have loved not wisely but too well. She is sounding the tocsin peal announcing the sexual revolution that will liberate not only her own sex, but everyone as well, from cramping repressions."

"I'm all for that," the man said. "I'll buy it."

"Well, I don't know . . . ," the wife said dubiously. "I'd have to know more about it."

Had Miss Doubloon seen me? I wasn't sure, there at the far edge of the crowd, and I didn't want to find out just then. I mounted my bike again and pedalled off, at top speed yet trying to avoid the sense of flight, wondering what I had witnessed.

Had she finally cracked up, or pulled herself together? Was this rather elaborate jape a healthy thumbing of the nose, or a buckling under the strain? Had she struck a blow, or been struck by one? Other questions pressed themselves urgently forward. How responsible was I, even as a minor not to be "held" responsible? Would I pursue this misadventure down every twisting road to its end?

Or might it pursue me to mine? How much of an equity had I in this muddle, and what was the "right" thing to do? Nobility is a great inconvenience, as you may know yourself if you've ever tried it.

"It's a watershed," my father said when I reported what I'd seen. "A watershed in contemporary morals. She's broken American literature in two."

Watershed or not, and whatever might be said of Miss Doubloon as a pioneer in the moral sphere, there was no doubt of her innovation in another. Because without knowing it, and whatever had or had not been done to old Hawthorne, I had been in on the birth of the twentieth-century T-shirt.

2

One Flesh

9

"*T*IPSY from salvation's bottle."

"Howling loudest who have drunk the least."

"God-intoxicated."

This was my father and me chatting about the Curator, and in doing so quoting, respectively, Dylan Thomas, Edwin Arlington Robinson, and I don't know. The Robinson was a shade off. It's "crying wildest" rather than "howling loudest."

There were certainly no half measures in Doc Mallard's conversion. He could be heard on street corners giving testimonials for Jesus, seen handing out evangelical leaflets, and exhorting everyone he knew to come to local revival meetings — at one of which he married my mother. Any prejudice against marrying a divorced woman dissolved in the Christian fellowship that would seal their joint assurance of heaven. One should not be too quick to condemn, much less deride, about-face fervors of this kind, which my father, not unkindly in his turn, had characterized with the Dylan Thomas quote, unknown to me but augmented with my allusion to Robinson. No, it's a hard world, and what people will believe is a measure of what they have to endure. And certainly impressive precedents for conversion abound (Malcolm Muggeridge is only one example in our time). I didn't take exception to Doc Mallard's particular obsession with the doctrine of the Last Days, or eschatology as it's called, currently very large, with the redeemed all but scanning the clouds in hopes and fears of apocalyptic descents. I was a little surprised though when, after looking at me for some time with a piercing stare, he said: "I think you're the antichrist."

"You're not just saying that?"

He set aside the Bible in which he had been perusing the book of Revelation while my mother was off in the kitchen brewing us all some tea. They lived together in the snug little cottage a wing of which he used for his dermatology practice.

"Your mother's told me about how even as a baby you'd pitch food and other assorted stuff at the sacred pictures and pious wall mottoes. Had you been Catholics you'd no doubt have desecrated icons likewise. Your mother had to move your high chair back to keep holy things out of range. When you were old enough to go to Sunday school you treated the Golden Texts you got for memorizing Bible verses the same way — chucking them flippantly into a hat as though they were playing cards. You 'baptized' the girl next door's little dolly by sinking it in a bathtub full of water, and there are only the sketchiest rumors of what you tried to do with *her* in there — thank God. As a growing boy, you were up to all kinds of mischief. You wedged cucumbers and yams into the exhaust pipes of people's cars, including Mrs. Clicko's poor old

Chevrolet. Your crowning iniquity to date: ruining your eighth-grade teacher at the age of fourteen."

"I was fifteen."

"A distinction hardly weighing heavily in the case of the antichrist. For that is the role for which you were grooming yourself all along, or maybe I should say being groomed. By whom, we don't know. Beelzebub. Lucifer. It makes no difference. People may not have been so far off the mark in hysterically thinking the devil had taken control of their cars when the clogged exhausts all but asphyxiated them. Mrs. Clicko was one."

"Have you heard the one about the car that was repossessed after they exorcised it?"

Pacing the floor, the Curator threw up his hands. "You see? Nothing sacred. How did you 'molest' that girl next door's little dolly? There were also reports of that."

"I have no idea what you're talking about," I answered truthfully, at the same time protesting only mildly, being inwardly curious about just how far this nonsense might go. I even encouraged it, which I suppose was perverse in itself. "Give a dog a bad name."

"My words fall on deaf ears, I see, but I'll finish as fast as I can because I don't want your poor dear mother to hear any of this. I haven't told her my suspicions. But the links in the chain are easily enough recognized now that they're all but forged, and the total corruption of the world festers and swells toward the Second Coming."

He paused a moment, thoughtfully pulling on his lower lip as he gazed at the floor. He seemed to me with each passing day a shade less sane, while at the same time progressively more confidently getting his act together, at least from his point of view. As much could not be said for me, whose affairs appeared to be hopelessly at sixes and sevens. My life seemed like a phonograph record with the needle stuck at a particularly cacophonical passage. I found I was furtively scratching myself again, thinking that if your new stepfather was a dermatologist who caused you skin rashes, it was time to light out. The Curator resumed both his biographical sketch of me and his travels about the room.

"Having turned an innocent and hard-working and no doubt up to now God-fearing teacher into the Great Whore of Babylon, you compound the offense by profaning a classic, inverting its moral with a joke. Because we have all the facts now and, as family, I'm in on them. You realize that. Your father, a decent man, made another trip to Kalamazoo to see how Miss Doubloon was doing, and again offering her financial aid — which she scarcely needs now, with the blessing Mammon has given her T-shirt business! She told him the A-Plus gag really originated with you. The 'grade' you gave her. An 'our' joke, like an 'our' song."

"I understand."

"Hester Prynne good in bed. Oh, my God. To what depths can we sink? Is there no shame?"

"I guess not," I said, beginning now to suspect there might be something to this antichrist pitch of his.

"At first she went into manufacturing the T-shirts just to support herself and the child, but it's boomed not only as a business but as a sign of the times — my God, if there don't go a couple of girls now." He pointed out the window through which he had glanced and there, sure enough, were a pair of teenagers walking along the sidewalk, their bosoms bobbing merrily under the now popular scarlet insignia.

"Of course I'm not opposed to the T-shirt craze as such, but the whole sex explosion it so defiantly and at the same time flippantly advertises," he continued after they had jiggled from view. "There's nothing wrong with a little humor, even suggestiveness. I'm not opposed to that. But the rampant permissiveness. Everybody rolling around in the sack, one-night stands, short-order nookie and what not. Girls hardly out of school emblazoning on their bodies that they're a good lay." He stopped in the center of the room and shook his finger at me. "You, sir, are the fountainhead of this abomination. From your sin and inspiration has issued this ever-ramifying blasphemy, like the ever-widening ripples from a stone cast into the water. With poor Maggie Doubloon as your instrument, just as you are, as I think and fear, Satan's, the curse unleashed is nationwide. Worldwide. And the stage is being set for the end of the world. I've been studying Revelation, and all signs point to it. Armageddon is due. The trumpet—ah, Jessie, tea and those beautiful cupcakes of yours."

I'm sitting in a park in Kalamazoo, thinking back on that scene. It's two months after the tea party in question, which in turn was two years after the summer Maggie Doubloon left Ulalume. I'm grinding my uneventful way through high school. My father has taught comparative religion at his alma mater in Iowa, but with no prospect of tenure has moved to New York and is getting rich doing television voice-overs, while threatening to do a little writing. Miss Doubloon is supposedly getting steadily richer on the T-shirt business for which the capital was furnished by her grandfather, with whom she lives. I don't know his name, and can't find her in the phone book. It yields no Doubloons. I have come here on spec, with a gnawing sense of responsibility as well as a deepening desire to see the child, a boy on whom she's steadfastly refused to let me set eyes, putting my father under orders not to give me her address or phone number, home or business. I'm glad she's prosperous, but T-shirts in general might well be considered a curse unleashed on the world, no quibbling with the Curator about that. He's probably also right about my desecrating the classics. I suppose it's in me. I'm profaning one right now, scribbling in a spiral notebook while aware of a cop watching me near the bench on which I'm sitting. At last he comes over, propelled by curiosity.

"You a poet or something?"

"How did you guess?"

"Way you gnaw your pencil and look off into space, like groping for a rhyme."

"A master of divination."

"What?"

"Nuttin'."

"My wife writes poetry. Goes to a writing class. I see what you wrote?"

"Sure."

I turned the notebook around so he could read it:

Leave us go then, me and you,
When the evening is dropped like an old shoe,
The first of what must inevitably be two.

He relinquished the end of the notebook he had been holding, nodding approval as I took it back.

"At least you can understand it. What would be the second? The second of the two shoes that will be dropped."

"Night."

"Ah, yes. First evening, and then night. It figures. You can understand it."

"At first I had 'When the evening is spread out against the sky, like a patient etherized upon a table.' "

"Oh, Christ. I'm glad you fixed that. At least you can understand it now. What's your name?"

"Prufrock."

"What kind o' Prufrock?"

"J. Alfred."

"Oh, part your name on the side. One of those. Like F. Scott Fitzgerald."

"And J. Walter Thompson."

I was glad some roughhousing youngsters, squirting water at each other from a public fountain by wedging their fingers into the spout, drew him away before our casual acquaintance could ripen into a lasting friendship.

Ambling through the park toward town, I mused on Eliot and his view that the rough beast slouching towards Bethlehem in Yeats's "The Second Coming" was simply the antichrist predicted in the New Testament, but decided that the poem was not all that amenable to interpretation all that simple, even given Yeats's theory that the human trend reverses itself in two-thousand-year cycles, making us due for an about-face from Christianity so called, whether amusedly or otherwise. Yeats's choice of Bethlehem as the site of the hideous new Incarnation was of course a pat symbolism, a handy use of poetic license. The polarized Nativity could occur anywhere. New Delhi, Paris, New York — or Kalamazoo. Or my stepfather might have been right in his belief that that dark mystery had already occurred, in Ulalume. He was absurd, but then who isn't. In any case, I improved the time by practicing my "slouch," as I had once my "trudge" as a forlorn lad on Christmas Eve. Ducking my head forward from the neck, I kind of shuffle-waddled along the path with outwardly splayed feet, duck feet, kicking up a thin spray of gravel with the soles of my shoes. The gait certainly needed work, considering its resemblance to that of Stepin Fetchit, the movie archetype now disapproved by liberal hearts. Grooming myself for the antichrist was suddenly shot out of my head by another project.

On a park bench I was passing sat a girl wearing one of my T-shirts — one, that is, of my Luciferian inspiration. I had decided on the rebel archangel as my patron because of still another favorite poem, Meredith's "Lucifer in Starlight." Among my fancies had been the notion that the galaxies did not swirl separately in the stinking void, but that they often collided, intermingling their awful gases and producing nightmarish new combinations of nebulae. Scientific theory has since caught up with my phantasmagoria, all but corroborating it. No matter. Lucifer or not, at our back is always "the army of unalterable law." These ruminations were dispersed because the girl in the T-shirt so illustrative of the amorality I had unloosed on the world had given me a plan for possibly discovering the name of the manufacturer, and thus, through it, Miss Doubloon's whereabouts.

Straightening out of my Bethlehem-bound slouch, I walked over and sat down next to her. I spread the arm away from her along the back of a bench otherwise unoccupied. I gazed idly about, humming to myself. I drew out the notebook and pencil I had pocketed, made a jotting or two, and stowed them away again. The girl, a blonde with a firm jawline, was bent over throwing fragments of her bag lunch to some pigeons — bits of bread crumbs, fragments of sausage piping, and the like — and out of the tail of my eye I saw that the T-shirt had crept up her back, leaving an area of white flesh exposed between it and her slacks. Most important, a label tag curled upward out of the hem of the shirt. Just laundering instructions? Or might it have the name of the manufacturer?

"Nice day, isn't it, Miss?" I said.

She darted me an upward look without materially altering her position, and resumed the Saint Francis of Assisi bit.

"Might I ask where you bought that shirt?"

She sighed, again still doubled over. "Can't you think of a better opening than that? 'Haven't we met before?' has even got that beat."

"No, really, it's not that kind of gambit at all. I'm particularly interested in this tag here. I'd like to locate the name of the factory that turns them out, and so if you'll just — if I might just —" I bent to lift it more clearly into view, causing my fingers to graze the skin of her waist just ever so. She straightened like a shot.

"Look, creep, if you don't get lost, and fast, I'd just as soon call that cop."

It was the one with whom I'd had the recent chat about poesy, again edging watchfully closer, this time twiddling his stick on its thong. I popped to my feet and hurried out of the park as fast as I could without giving the appearance of a degenerate in flight.

I returned to the problem of locating Miss Doubloon,

whom a descent on Kalamazoo seemed to be making scarcely less elusive. Her college could supply no leads. The teacher who'd been her roommate was off on vacation. What to do next?

I wandered into a big department store, hoping to find the shirts on sale, but was told "we don't handle that type of garment." That was in a Women's Sportswear section on the second floor. I was riding a down escalator when I was startled by the sight of Miss Doubloon coming up on a moving stairway next to it. Her face was in profile as she turned to speak to a woman on the step below her, so she didn't see me. I whirled around and began to run up the stairs away from her as fast as I could, forcing my way as best I could past other passengers. I squeezed by an old lady in a tartan cap who gasped out an explosive "Whell!" as I jammed her against the rail. Then a really fat man totally blocked my passage, so that I was borne back downward again, losing all the ground I had gained. Later in tranquil recollection I was to think of salmon battling their way upstream to spawn in native waters, but now the simple instinctive need to get away from Miss Doubloon consumed me utterly. Gripping the fat man's shoulders in both hands, I swivelled him forcibly around sideways and was able to just wedge past him that way, for he was broader than he was thick. A step or two later I knocked a parcel out of another old lady's hands, and after bending apologetically to retrieve it, resumed my flight. Then another sizable party blocked my way long enough to lose me further ground. So that it was like running as fast as you can to stay in the same place. The flight reflex had been quick, but, of course, not good, thinking. Or thinking at all. Just automatic impulse. A much better strategy for avoidance would have been simply to continue on down with my face averted, perhaps a hand to it, pretending to be scratching my nose or something, until I was safely past the Doubloon. Now, my obstructed bolt together with her own unimpeded progress soon had us abreast of one another, to say nothing of the attention I was attracting with this broken field running and the to-do it provoked among the other passengers, some of whom I was knocking the wind out of. Happily, she remained turned away from me in continued conversation with the woman below her, so that, while we reached the upper floor level simultaneously, she still hadn't seen me — or at least recognized me — and I was able to duck behind a display dummy and remain in hiding till she was out of sight. Then I resumed my descent, thinking to myself, "Whew! That was a close call."

I gained the main floor breathless, and naturally somewhat baffled by my behavior. I drifted aimlessly among the counters trying to sort out my sensations, and thus arrive at some comprehension of my clearly conflicting motivations. Obviously, I was more scared of involvement with the Doubloon than driven by conscience to seek it. Right? I wanted to be shut of her more than do the right thing. O.K.? Id versus ego would not be too pat or too glib a simplification, don't you agree? The latter could still carry the day, and humanly speaking, should, even allowing for her insistence that I and/or my family owed her nothing and we could forget about her. She could hack it alone.

Of course she was still in the building, and would have to come down again to get out of it, so flight would now be a cinch — if I wanted to be that craven, or that much of a "cad." I mulled all these intertangled elements over as I circled about the main floor, smoking a couple of cigarettes and watching the escalator, now from a distance, now close by. I remembered Miss Doubloon's once explaining to the class the distinction between continual and continuous. Continual might imply uninterrupted action but was now mainly restricted to what was intermittent or repeated. Continuous was favored for action without interruption in time (or unbroken in space, as in a continuous terrain). I liked to think my watch of the down escalator was continuous, always allowing for interference from the ever-moving crowds or having to put a cigarette out in a sandpot when ordered to do so by a security guard pointing to a No Smoking sign. I was behaving decently, a decent chap. A bit of all right. Then my heart bounced. I had caught sight of another set of escalators at the other end of the floor. That the view from here was of their undersides had no doubt caused their previous escape of my notice. Well. Now I had to keep an eye on two sets of moving stairs, necessitating a patrol of the entire floor, like a sentinel marching back and forth between terminal points. That naturally reduced my vigil from continuous to continual. Nothing to do about that, nothing to be ashamed of if my quarry escaped. Then on one such march I spotted another complication. A bank of elevators, naturally offering a third means of descent from the upper floors. My emotions can be imagined when I realized the near-hopelessness of this lookout. I shrugged. "Might as well call it quits," I said to myself. "You've done all you can. Go back home. You've taken every measure a decently intentioned chap could." Just then I caught a glimpse of Miss Doubloon approaching from the elevators. Or was it another woman wearing a yellow suit similar to hers? Who could say for sure from this distance? I turned and hurried toward the revolving doors and out into the street, coattails flying.

Retracing my way to the park, I thought I heard persistent footsteps behind me. A woman's heels clicking on the pavement at the same pace as my own. I turned into the park. They did.

"Anthony."

"This guy annoying you, Miss?" It was the same cop. "Look here, Prufrock, I've had just about —"

"Can't talk now," I said to him out of the side of my mouth, hustling on.

She caught up with me, and drew me onto a vacant bench. She set down a couple of packages she was carrying.

"Now what the hell is this all about?"

"I had to see you," I said.

She looked good and well both — another remembered distinction — quite attractive in the yellow linen suit, with the collar of a green blouse spread out over the shoulders. She had changed her auburn hair. Instead of wearing it in a billowing puff over her brow, she had gathered it into a ponytail, secured with a length of yellow yarn. Motherhood became her, as could be told from a flush to her cheeks not entirely accounted for by the pursuit. Of course she had gained weight.

"Thank God I found you," I panted. I gave a brief rundown of my attempts to locate her, emphasizing anew my determination to do the right thing. "I was about to get on the bus and go back home."

"You do just that. I'm getting along just jake, as Grandfather says in his true Midwestern style. He's put up the capital for the T-shirt line, which is also jake. And Ahab is fine."

"Who's that?"

"Your son. I've named him after my grandfather, whom I love. You know my mother is dead and my father is God knows where. He's practically raised me. Grandpa."

"I keep feeling the child should be legitimized, as well as have the benefit of a sound, normal father. I can marry you without a note from home when I turn eighteen, which shouldn't be too long. Later a divorce could be easily enough arranged."

"That's all going by the board, mark my words. I mean that there should necessarily be two parents. There's change in the wind. This is only the beginning of women's march toward independence. Call me an emancipated miss mother if you want. As for support, you've already made a great contribution with the gag that gave me the idea for the T-shirt, and T-shirts in general. They're going to usher in the new casual era too, is my hunch. We're raking in pots. Of course the *Scarlet Letter* television series gave us a boost, we sort of bounce off that. In any case I think I'm through with teaching. *That's* learned me a lot! But it's really Tony Thrasher who's delivered the coup de grâce to the Puritan ethic. It lies dead as a doornail at our feet, laughed to smithereens."

I lowered my eyes modestly without openly disclaiming the attribution. I murmured something about having had the benefit of forerunners paving the way, voices crying in the wilderness well in advance of my advent, seminal as that might have been. Hawthorne himself might conceivably be considered one of the long preparatory line preceding me, implicitly criticizing, as he did, the harsh rigidity of the custom he was delineating, at one juncture of the story even pointing out how Hester's very punishment had set her apart, freeing her mind for latitudes of speculation beyond the reach of narrow-minded censors to whom, in fact, the scarlet letter had in an odd reversal become a badge of honor, like the crucifix on a nun's bosom. One must be fair, one must not hog all the credit. Spadework had been done — much, much of it. Hundreds of years of it! And were I the antichrist himself, that too had a tradition. Nero was thought by the early Christians to be the Beast, as he was sometimes called. Then Mohammed. Later the papal supremacy was held by such as Luther to personify the antichrist collectively. So it ran. A bunched field. Now a new nominee tapped for informed conjecture. One from whose lips had not yet been heard, "If drafted I will not run. If elected I will not serve." No, that had not been heard, not by a long chalk! No siree, Bob.

"It's just that I thought I should do *something*. Contribute something," I said. "Be on the scene, part of it, somehow. Maybe get a job here for the summer."

The Doubloon drank me in for some moments, her head characteristically cocked to one side as she regarded me with what I had become accustomed to thinking of as an affectionate exasperation. Or exasperated affection. She drew a long breath, as though collecting a fund of impatience to be discharged in as lengthy a sigh.

"You want to stick around? You want to see Ahab? You want to be on the scene? You want a job? All right, you asked for it. I remember from your themes your typing was always first-rate. My grandfather keeps saying he wants to hire a private secretary. Come on. Let's go. It may not be all beer and skittles. His name is Stubblefield."

Running a step or two to draw abreast of her as she up

and led the way with her purposeful stride, I wanted to tell her, as I had wanted to mounting Mrs. Clicko's stairs behind her on that fateful night, that she had what Heine has called "the requisite plenitude of posterior," but couldn't find the words. I just couldn't find the words.

10

My secretarial duties were not as sedentary or office-bound as I had feared. None of the monotony of "relating to paper" that I remembered as the declared bugbear of our parsonage secretary. The first job to which old Stubblefield set me was spreading around a two-hundred-foot house driveway three or four tons of gravel some "idiot of an imbecile" making the delivery had dumped in a mountain near the front porch, instead of distributing it himself. All he'd have had to do was traverse the length of the driveway in low gear, with the dump truck tilted at a slight angle allowing the gravel to dribble slowly and evenly outward under a tailgate dangling loose from its top hinges. I'd seen it done myself. Five minutes and the thing is done. At the rate I worked in the broiling sun, disseminating the stone with a wheelbarrow and shovel, then smoothing it out with a rake, it would take me more like five days.

A codger of eighty-three, Stubblefield had sunk a good deal of his amassed capital into T-Shirts Unlimited, and with a hit on his hands he enjoyed the paperwork he could do in his den, letting Maggie go to the office downtown, and his private secretary relate to gravel, dirty windows, car washing, and the like. He made *you* live each day as though it was his last. When you greeted him with "Hi, how are you?" his answer was almost invariably "Extant." That was as high as he would put it. Farther than that he wouldn't go. He was on the brink of disappearance. But daily, in a fine leather armchair in his office-den, he would pore happily over the memos and other paper to which I now longed to be soul-crushingly confined. Every once in a while he would poke his head out the window and call out some words of encouragement, or join me in cursing the idiot of an imbecile who made such fine deliveries for others to cope with. He, Stubblefield, had missed him only by minutes. I must not mind too much the bleeding blisters — they would soon be calluses, and I would have the horny hands that went with the beautiful physique I was developing. A slight limp and cutting edge to his soprano voice sometimes gave me the illusion that I was working for Walter Brennan, but it would pass when the sun fogging my vision disappeared behind a welcome cloud.

After a week or so of relating to gravel, the prospect was that I would next relate to roof gutters, which testified to the heap of maintenance required around the old place. Soggy masses of dead leaves must be clawed out of them, fresh basket shields be placed in the downspouts to catch the new ones come fall, and the like. These duties called for a secretary with the agility of a mountain goat, and good Top-Siders to ensure firm traction on slate surfaces with a steep pitch all around. Extant would come bodily out of the house to encourage me in this function, squinting upward with a hand shielding his face against the sun as he shouted heartening sentiments, to say nothing of words of praise. I was a find. A treasure. The dexterity with which I scooped glop out of the gutters and deposited it in buckets to be carried with maximum caution down a ladder for disposal elsewhere was all that could reasonably have been hoped for in a secretary, and that one with no previous experience!

"How much do I pay you?"

"Three fifty an hour."

"Make it four."

Extant professed harassment by the hit he had on his hands, indeed an entire new industry of which this secretary of his was reported to be the fountainhead. Some toils were more onerous than their fruits were felicitous. He would have preferred spending his last days sitting on a park bench smoking and tippling and waiting for Amy Lowell to come back. When he thought of all the yard work still to be done when the house itself was again shipshape, such as the cordwood to be chopped from a fallen oak, the good trees still to be pruned and their wounds dressed with creosote, he wondered why he hadn't hired a secretary sooner. Add to this the gutting by fire of the motel where I was staying, two days after I moved in, and the consequent loss of my personal effects, necessitating my moving in with my employer, and you will have some sense of my summer's idyll. He seemed to have no idea who the father of his great-grandchild was, nor any curiosity about it. Or maybe he didn't want to know. In any case, he showed no disapproval of Miss Doubloon's lifestyle as a "miss mother." Whether in his head he was putting two and two together I never knew. I was just a pupil of his granddaughter's working my way through summer vacation. Since she occupied one of the three bedrooms, the baby's nurse another, there was nothing for me to do for the moment but sack out with Extant. Were these collective circumstances the wages of sin, with time and a half for overtime? Or the first fruits of reform? One never knows, do one.

And now for Ahab.

Ahab seemed suspicious of me from the first. At age two he appeared to have developed in full the gift of skepticism, at least as far as I was concerned. He eyed me dubiously — or so I imagined — whether sucking a bottle of milk or fruit juice, or glancing over his shoulder as he toddled about the floor in search of electric sockets with which to excite alarm. He had a jaundiced eye, however blue, and curls of yellow hair like pine shavings, similar to mine though much lighter in color — the color mine were at that age, I guess. The dubious view of me was most in evidence when he was being fed, bathed, walked, or wheeled around by the nursemaid, a high-school student my own age known as Bubbles Breedlove. Nobody likes to have a dim view taken of him, especially in the presence of a third party stunningly attractive to oneself. She was a buxom girl, with whorls of honey-colored hair to her shoulders, and a mouth like the inside of a jelly doughnut. I don't mean to offer that as a simile, only to report a mental association. No grossness is implied, such as the overapplication of lipstick. Far from it. Only a crimson sumptuosity. We had here a wide, generously molded, rubbery orifice, such as made one think of long, drenching kisses draining the sap from one's bones, hours of slobbering bliss. What a swine one is, one thinks, loftily. And do one's rippling muscles remind her of writhing adders as one toils, shirtless, in the blazing sun? A youth glistening in the morning of his manhood? A mouth like the inside of a jelly doughnut.

"Some job," she said, pausing with her charge in his stroller.

"I'd rather be the cretin who dumped the load here. *He* can keep cool, there in his truck."

She surveyed the scene, resting her weight on one leg, a hand on the stroller, the other on her hip. "As the parts of the driveway you've covered get closer to the pile itself — O.K.? — as that happens, it might pay you not to use the wheelbarrow at all, but just I mean kind of spray the gravel around with the shovel. Like the sower going forth to sow his seed kind of thing?"

"The point is well taken," I said, catching a whiff of some floral scent that made my senses reel. "I may do just that. I think we make a sort of beauty-and-the-beast scene. The toiling Caliban and the pure Lenore."

"Hey, I like the way you talk. Just listen to the way he said that, Ahab. You wouldn't think anybody shoveling gravel would have such a way with words. You can spread the malarkey, but don't let me stop you."

Sucking a bottle, Ahab watched me as we chatted, storing up impressions of a conversation about which he would have something of his own to say as soon as he had himself fully mastered the speech with which such inanities were apparently exchanged. I fairly clung to the handle of the shovel on which I leaned as, catching another whiff of the scent I was in noseshot of, I closed my eyes in a fresh spasm of desire.

"May I ask what that perfume is you're wearing?"

"I'm not wearing anything. Probably the dusting powder I use on Ahab after I bathe him."

Another shabby moment in the mounting toll of one's life, one hardly calculated to lessen the disesteem in which one already held oneself. The negative spell was broken when there was a crunch of tires on one's handiwork and Stubblefield came bowling down the driveway in his old Buick. He climbed out from behind the wheel, clutching a bag of groceries.

"Bought a rib roast for dinner," he said. "It weighs eight pounds and three ounces, just like a newborn baby."

"How are you, Mr. Stubblefield?" Bubbles asked.

"Extant," he said, the usual reply accompanied by the customary shrug.

"Isn't he the all-time blast."

"The butcher said I was lifelike, and the checkout girl said how natural I looked. That gave me rather a turn. How's the Cupid here? How's that for cherubic? Give him a bow and arrow and he's in business. Has he drawn a bead on you two yet? Just look at this creature, Tony. Bubbles, show him why they call you Bubbles."

"Oh, come on, Stubby."

I imagined it well enough for myself. A specialty dance with a large balloon covering her midriff, done at parties when the hour was late, not lewd, but sweetly suggestive.

"It's just her effervescent spirits," I said, to dispel the apparent embarrassment.

Stubblefield shuffled toward the house, trailing praise of her. "You're an unplucked daffodil, my dear," he said, "meaning no offense." And to me: "Take the afternoon off."

At twenty minutes to four, that didn't add up to much largesse, especially considering that I was being paid by the hour, but the thought was welcome. The only drawback being that, before there was any question of my taking a stroll with Bubbles and her charge, as Stubble-field seemingly intended, I would have to shower and change from the hide out. So the best that came of it was to exchange waves with her the length of the drive, as I plucked my blue denim shirt from a bush where I'd hung it. If this was another leitmotif in the making, I wasn't jumping for joy over it.

Stubblefield's show of matchmaking Bubbles and me was a development of which Miss Doubloon could only take the dimmest view. On the surface preserving the fiction of Ahab's anonymous paternity — certainly the implied denial that I had anything to do with it — pre-tending that she "couldn't care less" what shenanigans her ex-pupil conducted during his vacation stay here, she must inwardly bridle at any fancy he conceived for the luscious sitter-in-residence. Not that I was such a goon as to show any. But it must obviously be taken for granted in these close quarters, especially with Stubblefield talk-ing it up, in what one sensed to be an old man's under-standable taste for a little valedictory chaos. Maybe he was playing a sly game here, only pretending to believe Ahab to have been fathered by an ex-lover in whom Miss Doubloon had now lost interest, while secretly suspecting me, and trying to smoke his granddaughter out by needling her emotions to the surface. In any case, while there was nothing more "between" her and me, in keeping with nature's law that nothing is either permanent or pre-dictable, jealousy can find embers in what are thought to be ashes, and I must clearly cool my hots for Kim Breedlove, known as Bubbles.

Now that the Nightie Night had burned down, the nearest motel was five miles away, but walking to and from it might still have beat climbing into bed with

Stubblefield, wearing, into the bargain, one of his extraordinary flannel gowns pending the acquisition of fresh jammies for yourself, there to lie, hands laced under head, while he played Scheherazade until at last he fell asleep. Most of his tales were reminiscences of erotic feats to which my woolgathered ravishment of Bubbles in the boxroom overhead would have run a poor second, and I had the feeling that, over the years, they had gained in translation from fact to fantasy. Yet in all his chronicles I sensed a distinct strain of the misogyny that often accompanies wholesale womanizing, and may even in some measure motivate it. "Safety in numbers" is an insightful old wheeze; but he seemed not to have found much shelter in it. He'd had three wives, sex with the first of whom had been like "chewing on pine cones."

"We went to visit her people in Anaheim, California, on our honeymoon," he related. "On our bridal night we slept in a tent in the back yard. It was like being in that sleeping bag in *For Whom the Bell Tolls*?"

"Did the earth move?" I could only decently inquire, being on cue.

"Oh, yeah. Shortly after midnight there was a quake registering four point five on the Richter scale." He gave me a jocular kick in the shins, a bed version of the nudge in the ribs more popularly associated with pals sharing a laugh. Throughout the tapering sequence of chuckles and cackles that followed, I smiled to myself, there in the dark, not so much at the gag for which I had been set up, probably a creditable enough one in relating a First Night with a pile of pine cones in Anaheim, but in a kind of secret self-satisfaction of my own: a month of this kind of suffering and I would not only have paid my debt to God Almighty but have left over a substantial moral balance to squander in some direction of my own choosing, possibly even that of making Bubbles Breedlove my main squeeze. In Puritan America we sweat so much guilt over sex that our pleasures come prepaid. I could hear the mouse-squeak of her footsteps overhead. And I myself a sterling lad . . .

Stubblefield continued his saga, gradually crowding me toward the edge of the bed with the kicks and pokes that accompanied the zingers and payoffs toward which he systematically built. It was dated stuff, but not the worst of its kind. He was of that vintage of worldlings who called an umbrella a bumbershoot; of whose gaieties midnight sailings comprised no small part; who tipped their hats to ladies travelling alone and asked whether they might be of service. It had been aboard ship that he had met his second wife, while his first sulked in her stateroom below. Once aware of his habit of bulldozing you steadily across the mattress as his narratives unfolded, I tried to get to bed first as often as possible, to guarantee a position next to the wall. Being ultimately wedged against it was hardly a pleasure, but it was preferable to the anxiety of being shoved onto the floor. I had once or twice offered to sleep on a parlor couch, but this so clearly vexed Stubblefield that I knew continuing to insist on it would jeopardize my post as his secretary, and arduous as all this was, it beat returning to what I must now call home before absolutely necessary.

The one other member of the household was an Airedale named Chuck who barked at me perpetually, whether spreading gravel, chopping wood, or engaged in any other of my secretarial chores. We know dogs can smell fear. I shouldn't wonder but that they can also smell Weltschmerz, which was my prevailing mood that summer, indeed those years. Being progressively more saturated in Camus, Beckett, Kafka, and Kierkegaard must have left on me a thickening odor of existential dread that any dog with a sense of smell worthy of his species could pick up — and recognize as so close to angst as made no matter. My misery had its greatest specific density at the dinner table, where sexual frustration over Bubbles mingled most acutely with the sense of imposture inherent in my enjoyment of this family bosom at all. Here the dog growled steadily at the pessimism I spouted as a consequence.

"In the beginning the earth was without form and void. Why didn't they leave well enough alone? It's been all downhill from there."

"Now, Tony," Miss Doubloon scolded. She had come from the office bursting with pleasure over a flood of orders for a new line of shirts. "Don't talk like that. You don't believe such rot, do you, Ahab?"

"Of course not," Bubbles put in. "We don't want the naughty man to talk such pessimism, do we, honey? Such talk is not for him's little ears, is it? Oh, honey, don't do that. Naughty."

My hands under the table gripped my kneecaps, as though they were the lids of jars to be unscrewed, as I watched Ahab squeeze a banana in his fist. Clucking reproachfully, Bubbles rose and went into the kitchen to get a towel from the day cook, Mrs. Bender, who came in to get dinner and wash up. Mrs. Bender put her head in the doorway to ask whether there was too much nutmeg in the stringbeans. "They can boss the taste." We assured her they were fine. The nutmeg wasn't bossing the taste.

After dinner I might take in a picture at the local movie house or shoot a game or two at a nearby pool hall, then it would be home again with the dog barking as I entered, or even snapping at my heels as he sniffed Weltschmerz on my pants cuffs. A race to bed to get the wall position, for a fresh installment of Stubblefield's sexual autobiography. Let's see, is this the third wife we're on? No, we're being filled in with some omitted material on the second. "The countryside there was a series of rolling foothills accented by jagged granite outcroppings, and so was she. Well, sir, this one was a writer, that is, wanted to be, and she asked me for a couple of thousand bucks so she could go to Acapulco and polish up her perceptions . . ."

We are now speaking of a Dorene Bradshaw, whose literary aspirations no amount of returned manuscripts could squelch, nor whose determination to marry any amount of rejection could daunt. She stood six feet two in stocking feet, and weighed two hundred and thirty pounds without makeup. Certain investments having turned putrid, Stubblefield had ruled out a second marriage, at least for the time being, but the Bradshaw was persistent. He called the situation one of sleeping with a woman you might marry, or "renting with an option to buy." After a bath in the market, his fortune was recouped with money sunk into a garment business that flourished like the green bay tree of Scripture, and he did marry her.

"This marriage was worse than Abraham Lincoln's," he said. "Much as she kept talking about losing weight, she kept eating bonbons while she wrote, which she called bawbaw, giving them the French pronunciation. She'd complain of gaining weight and there on the table would be succotash, and you know what that is. Corn and lima beans, which between them have got more starch than your mother's lace curtains. The time inevitably came when, like every wife who ever lived, she was going to starve herself back into her wedding dress. Or in this case suit . . ."

I sensed the story building to its climax by a gradual, preparatory shift in Stubblefield's position on the bed, the almost automatic readying of his hands and feet for the convulsive lunge which something in his nature dictated must accompany the zinger. As a counter-preparation, I hoisted my knees against the wall in order to brace myself for the blow, and held my breath. While not without drawbacks, this at least beat hearing the creak of Bubbles's footsteps overhead *without* ameliorating distraction.

"Finally I came right out with it. I couldn't stand this anymore, says I. And says she, it was just as hard on her, the attritions of marriage and the what-do-you-call-it, the atonality she called it of close harmony and one thing and another, somehow dragging Stravinsky into it and somebody named Villa-Lobos, but she had decided she didn't want children. They might hold a union together but they destroyed your figure. 'Yeah,' I said, 'there is a destiny that ends our shapes,'" and he gave me a shove that unbuckled my knees and sent my head against the wall.

This was only penultimate. A warmup for the real snapper.

"The argument continued with me frankly saying, stating, asseverating, averring, what have you, that I wanted to be single again. And damned if she doesn't come through with an epigram I'm going to have to top if I expect to win this one. Because this is for all the marbles. You understand?"

"I understand."

I settled slowly around onto my back, feeling the supine

position probably more protective all things considered than lying on my side, when the kicker came — kicker in this case having literal connotations. He cleared his throat for the homestretch.

"'A single man is like one of a pair of cymbals,' she says. And quick as a flash, you know what I says?"

"No. What was your comeback?"

"I says, 'Yeah — there's never any clash.'" And my right hip struck the wall with a force that shook my confidence in myself as secretarial timber.

Did I believe his stories? I lent them credence. You will note my choice of words. I only lent, not gave, them credence. I might want it back, the credence, indeed reserved the right to foreclose without notice if any of his rigmaroles revealed the slightest discrepancy or gave the least sign of coming out at the elbows consistency-wise. Oh, exaggeration was to be humanly allowed for. We're all guilty of that, if indeed guilt is the right word for embroideries of which the listener is as much the beneficiary as the teller. Life must be given a shine, gussied up here and there. You've been told how it's been all downhill since the spirit moved on the face of the waters, what a pail of worms we've got on the table after twenty trillion years. Biomathematical product of an equation stretching out across the cosmic blackboard from here to Andromeda, over space we are asked to believe is *bent yet* . . .

Doze. Dream. I am pursued by raconteurs from whose threats of systematically spun beginnings, middles, and ends I flee down a long Utrillo street, within whose narrowing vaginal cleft I vanish at last, swallowed in a half delicious, half nightmarish protoplasmic twitch by which I am again unborn, no more than one of uncountable soundlessly bursting bubbles . . .

The next morning a mirror check reveals a body bruise on one hip, and, in the middle of my forehead, a vague circular blue mark like that left by official government grading stamps on dressed beef. These and the vague memory of a dream of effervescing as one drowned are all that remain of a night as restful as could be expected.

One hated to leave all this, but the summer wound to its appointed close and home one must go, and back to Central High. Thoughts of seeing my stepfather once again brought a revival of my skin rashes, and I wandered into a local drugstore to see if the pharmacist there mightn't have something new to recommend. Shades of Mr. Patterson and the quest for capsules one must be glad had been in vain, now that one had seen Ahab and knew he was in the world and of the world, despite what one knew and would always know to be "the sorry scheme of things entire," never to be remolded nearer to the heart's desire, etc. Miss Doubloon was ecstatic that she had him, and as a great-grandfather Stubblefield couldn't have been more doting. The boy was already snug in the old man's will. . . .

This apothecary's name was Lester Brader, according to a shingle so specifying, and since he too remained on his dais while waiting on me, I had again the sense of addressing a tribunal. If there were such a thing as a square tomato, that's what I would compare his face to, as regards shape and color. The last thing I could imagine coming of my confrontation with it would be the true commencement of my entanglement with Bubbles Breedlove. He continued filling some prescriptions while taking care of me, which required my talking, again, across a counter, an intervening aisle, and the shelf at which he worked, to say nothing of the aforementioned difference in sea level.

"You say you itch," he said, typing something from the standing position for which pharmacists are famous, presumably the label for a bottle.

"That is correct."

"Where?"

"Everywhere."

"What do you mean, everywhere?"

"Kalamazoo, Chicago, the city, the country," I said, avoiding his pitfall with a humorous evasion, for I noted that a lurking female clerk and one customer had been suddenly augmented by the arrival of two more of the latter, all affecting immersion in sun-goggle racks, candy displays, and toiletries while obviously hoping to overhear some unsavory intimacy. Brader tabled for the moment the question of anatomical locale and dwelt on the particular type of pruritus we were up against. He needed much, much more data.

He enacted a series of gestures appropriate to the exploration of variously branching thoroughfares of possibility. First of all, was it a contact dermatitis, and if that, what had caused it. My soap, a lotion of some kind, poison ivy or oak, sumac, "or et cetera." He seemed to display more than any pharmacist I'd known the satisfaction of operating from a dais, which is the simple advantage of all people elevated if only by a few feet. Ministers on their pulpits, judges on their benches, conductors flailing the air on podiums from which they will presently drink their drafts of applause. Desk sergeants, department store demonstrators, song pluggers. Anything from which to hold you at a disadvantage. If there is no platform, the tailgate of a truck will do.

"Is there an infection, and if so, how far has it gone?"

At this a backup of now *six* eavesdroppers really pricked up their ears. With such an area of speculation opened, anything might be hoped for. Possibly even an indiscretion in a Paris brothel. What do you do in a case like this? Hew to standards, or give the people what they want? If so, should it be PG or X-rated? These were adults, maybe deserving a little something to enliven their humdrum lives. The exposure of another's shame would do it.

"There is an infection," I said.

"Blisters?"

"Yes, there are blisters."

"Are they weeping?"

"I believe they are about to."

"The important thing is to keep from scratching, though you probably have, if there's infection. Another question we might ask — is the cause an allergy?"

Here my heart leaped up. "I'm allergic to my dermatologist," I could with almost total validity answer. But the lulu was not to be. The moment passed, unseized, as Brader went on: "Often the causes are psychosomatic. I think they are in the majority of cases. I mean, think of those millions of tiny nerve-ends capable of being inflamed by emotions that are almost never quiet. Are you uptight about something?"

"Aren't we all?"

"That's too general. I mean something specific."

Again, I could honestly have told him I was tense at the prospect of facing a dermatologist who happened to be my stepfather, or vice versa, but I figured that that — however founded in actuality — might be a little baroque for him, not to say our hearers. Who seemed to grow restive at being cheated of a reasonably expected tidbit. "As a kid I was excluded from stuff," I said.

"Again I ask, where is the itch?"

"Everywhere, principally. Just at the moment, it's the backs of my hands. And my ankles, some. It varies. Clears up here, starts up there."

The other customers turned away, no doubt muttering resentfully under their breaths about being built up to such a letdown by an obvious imposter, and as they scattered they brought into view a young woman with a baby in a stroller, browsing at the toothbrush rack.

"Hi, Tony," Bubbles said. "Fancy running into you here."

"Yeah, a block from home. I was just . . . and the druggist here seems to . . . it's really nothing much that . . . well, hello, Ahab. I like your shirt."

"Kinda wow, isn't it." Bubbles was about to amplify that when the druggist came over, holding out a boxed tube of something.

"This works for a lot of people," he said. "It has an anesthetic ingredient in it, as strong as you can get without a prescription. It works especially well in such sensitive areas as —"

"Swell," I said, taking the preparation with an amiable smile precluding any intention to sue him for practicing both dermatology and psychiatry without a license. I paid the clerk, waited for Bubbles to make her purchases, and then we went out together, licking ice cream cones as we strolled the long way home, through the park.

Of course I fancied that we were a family as we sauntered under the rustling maples. Would it not have been less than human not to imagine that I was married to this toothsome lass, and that we were taking our issue out for a promenade in the summer afternoon? Oh, to be sure we might have found we must wed in haste, but that we had loved well but unwisely could only have added charm to our sweet circumstance. The fantasy unfolded with each step. This was but the first of two children we would have, the other a girl, taking even more after her buxom mother. I savored the glances of passing folk, turning to smile their blessing on the scene. Such a personable pair, and so brave to be taking on at such a tender age the responsibilities of familyhood. Would that there were more like them, and less of the feckless libertines of the New Freedom. Liberty made license! Gives you hope for the world after all.

Bubbles said: "My sainted father itched in places you wouldn't believe either. Like — wait for it — like between the toes, of all places. And after a hundred salves like this bird probably sold you, you know what did the trick? All right, give up? Cornstarch. It's a born lubricant, like this dry whatchamacallit. A powder that you squirt on for oil."

"Graphite. But I didn't realize your father was dead, Bubbles. I thought he was alive, living somewhere like Idaho or something."

"Who said he was dead? Of course he's alive, and I adore him."

I was about to point out that people weren't sainted, or so described, until they were gone, but held my tongue. Why mar the beauty of the hour? But my fantasy was sorely strained. I had again about given up on her when again she redeemed herself, this time with a story about some neighbors with a parakeet that got caught in a mousetrap. That was typical of the effect she had on me

— lighting a fire the next minute quenched, and the next rekindled. She had me crazy, oscillating between extremes of impression, now dismayed by her scatty side, now taken by her endearing qualities, though the latter might be regarded by the superficial observer as, more or less, the sum total of her body surface. Ah, welladay. When the lad for longing sighs . . .

We were leaving the park when she suddenly jerked the stroller around and went back into it, obviously to avoid someone she had spotted coming toward us up the street.

"Hermie Balmer," she said, recognizing the need to explain her military-drill behavior. "He just won't get lost. Those phone calls that keep coming for me at the house? Hermie, not taking no for an answer. You at least could do that."

"That I could, that I could," I said, in an Irish brogue I would have been powerless to explain. People never cease to amaze me.

"He's a slurm."

"Why do you say that?" I asked, hoping to learn from her answer what the term meant. It was so hard keeping up with the new slang. Or was I in at the birth of another coinage?

"First off, he has the kind of flesh that when you poke it it stays poked?"

"You've jabbed a forefinger into it on occasion?"

"No, no, it's just a for-instance. The feeling you get about some men, especially when they come complete with freckles and pink hair and white, bllllech, eyelashes? It's just to give you an idea of what you think it would be like if you *did* poke them. You know what I mean. Don't go being a blob on me, Anthony Thrasher."

"That I won't, that I won't." More Irish brogue. Incredible. And was Hermie Balmer getting a load of us from the street, after noticing the about-face?

"Because you're different. You've got style. Ego style. You'd take no for an answer with a pizzazz that would sweep a girl off her feet. You're swave, as my sainted aunt pronounces it, the one I live with. Swave and blaze. You must meet her. Of course you haven't seen and done everything, you're too young, but you have the poise of somebody who's confident he *will*. Browse at the book-stalls along the Seine, go to like Barcelona and Istanbul. So I mean like you're world-weary on *credit*. Using it up in advance."

"The dog can smell Weltschmerz on me."

"Jesus, you've got everything. Look, the collar of my coat is turned up and you're going to straighten it, and while you do, look back and see if he's following us."

"But I don't know him."

"Then see if somebody *is* following us. And I think you'll know him. If you cut his throat, he'll lie there in a pool of ketchup. Slowly, slowly . . ."

I did as bade, giving a quick gander all around, but saw no one behind us except the familiar police officer, now doffing his cap in order to scratch his head at the sight of us, like a cop conveying befuddlement in an old movie. Yes, it's me, officer, a sterling lad after all, with a lovely wife and growing family, taking the afternoon air — not the raunchy poet accused of annoying girls on park benches. No sign of the slurm, though through a gap in the shrubbery I thought I could see an almost indistinguishable youth watching us from the street.

Safe at last from pursuit, Bubbles fished a camera from a bag hanging on a handle of the stroller and began to snap pictures like mad. Of Ahab, then of me holding him with the familiar blend of stunned excitement and addled awe. Don't we all have it in any case as we wrap our arms around this mysterious, inscrutable, come-from-nowhere bundle of wriggling pulp, clutching at our nose or ear, striking us each time anew with the incredible audacity of birth? How much profounder this blank wonder when the object is our own. Something we've had everything to do with, but has nothing to do with us. The sense again that Ahab had my number made me feel relieved to hand him over to Bubbles, for a shot or two that I would take. At last she strapped him back into the stroller, and home we went.

A camera nut who often spoke of making photography her career, Bubbles started the same damn thing all over again in the front yard. I was clowning around trying to get a grin or two out of Ahab, making faces, finger-waggling with thumbs in my ears, tossing a rubber ball to him, when I heard footsteps on the gravel, broken off in a manner leaving no doubt it was Maggie Doubloon stopping cold in disapproval. After taking in the scene, she resumed her march toward the house, swinging the briefcase inevitably marking her return walk from the office, but beckoning me inside with the slightest jerk of her head.

"Keep him in the sun for a while, Bubbles," she called from the door as we disappeared.

She told me to feel free to sit down as she paced the parlor floor.

"It was a mistake to ask you here, even for so short a time. You've become much too fond of Ahab, and maybe of others I could mention too. But I did it in good faith and with the best will in the world, seeing that you had plunked yourself down here in town anyway for God knows what kind of siege. Tony, you and your family have behaved absolutely commendably toward me. I have no complaints on that score. Your parents and you — but it's no use going through all that now. I'm satisfied with the outcome. I'm even glad for the — mistake we made. I had never wanted children, but I'm ecstatic with Ahab now that he's here. No one seems to suspect, and if they do they don't show it, so that's that. I think now we owe you a little something. I've talked it over with Grandpa, and he agrees we should give you a little piece of the business."

"Absolutely not."

"But it all came out of that woolly little noddle of yours. That started the ball rolling, even snowballing. When we're through with our present series of shirts we'll start another. I have a hunch T-shirts are going to be an even greater craze in the sixties and seventies than we thought. Maybe even for our lifetimes. So we'll see that you get a few shares — maybe a hundred or so — of T-Shirts Unlimited. If we keep booming, the dividends might even see you through college. But this must be goodbye, for the good of all concerned. You plan to leave the Friday before Labor Day, and have your bus tickets, I understand. That'll get you home in time to get ready for school. Anthony, my dear, foolish, bright, crazy, lazy beamish boy, how I shall love and hate to see your back."

"Would you like me to leave sooner? Do you object to me staying till then?"

"Object to *my* staying. The subject of a gerund is modified in the possessive," she said, and burst into tears.

Watching her run out the back door and into the yard,

I knew that my following her would have been not only useless, but inexcusable. I knew now and for all time what we meant and would mean to each other. But trying to comfort her as she wandered among the last of the summer flowers, my heart wrung like a dishcloth, would have served no purpose for either of us. I was grateful for the interruption that distracted my attention, however much it might have implied in the way of an eavesdropper.

A faint scuffing on the stairs made me turn in time to see Stubblefield descending them, fresh from a nap. These days, he tended to drop off with a copy of *Tender Is the Night* that I had given him, the snooze generally completed with the volume reposing on his chest. He was dressed in lemon-colored slacks and a blue T-shirt reading "I'm in the book." More evidence of the sex explosion of which T-Shirts Unlimited was a supposed exponent and I the presumed detonator. Pink sneakers with white laces completed his plangent getup.

"Why," he said, "your Fitzgerald has your Dick Diver telling your Nicole he feels badly about something. Tsk, tsk. Should have thought Maggie would have corrected him by this time. Makes me feel bad — recognizing as I do now that it's an adjective, not an adverb. Diver don't talk very well English."

"Guilty as charged."

Stubblefield shuffled farther into the room.

"Bubbles says she feels badly too, but I reckon you can correct her on that, what?" Here he jabbed me in the chest and winked. The eye in question remained shut for a moment, as it often did, owing to a rheumy condition often accentuated by a period of sleep. When he became

151

arch and winked at the breakfast table, the eye sometimes stayed glued shut until he pried the lids apart with thumb and forefinger. Which was the case now.

"Well, sir," he said, sitting down on the bottom step in a manner leaving no doubt that he was beginning another ramble, and that as his private secretary I should join him there, which I did, wishing I had on my flak vest for his sly nudges, "I'm riding on this bus, sitting behind these two women, and they're talking about some friends of theirs, analyzing their sexual habits and what they signify? One of them, Fritz, is going out with so many women, and prides himself on so many conquests, that he's obviously fighting homosexuality. On a bus, mind you, to Grand Rapids. Fighting homosexuality because omnivorous — that was the word the woman used, omnivorous — omnivorous erotic athleticism is the precise opposite of what it appears to be. That's supposed to be a truism of psychiatry. On a bus to Grand Rapids."

"There seems to be no end."

"All right. Then they start an another friend —"

"Vivisecting our friends is a major pastime these days."

"This one's a woman, and I'm a sonofabitch if she doesn't date men right and left because *she's* fighting *lesbianism*. Well, we bounce along for a while . . ." Early suspicion that this was a cooked-up routine and not an embroidered reminiscence based in fact served to sharpen my interest rather than otherwise, because efforts of Extant in this genre were generally more rewarding. But I steeled myself all the more for the payoff shove, because the snappers in this case had more the how'm-I-doing, pride-of-creator zest. ". . . and they give her a going over along the same lines, until they've exhausted the subject, and the gossip turns to a third friend. A rich man-about-town, I gathered, and so I keep an ear peeled for any sign of dating on his part." A pause made me turn my head inquiringly, more or less on cue, and Stubblefield shook his own. "Negative. No use even asking him to dinner as an extra man, because he's not available, and to the theatre and opera he goes alone. He doesn't date anybody. He doesn't go out with *either* sex." Another pause, just long enough to meet the comedian's sense of timing. "So I figured he must be fighting bisexuality," Stubblefield said, and he rammed me against the wall with a force that not only threatened to dislocate my shoulder but also clipped my right ear on the edge of the banister.

Stubblefield climbed to his feet. "I take it you're not averse to a stroll around the back yard before dinner?"

Secretarial diligence had in the closing days called for a summer's-end burst of attention to what had become rather unkempt grounds, and we took a turn through a small garden, by now vacated by Maggie, and then on into a woodlot where I had been clearing brush into piles for later disposal. He began a conversational rigmarole so studded with literary allusions that I could only marvel again over where in God's name he had picked them up — however chaotically. How he got onto Chekhov I can't remember, but his ramble revived suspicions that the mots he pulled off, some of them, may have been steals, though I have no proof. The finish for his last routine was certainly original. I knew for a fact that he had never seen or read any of Chekhov's plays, the extent of his familiarity with them being a movie he had seen of *Uncle Vanya*, starring Franchot Tone.

"This might be weeded here, so the myrtle has half a chance. I always think it beats pachysandra for a ground cover, and certainly creeping Charlie. Why, Chekhov wrote those plays as comedies, and so he used to say that if any crybabies wanted to shed tears over them, it was none of his business. And he was right. The purpose of art is to keep the guts tucked in, not spill them. Don't you think?"

"I couldn't agree with you more."

"That's why Thomas Wolfe gives me the heebie-jeebies . . ."

Switching off half my attention, I pondered Stubblefield's conversational method. The inevitable progression toward an epigrammatic finish was all right, but why must it be accompanied by an almost convulsive assault on the listener? Was that the simple discharge of an accumulated psychic energy? A form of collapse brought on by a kind of momentary exhaustion? That phenomenon was even more noticeable when you were out walking with him — which was why I kept a wary eye on a pile of brush toward which he softly but steadily bumped me, mostly dead branches and uprooted honeysuckle I had raked into a mound on the edge of the woodlot. That strolling chats were even more hazardous than bedtime stories was indicated now. This one had come to focus on the difference between art and religion, as to their respective roles in human life. "They're both protective. Similar in one sense, yet completely the opposite. Art is a parasol. Religion is an umbrella," he said, and pitched me headfirst into the pile of debris.

As I got to my feet, brushing off twigs and leaves, I noted what a headful of Stubblefield's obiter dicta I was going home to Ulalume with, enough to dine out on, there and elsewhere, for a long time to come. One was coming away from old Kazoo with an assortment of aphorisms, snappers, gags, and epiphanies rattling around in the old dome like a bag of marbles. That brought in its train thoughts of departure itself. Sad thoughts. End-of-summer thoughts always pensive enough in themselves, without darkening by these particular looming goodbyes. Goodbyes to Maggie Doubloon and Ahab, to Stubblefield — and goodbye to Bubbles Breedlove. Goodbye, goodbye, goodbye.

"The less you like women the more of them you're going to need," Stubblefield said, and was a moment unsticking a wink from a rheumy left eye. A last paradox to tuck into a nook of my mind, like the socks I was wedging into a corner of my suitcase. He seemed to be summing up his own life as a womanizer, with its quantitative quest to fill a qualitative gap, and I was glad he was watching me pack from a far corner of the bedroom, because normally the *aperçu* would have rated a healthy thump in the sidegut. The thought thickened an already enveloping gloom, and I snapped the brand-new grip shut and jerked it off the bed, eager to be off.

"People are at their best when they're saying goodbye," I seemed to have read somewhere, but now I wondered. My mood turned from murky to foul. What the hell did I want? Nothing, alas, that I had. Polarized regret and relief over departure produced a tangle of emotions hardly unscrambled by the reflection that in returning home I was only going to half a home. Stubblefield was to drive me to the bus station, and as he shuffled downstairs to get the car out of the garage and around to the front door, I hurried up a flight to say goodbye to Bubbles, the first and not the least of the ordeals of farewell. I knew that, coming down, I would feel rottener still, whether I had kissed her or not. I mean really kissed her, as I had longed to for so long. How the flesh wishes what the spirit disallows! Or put in one of Stubblefield's dipsydoodles, the spirit is willing but the flesh is strong.

She was at a small desk crowded into a corner of her tiny room, writing a letter to a girlfriend who had moved to Wisconsin.

"Will you write me?" I asked.

"If you write me."

"All right," I said, sidling cautiously into a blunder of prime quality. The old Adam had made me wait till she was alone in her room when I could just as easily have said goodbye as she passed my open door awhile before.

When she rose, I spread my arms in a jovial expression of friendliness, but they closed hungrily around her, as though in some kind of local autonomy of their own, and the embrace became something altogether different. What a lusciously ripe creature she was. Those beautiful billows of flank and bust and back. The kind of girl a previous generation called stacked, but that we blades in Ulalume called a crate of melons. This in the tradition of Spuds Wentworth, whom you will remember as our ranking amorist and linguist of the heart. Possibly even another of his coinages. If your main squeeze was a crate of melons, you were the envy of Central High. I tried to think of some pretty compliment to leave in Bubbles's pink shell of an ear, but nothing came except a husky "You're so lovely." I wanted her to say something deflating, like that I was kinda wow myself, to break the spell swelling the room with perfidy. All she did was take the mouth hungrily pressed to her own. A First Kiss drunk in farewell is a crazy experience indeed! Something both rapturous and absurd. In the midst of this one, the sound of Maggie Doubloon and Ahab playing in the back yard could be heard, followed by that of Stubblefield bringing the car around to the front, scrunching over the gravel I had so painstakingly spread. We ended it with a sort of laughing gasp, shaking our heads. Bubbles returned to the desk and scribbled the name and address of the aunt with whom she would again be staying, now that high school would resume, necessitating other arrangements for Ahab. We kissed again, more hastily, and I fled, wiping my mouth with a handkerchief and with my other hand plucking my suitcase off the lower landing as I dashed on down to the vestibule where Maggie and Ahab waited to be bade goodbye, farewells to be made brief for the good of all, then out the door in a deranged state of mind, to where Stubblefield sat in the Buick with the motor running. It had been a wonderful summer, it had been a glorious mistake.

I listened in a daze to the resumed saga of Stubblefield's married life as we ground through morning traffic toward the bus depot. I did so with half an ear, which was about all I had left after the blow against the banister.

"One trouble was too many visits from her brother, an oaf I didn't like from the start. What Bubbles would call a slurm."

"What exactly —?"

"He came by it honestly enough, since the father was the same way. Looking back on it now, I see that he constantly used 'epitome' as a superlative, as though it means the height of something. If I'd known then what Maggie's told me since, I'd have corrected him every time he opened his mouth. What did he do, you ask. Well, sir, he knew that as a prospective young son-in-law I was worried about shouldering the medical bills for someone about whose health there was some question, so he offers to give me a two-year guarantee on the bride."

"Like a car or something?"

"You got it. All doctor and/or hospital bills up to that point he'd pay. Just to see how far he'd go with anything so gross, I asked him if he'd put it in writing, and damned if he didn't. I could see that it gave him a sense of power to be able to dish it out like that. Just as our sincerest laughter with some pain is fraught, if I've got that quotation right, our benefactions have a self-serving element in them. It's the strontium ninety in the milk of human kindness," Stubblefield said, and gave me a cuff on the shoulder with his fist. He'd had to reach over to do it, as I was wedged as far against my door as I could get to avoid his elbow in my ribs. "Where was I?"

"You have it in writing."

"Yes. He even went so far as to stake us to a preliminary thorough checkup, where I was shown the X-rays. Have you ever looked at pictures of the human insides? It's like degenerate bourgeois art. So I married her, and by God if she didn't develop gallbladder complications requiring expensive surgery three days after the warranty ran out on her. How do you like that?"

He swore at a motorist he'd had to swerve around to avoid and after passing him settled back into his narrative stride. I had lost my grasp, if I'd ever had it, of which wife this was in the doleful roll, but probably the woman marriage to whom had been worse than Abraham Lincoln's. He shuttled back and forth among his squaws, as he called them, so freely that there was really no keeping them apart. And I realized now that I had never got quite straight which of them was Maggie's grandmother. Which was just as well.

"It took only one Christmas to show that there was a gap in taste here. Under the tree was a tweed jacket that I could hear clear through the wrappings. Every color you could name was in those hound's-teeth, and some you couldn't. And vulcanized at the elbows, as though sheer color strain had caused it to sustain a couple of blowouts. Finally she asked me what I thought of the present, and I says, 'It's more blessed to give than receive.'"

Fears that traffic snarls would make me miss the bus proved groundless. We arrived at the depot with a good ten minutes to spare. We parked the car with Stubblefield still winding up his story. "Like Newton seeing the apple fall on his cousin's head, I thought, 'I wonder if she realizes the gravity of the situation.' Well, sir, we moved into another neighborhood, a street noted for its literary lights," he rattled on as we walked toward the terminal. I noticed a lot of empty cartons stacked against a wall we passed, and as I allowed myself to be steadily canted toward them I wondered if this mightn't be a penance for my seeing the gag coming a mile off. No one listening to him set it up could have failed to spot it. "A novelist here, there a couple of cohabiting poets, a local journalist across the street. So you know what I called it?"

"No," I said guiltily. It was like letting your grandfather win at checkers.

"I called it the writer's block."

As I went sprawling into the stack of cartons, bringing them down in a jumble around my head, it struck me that Stubblefield's zinger reflexes might involve some kind of motor instability, brought into play in spasms of mirth timed for participation by his companion. This was food for later thought, I reflected as I picked myself up, recovered the suitcase I had dropped, and made for the depot.

We parted at the open door of the throbbing bus. I thanked him for everything as we wrung one another's hand, promising to keep in touch. Then I sprang quickly aboard, and soon I was bowling toward Chicago on the first leg of my journey back to North Dakota.

So it was "home" again, "home" again, jiggety-jig. I slumped against the window to watch the city limits and then at last the open country scenery rolling hypnotically by. For distraction I did a little work on the "Prufrock" pastiche:

> We'll mosey on through fly-infested streets,
> And maybe lift a few at Sneaky Pete's.

But my heart wasn't in it. I had the uneasy conviction that I was a slurm — whatever that was.

11

"And so I had this idea."

Mother and I were taking tea in the same room in which the Curator had called me the antichrist, the little glazed alcove off the main parlor, now made doubly pleasant by the house plants in which she had enveloped it, as she had a room or two even in that cold parsonage, the memory of which to this day is like leftover parsnips. It is from Dearest that I have derived my own fondness for domestic flora, and my understanding of them too. Their so varying individualities! The bloodleaf with its Slavic temperament. The Episcopalian prissiness of the poinsettia ("With leaves like these, as you think them, you klutz, though they are in fact bracts, with leaves like these, who needs flowers? And yet I give you such pretty little blossoms too, you undeserving clod"). The jade plant as your butch fag, with its leathery foliage and muscular boughs. The tarted slut known as eyelash begonia, every leaf different and all things to all men. The spider plant copiously proliferating with no redeeming social value. . . .

The Curator was in his office quarters, holding the local

epidermis *in statu quo*. Faint sounds could be heard through the intervening wall. A low drone of voices, a ripple of feminine laughter, like a flute arpeggio over his own bassoon. A door shutting and a car starting up in the driveway beyond. I didn't dislike my stepfather so much as resent the dislodgement entailed by a new domestic regime, the transfer of executive power however orderly. Was I cracking those high-school books to ensure acceptance by a decent college! Leaves falling on the lamplit Quad, girls, mixer dances, limburger set by wits on the dormitory radiators. . . . As far as the religious end of all this was concerned, I saw my stepfather as a lapsed atheist rather than a Christian convert. Someone who had suffered a failure of the nerve my father had recovered. Temperamentally, I leaned more to the free-thought conviction that there was none in heaven — that my father who was on earth had scrapped what we both saw as superstition.

My mother was talking about him, in a little digression I knew was a circuitous route to this "idea" she had, for what God only knew.

"I suppose he's happy enough. And miserable enough along with it, like me. Like all the rest of us. Like everybody, I suppose."

I prowled the alcove, looking for dead leaves to pinch back, a large wedge of walnut cake in my free hand.

"We're still on friendly terms, all of us, and he seems to be making lots of money with those TV commercials. Living it up. There was always this man-of-the-world side of him, dying to burst out. Conscious of how he should dress for sick calls, for deathbeds. But I don't see how — even raking in pots, as they call it in that English novel you gave me to read — how he can be happy for very long with this" — she cleared her throat in preparation for what must now be broached — "this bit of froth he's living with in New York. I believe that's what they call it."

"Bit of fluff is the expression, Dearest. Where did you learn about her?"

"From him. Oh, not that he called this Abby girl of his that. But it's what I'd call a twenty-three-year-old floozy who looks like this, as he probably would too if somebody else had her."

I examined the colored snapshot she handed over. It showed a pretty ash-blonde girl in a pink dress posing against a bank of rhododendrons in purple bloom. She flashed a bright smile as she cocked her head coquettishly to one side, a picture hat with a long ribbon hanging from one hand.

"Wouldn't you call that a bit of fluff?"

"I'd have to talk to her. I could go and check."

"She may be a nice enough girl. I understand she wants to be an actress and probably thinks Pop can help her break in. He may have given her a snow job about that — no, I take that back. I really must," Dearest said with a self-reproachful shake of her head. "Your father is nothing if not honest. He would never do a thing like that. He's just another" — sigh — "man staving off middle age with a girl young enough to be his daughter. A fling at the fleshpots and all that. They say her family lives in a place in Connecticut called Fairfield County that's supposed to be pretty fleshpotty." She shook her head again. "I don't know what I'm saying."

"What was this idea you said you had?"

Mother heaved another long sigh, this time staring at the floor as she rubbed her palms together between her knees — an old idiosyncrasy.

"I'm perfectly content with Humphrey Mallard here.

No, that's not an entirely truthful beginning. I like him fine, and I share his Christian faith, as I shared your father's when he had it. I'd not have left him if he hadn't left *it*. That's the whole thing in a nutshell, or most of it. So secretly, a psychiatrist would say, I resent Humphrey's having undermined it, as I'm grateful to your father for having passed his along to Humphrey. *This* is better than staying married to your father as he is *now* would have been. But it's not quite as satisfying as life with him the way he was *then*. Before the Great Debate, which I wish to God had never taken place. The two parts of my nature — my two basic needs if you will, faith and a relationship — were in better balance then."

I returned to my chair, and without looking at her said, rather riskily, "So deep down you'd like to dismantle what happened and go back to life with Pop. I mean if you had your druthers."

"Does this make sense to you, Tony?"

"Perfectly. But what's your idea?"

"You just said it. That they could have a return match and switch each other back to the way they were."

I was a long time ruminantly chewing a mouthful of the walnut cake — probably virtually Fletcherizing it like Ma Pettigrew — as I turned this proposal over in my mind. It was certainly something different.

"I don't think it's very practical, Dearest," I answered at last.

"Why not?"

"Because I don't think it would work. Or I doubt it would."

"It worked before. They're both very persuasive men. I had this dream the other night where the two men in my life were sitting on opposite ends of a teeter-totter, going up and down, and as I awoke it came to me in a flash that that's what it meant. That's what the dream was telling me. They should debate again and persuade each other to switch back. Reverse their thinking on a question you yourself say has two sides."

"Yes, but with this difference."

I rose and walked the floor again, this time with teacup and saucer in hand.

"I think that in the first case each won the other over to a conviction he secretly harbored anyway. He was ripe for the reversal. You yourself spoke of this other man trying to burst out of the minister you married. The same held true of Doc Mallard. The deep-seated longing to believe. That situation no longer holds. The alter egos have emerged to stay. The infidel hiding in the Christian, the believer inside the Ingersoll-Darrow overcompensating cover-up. They're out — for good!"

"How do you know? You make it sound like a Jack-in-the-box popping out. You stuff him back in and clap the lid down."

"This isn't like that. This is more like trying to run water back into a tap, I'm afraid. Where would you hold this match?"

"Right here again. People would come from miles around. The first one is still the talk of the county. It would be like Joe Louis fighting Schmeling again — and turning the tables. How thrilling!"

"Have you suggested this to Doc?"

Mother frowned studiously at the floor. "No. I was hoping you would."

I had a wild vision of such a return debate, in a packed house with fresh listeners augmenting the repeaters hungry for another show. The bit of fluff, brought west in tow, beside the crate of melons squired by none other than yours truly. Maggie Doubloon on my other side trying to shush precocious Ahab, now three, or four, or eight, then Dearest rooting, this time, for the Curator, as the religio-philosophical warrior who alone could bring Father back into the fold, and the state of grace qualifying him again for the cloth he had voluntarily shucked, and as a compatible mate for her. Farther down the line might be Stubblefield, fracturing a neighbor's rib or two as one or the other of the disputants got off a good one. It was a heady dream I saw little hope of being realized, but Mother continued so wistfully to nurse it that I thought the least I could do was broach the subject to the Curator.

One Sunday afternoon in Indian summer I came in from a pickup baseball game to find him in the parlor listening to his favorite television evangelist, and when the sermon was over, he turned the set off with such an expression of spiritual surfeit, a beatific version of after-dinner glut, that I thought this might be a good time to put forward the proposal. The filial satisfaction of doing my mother a favor she very much wanted me to stood in precarious counterbalance against the Beelzebubian realization that in doing it I was furthering a device for the possible dismantlement of his marriage as well as the loss of his faith. But then that wasn't any of my beeswax, was it, and besides, as Frost tells the orchard trees, something has to be left to God. Despite all that, I entered the living room to join him with my slouching-towards-Bethlehem gait, secretly observing that it was after all he who had put the bug in my ear. I still wore my baseball cap, the bill switched around to the back. I took a last drag on a coffin nail I was smoking and, with a sneer curling one nostril as smoke issued from both, I punched the butt out in an ashtray and plopped into a chair, slinging a leg over its arm.

"You ought to watch your posture, Biff."

"Arrrgh."

"Put your shoulders back. Throw your chest out."

"It's the only one I've got," I said, as thousands sang in the streets and bells tolled as one to mark the hundredth anniversary of the gag.

"Aren't you in training for something?"

"Bet your sweet buns."

"The basketball squad, I believe."

"Can de sermon."

"And smoking will do you little good for that game. You can't star round-shouldered and with a hacking cough. Or get the lead in the high-school play. Your mother's worried about your posture too. She —" He leaned forward in his chair to peer toward the kitchen where she could be heard preparing dinner, to make sure he wasn't overheard. "I found her cutting the mail-order form out of a newspaper ad for shoulder braces. Harnesses, sort of, that you strap around your back and chest. She wants to send for one of those rigs for you. We don't make the best impression with a poor carriage — especially young people. We all like to strut our part. The world's a stage, and we're players on it."

"Yeah, and the show's in trouble out of town. Has been for a million years. They'll never bring it in. No doctor can get the lousy thing in shape."

"But one. Christ. And he will. In the fullness of time. And there's evidence that that time is at hand. I don't know whether you caught anything of what Reverend Melton said just now, in his sermon on the text from Revelation. All things point to the end being near."

167

I nodded, keeping my own counsel as to the role in the great Windup which I must personally play. If it was written, how could I be held responsible? Looking off, I felt the Curator's eye on me. He cleared his throat to say something more, but I cut in. Again with the sense of obliging Mother and that of doing the Devil's work in perfect equipoise, I asked: "What would you say to repeating the Great Debate with Pop?"

He was at first taken aback, quite naturally. Stunned by a suggestion bound to take him by surprise. Then he raised his eyebrows, cocked his head, shrugged his mouth and so on, with the expression customary to second thoughts. He gave a slight laugh.

"Well, it would be an interesting idea."

"You yourself give what are called testimonials to Christ everywhere. This would be your chance for a big one, as it would be for Pop to make his pitch. The preacher is still there, only turned inside out. It would be a thrilling event. Two forensically skilled adversaries in a rematch arguing the opposite positions." Like boxers switching trunks, I thought without saying so. The Serpent is too wily to undermine his cause with debasing comparisons likely to let victims escape his clutches. "Well, what do you say, Doc?"

"I say this. That I couldn't very well say no to a challenge your father issued. But I wouldn't challenge him. You'd have to put the bee in his bonnet yourself."

"Very well then, we'll see." I rose, content for the moment with having planted the seed. "No rush. We're in touch with Pop of course, so we can see what we'll see. Something to keep on the back burner anyway."

It was still on the back burner that Christmas, when I

went to service with them to please Dearest, as I did from time to time against personal disinclination to church-going. Shuffling down the aisle behind them, I Yeatsed it up as best I could with the mail-order harness on, which Mother had sent for and which I wore now and then, also to please her. The rig certainly cramped my style as the antichrist, forcing on me a kind of clean-cut-military-academy-chap carriage, but what I lost on the one end I made up on the other, scuffing along in my no-account waddle all the way down to our pew.

I had spoken on the phone with my father several times, but the conversation never seemed to provide an apt open-ing to broach the subject of the rematch. In no case did I speak with the bit of fluff, though once I caught her voice talking with the operator putting in our person-to-person call. "Get him in a sec," she could be heard saying. She sounded like a wonderful human being. The idea was still on the back burner that Easter, when, again to satisfy Dearest, I traipsed along to divine worship, this time suc-cessfully slouching down the aisle behind them without the braces, hands in pockets for an additional touch, and when the congregation rose to raise their voices in the famous Easter anthem, I muttered my own profane version under my breath:

> Low in the gravy lay
> Meatballs and onions . . .

While the subject of the return bout simmered on the back plate, others of more immediate consequence sud-denly boiled up on the front.

Correspondence begun with Bubbles Breedlove had

soon petered out — the "out of sight out of mind" principle prevailing over "absence makes the heart grow fonder" — but shortly after that Holy Week I got a letter from Stubblefield offering me again the post of personal secretary, come summer vacation. He had had to fire a knucklehead with apparently no conception of the duties that involved — the multiform challenges *and* opportunities they afforded. A follow-up telephone conversation, made on the sly I was sure behind Maggie's back, gave me a chance to fish out some details as to exactly what these might be.

For one thing, heavy winter snows had called for so much plowing out that all my newly laid gravel had been bulldozed along with the white stuff into the lawn, from which it had now to be raked back onto the denuded driveway. As one who had done some of that "lice picking" on the church and parsonage drives, I knew what it entailed: stoop labor compared with which short-hoe chop cultivation of vegetable farms, as depicted in protest novels, was fun. To do a perfect job you had to practically pick the last remnants out a stone at a time with a pair of tweezers. It was more tedious on balance, and might take longer, than the original distribution by wheelbarrow and shovel had. But there were other things, Stubblefield hurried on to assure me when he sensed a tepidity at the other end. He had decided to overhaul his Buick, an education in itself to a youth who expected to drive a car the rest of his life and therefore might want to know what an internal combustion engine really was and how it worked. Lying on my back or draped over a fender, I would relate to automotive giblets in the richest sense. Then there would be more paperwork — I liked the "more" since I couldn't remember any interrupting the muscle-building of my first tour of employment — because his eyesight was worsening, so that were he a hawk on the wing he couldn't have spotted a field mouse more than a mile off, and though I admittedly used the hunt-and-peck system, he heard my typing was O.K. Some subtle fishing confirmed suspicions that he was indeed doing all this behind Maggie's back. "I don't think she wants me underfoot," I said, without going into essentials. But then the normal wish to see Ahab again made me quickly add, "Of course the motel must be restored by now?"

"It soon will be."

"*Will* be? It's been nearly a year."

"Legal entanglements over the new corporation that's taking the Nightie Night over. But they're about to resume construction. Meanwhile you can stay here again. My bed in yours."

Very soon there arrived another letter, saying nothing about that at all, but ending:

And now they've found gravel in my kidneys. What do you think of that, pal o' mine? It doesn't seem too serious, no talk about an operation or anything, but I do have to take it easy and so will need an amanuensis to take a lot of the clerical this that and the other off these old shoulders. What do you say to that, keemo sobby, or however they spell it. And with the glims going, I'll need a sort of companion to read to me, and with my catholic interest in just about everything, you could work in any school stuff you have to brush up on. Two birds with one stone. And speaking of stones as we seem to, again don't worry about that on my

behalf. They can dissolve those things if need be, so
buck up. Just if you could get here as soon as possible
after school is out and your vacation begins. You never
know.

Your friend,
Stubby.

P.S. Bubbles Breedlove will be on the scene again, and
guess what else. We seem to have a ghost in the house.
Fact. A poltergeist type of thing. I'm no longer an
atheist after seeing china pitchers and other bits of
crockery lying around the floor. More things in heaven
and earth, eh, Laertes? Or is it Horatio? Bubbles runs
around here half naked half the night trying to get a
picture of it, and claims to have one, though I think
it's a flaw in the negative. She claims to have seen a
"milky luminescence" on the stairs. Can you tie that,
old buddy? See you soon then.

S.

Eventually Stubblefield was caught phoning me when
Maggie picked up another extension to make a call of her
own, and, recognizing my voice and guessing what was up,
asked him to get off so she could "chat" with me. I told
her what was up and that I "leaned toward" a return to
old Kazoo pending her approval. She heaved her pedagogi-
cal sigh and said, "I suppose it couldn't do any more harm
than was already done the last time. How do you feel about
all this now, Tony?"
"How the hell do I know."
"Well, we mustn't risk talking about it now. Grandpa
may pick up the phone again. The motel isn't quite fin-

ished, but they're resuming work on it and it should be ready by the time you get here." Her tone turned discernibly mischievous when she asked, "How is Mrs. Clicko?"

"One of her new boarders is my civics teacher, a bachelor named Mr. Coburn. They say she has her cap set for him. I think you should send her a snapshot of Ahab."

"He pointed at one of you the other day and said, 'Nope.' But there was nothing personal in it. No one meets his standards."

The defacement of both mine and others' likenesses had been effected by the distribution of ketchup and mustard over the picture album, by the time I arrived shortly before the Fourth of July. Apparently thorough enough watch had not been kept by an interim nursemaid given to putting the "all boy" label on the mischief wrought the minute her back was turned, and whose back they were glad to see when Bubbles Breedlove was through school and free to join the household once more. "He's into everything" was another jolly construction put on Ahab's depredations. Peanut butter massaged into the dog's hide, soup poured on the family Bible, and apples pitched at the electric fan, together with such things as an attempt to put the cat in the dishwasher, all testified to a gift for improvisation more than recalling my own wanton babyhood. Did the antichrist, too, rate a forerunner, so that I was only playing John the Baptist to the real article? When I arrived, on a Sunday, it was to walk into a tizzy over a shambles made of the morning paper. It had been found lying in shreds on the front porch.

"Surely he couldn't do a thing like that," I said. "It was neighborhood vandals."

"Oh, he could climb out of his bed and steal downstairs," Stubblefield said. "He's done it before. That kid's full of the Old Nick. Well, let's take your stuff up to our room."

" 'Our' room?" I had come from the bus depot by cab, which I'd dismissed on the assumption that someone here would drive me to the motel. Now it turned out that the Grand Reopening had again been postponed, for an interval in which again bunking with Stubblefield would be a main feature of my reentry into the family bosom. My protestations were tempered by the knowledge that that would once more include Bubbles, the sight of whom set me tingling. My voice was hoarse with passion as, lugging a suitcase up the stairs behind Stubblefield, I said, "You say you've redecorated your room?" He toted the other with no visible sign of the reported infirmities.

"I never liked the old wallpaper. It always gravelled me." The thematic recurrence of gravel had already begun to seem like persecution, and here it was surfacing as a verb. Spiritually stuffing my mouth with one then the other of Bubbles's breasts had left my mouth hot and dry, so that my tongue seemed like a piece of cork manipulated only with great difficulty into the shapes necessary for speech. What in God's name was I doing here again, if not in some blind pursuit of self-torture? Perhaps I would get the hang of it someday, human life, but likely not this summer.

"Well, here are the old digs. How do you like the wall-paper?"

It depicted supposedly authentic historic battles between Indians and white settlers in the area, with some hatchet mayhem of women and children systematically recurring from panel to panel. A lighter note was struck by many village dogs barking at intruders and dead horses swirling downstream, while true comedy relief was supplied by pale-

174

faces smoking peace pipes with visible nausea. I didn't see how anyone could sleep amid all this carnage even with the lights out, but that was academic in view of the fact that the thought of Bubbles lying, possibly in the raw, just overhead was going to keep me awake anyway. I was by now so racked with ambivalence (my métier) that I wasn't sure whether I wanted a motel room made available after all. If I did move into one, would Bubbles be lured there as part of my rightful share of the sex explosion I was supposed to have touched off?

"You remember that dreary ornithological paper. All those grice peering at you through the underbrush."

"Grice?"

"Isn't that the plural of grouse?"

"Why not?"

I waited for Stubblefield to leave, but he sank into his favorite armchair to keep me company while I unpacked the suitcase heaved onto the bed. He lit up a cigar with the assurance that even people who eschewed them enjoyed the aroma of one smoked by somebody else, and having done so, and seeing that it was drawing well, he resumed the saga of his own love life.

"I submit that there is a subtle difference between kicking a cat out of the house and brushing it across the threshold with your foot. But that is a distinction that cat fanatics will not recognize. That was all I did. Oh, I may have brushed it *vigorously*, so that it kind of sailed over the doormat, but brush it is all I did, with the side of my foot, not booted it out of doors with the pointed toe of my foot. But no, says she, 'You kicked Tannhäuser out into the rain,' was how she would have it. That was another bone of contention, the rain. It wasn't that, really, only a light drizzle, if that. The Guy Upstairs was squeezing the atomizer bulb. No more. But to punish me, she went Out Into the Night to rescue the cat she had a perfect right to keep in the house. That was her refrain. A woman had a right to this, a right to that. You're going to find that more and more as you get out into life, married or otherwise. Women's rights. The movement is in its infancy now, but wait. And their rights are part and parcel with their wrongs. Them they cherish even more. Two sides of the same coin."

Here he rose and drifted slowly toward me, and, sensing the snapper was imminent, I edged around to the foot of the bed, to try to put some protection between him and me. He had set the cigar down in an ashtray, to free his hands for some sort of supplementary pantomime. I had a couple of shirts in my hand, to put into a bureau drawer, but he had me hemmed in. He assumed a boxer's crouch, and came in weaving and bobbing, dukes up.

"What they do is give you the old one two," he said. "They lead with their right and follow with their wrong," and, suiting the action to the words, dealt me one in the shoulder and another in the ribs, sending me into the ropes — that is, against the foot of the brass bed, a rail of which caught me across the small of the back. It was like old times.

"How is Bubbles these days?" I asked, on being let continue to the bureau.

"Fine. Her father is around just now. Maybe for the summer. A character."

In talking about him, Stubblefield sketched in some essentials of Bubbles's background of which I was still ignorant.

She was an Idaho-born girl whose widowed father had

arranged to have her live with this aunt in Kalamazoo, so that she might begin in her high-school years to acquire a little eastern polish. There was a suspicion that part of his motivation had been the courting without family encumbrances of an also-wealthy Idaho widow, a project now fallen through, leaving him "on the looserino," as Stubblefield put it. After a pause replete with self-explanatory hesitation, he said, "He's interested in Maggie. And I think she cottons to him. You'll see. As the widow out there would have to take Bubbles, he'll have to take Ahab, but what the hell. The world is full of stepparents and stepchildren. You're one yourself now. Minced families is large these days. There he is now."

A great honking outside drew me to the window through which Stubblefield was peering down into the front yard, where I saw a magnificent Lincoln-Mercury station wagon with an Idaho license plate draw to a stop. A forty-year-old man wearing what might be called a five-gallon hat ducked in order to climb out from behind the wheel. He stood six feet two in glittering black boots, tan chinos, a blue shirt open at the throat, and a brown safari jacket. A thumb hooked into a three-inch silver-buckled tooled leather belt, he strolled toward the stairs down which Bubbles in her red summer frock bounded into his arms — or into his free arm. It was obvious from whom she had got her bursting vitality. They were blond variations of one another, smiling their three-hundred-watt Breedlove smiles. I must have my teeth checked.

"Come on down, you can unpack later."

We all converged in the vestibule, including the Airedale, for whom my existential dread seemed satisfactorily submerged in the general animal health, judging from the way he capered and panted and snuffled without prejudice. Maggie introduced me.

"Hank, this is Tony Thrasher. Hank Breedlove."

"The erstwhile pupil. Well, I've. Heard a lot a. Bout you, guy."

From the expectant smiles on the faces of the rest, I sensed some kind of ritual, or initiation, was in progress. They all seemed to step back, forming a circle of attention, as Breedlove went on:

"Any guy from. North Dakota's that much. Closer to Idaho and. That's O.K. with me. Put 'er. There, fella."

As with his right hand Breedlove made soupbones of the metacarpals in my own, all but bringing me to my knees with a cry of "uncle," the others continued to watch me for signs that I dug the bit. At last I tumbled. Of course. A John Wayne imitation by a professional Westerner. Apart from the sinister banality of all movie-star impressions, I had to admit a valid strain of satire in this one. The voice timbre and the cadence were all right, but what took the cake was the send-up in the pacing. That was exactly how John Wayne talked, in fractured sentences as though the script were punctuated that way. The only question was how long this would last, for well after we had reached the parlor Breedlove was going on with the bit. I wanted to say, "Man, you've got it in your teeth."

"I understand you. Had the entire house done. Over recently, Maggie. I must say it. Meets with my hearty a. Pproval, ma'am."

He seemed not to have heard that enough was too much, and I wondered whether there was a repertoire, and we were next to be treated to doses of "You dirty rat," "Meet me at the casbah," and "Here's looking at you, sweetheart." But anxieties proved groundless, at least for the moment. Presently he was talking in his normal tone, a semidrawl not all that far from Wayne, and which I wasn't qualified to authenticate as Idaho or criticize as not. Maybe it was an eclectic synthesis of his born diction and Plainsman yearnings, the latter cinema-fed if it came to that. There was no trace of it in Bubbles's by-now standardized mid-American inflection. He sometimes seemed a bona fide Texan, his having been raised in Potlatch, Idaho, a dismissible technicality. You expected him at any minute to deny that he grew baking potatoes and reveal himself as an oil tycoon. He told us about the meaning of the town's name at dinner, for which he and Bubbles stayed.

Mrs. Bender still came in by the day to cook the evening meal and clean up. Tonight there was roast beef and Yorkshire pudding, with a horseradish sauce in which we all assured her that the horseradish didn't "boss the taste." We did collective justice to it all while Hank Breedlove explained what a potlatch was.

"It's a ceremonial feast among Indians of the Pacific coast, at the end of which, the grand climax — well, no, first off the host passes out expensive presents to his guests from other kin groups. That's just for openers. Then the smash finish. He hasn't gone far enough to prove how well off he is. Now he starts destroying valuable property to show he can afford to do so. He'll build a huge bonfire on which he chucks articles of furniture, rugs, pottery, clothes, you name it. Anything to impress neighbors he's got it made. He's got to outdo the friend or relative who threw the last potlatch he went to. Top him, you see. You talk about keeping up with the Joneses. This is conspicuous consumption. Like you ain't seen since — since —"

"Garbo in *Camille?*" I piped up.

"What? Oh, I see what you mean. All those expensive gowns, box at the opera, holidays in country houses."

"And somebody having to cough up for it," I plowed doggedly on, wishing I was dead and in hell.

"That's for sure," Breedlove said. "But insane as it might seem to us, at least it wasn't stuff bought on credit, like our cars and houses and hi-fi stereos. These were possessions they owned, maybe even made themselves. Maybe *needed.*"

"I seem now to remember hearing the word. Have you any idea what it comes from, Mr. Breedlove?"

"Please. Hank me. Any more mister and I'm. Likely to haul off and. Call you sir, fella. And I don't think that'd. Set very well, eh, Tony?"

"Don't do that, you dirty rat." Would nobody stop me before I committed suicide?

"Why, I think I can answer that. I believe it's a Nootka word, something like 'patshatl,' which means gift, or giving. Got corrupted. The Chinooks got the word from them, is my understanding. Maybe all the Indians in the Columbia basin and around there gave these wingdings, but the Chinook bashes are the ones I'm familiar with. They're mainly Washington and up north into Canada and Alaska, but of course Potlatch is as far west in Idaho as you can get and still be in the state. We're smack on the border. Maybe when Bubbles gets married I'll have to throw a potlatch myself. Chuck everything on the pyre including the Mercury station wagon."

"In that case I'll just live in sin with somebody, Daddy."

"Heyell you will," Breedlove said, darting what I fancied to be an involuntary glance in my direction. His bright blue eyes made me lower my own pale blue imitations to my plate, my head bobbing agreement at inscrutable lengths as I knifed away at my roast beef.

"Throw a potlatch, but stop at the giving of presents. Don't build a bonfire," I suggested. "But if you do, I have dibs on the Mercury. She's a beauty. Uh, do you suppose our 'potluck' comes from there?"

Breedlove shook his head, chewing. No, there was no connection. Potluck was self-explanatory, meaning just what it said, a meal made from whatever food is around.

Throughout all this I had kept half an eye on Ahab. He was not only allowed to eat with us, sitting on a chair augmented by a Webster's Unabridged, but was let drink his milk by squirting it into his mouth from a water pistol, a decadent pleasure recently cultivated, and giving promise of an early Byzantine decline, no doubt marked by the consumption of spicy foodstuffs while luxuriating on furniture of overstylized design in quarters characterized by the lavish employment of gilt and excessive use of mosaic. He would dip the muzzle of the pistol into his mug of milk, poke it into his mouth, and fire away, to the delight of all.

We were served coffee with our apple pie, for which we were urged to "save room" unless we wanted to plunge Mrs. Bender into belligerent gloom. Stubblefield was given decaffeinated, which Breedlove called platonic coffee. At the remark, Bubbles gave me a secret wink, whose relevance to our cause I was left to puzzle over, supposing that the subject of sex had thus indirectly come up, and that it would be our early concern. I began to shimmer with excitement as I held up my end of an exchange of melting glances, finally dropping my eyes to the rim of her red dress, cut just low enough to offer a glimpse of the sweet mounds within, at whose coral tips I nibbled in spirit until I must have begun visibly to salivate, because I was again aware of Breedlove's stare. I made a diversionary face at Ahab, who then trained his pistol on the dog, to everyone's amusement except his mother's. I was powerless to form an opinion. I had everything to do with this, but it had nothing to do with me.

A chance to be alone with Bubbles eluded me for the time being. Breedlove drove her to the aunt with whom she stayed, to pick up her things, Maggie riding along, Ahab beside her in the back seat. Stubblefield being occupied elsewhere, it gave me a chance at something high on my list of priorities: to be alone with the family Bible.

I carried it from a parlor table on which I had spotted it for the first time, to an armchair, eager to have a look at the genealogical tree I suspected it contained, particularly to see whether in that case the newest member was recorded there. It was certainly the biggest Bible I had ever hefted. It had two clasps, with hinges the size of those on a barn door. I swung it open and there was the pedigree, with no Ahab. It stopped with Margaret Inez Doubloon, daughter of Carlos Doubloon and Sarah Stubblefield, daughter of Ahab Stubblefield, etc., etc., and so on back roughly halfway to Adam and Eve, the "mists of time" in which the forebears were lost being symbolized by diminishing legibility in the ink. Only one of Stubblefield's three or four "squaws" was listed, the Marie Aumont who was Miss Doubloon's grandmother. I associated her with none of his narratives, which were by now nothing but a grand mishmash in my mind anyway.

I found three more Ahabs up the line. Apparently the name was regarded as reflecting a rock-ribbed integrity in the clan. But had the ancestors in question used this Bible for anything but recording their lineage? Had they read it? The Sarahs and Ezras and so on were fine, but why Ahab? He was one of the wickedest kings Israel ever had. He had married Jezebel, and of course it was a good job that he had, since, as we say of dislikable couples, that way they wouldn't spoil two families. I wondered if some forebear's enthusiasm for Melville mightn't have accounted for all the Ahabs, but no; the first was entered in 1802, and wasn't that some fifty years before *Moby-Dick*?

Hearing a car pull into the driveway, I quickly scrawled my name beside Maggie Doubloon's with a forefinger serving as an imaginary pen, and Ahab's under that, and clapped the Bible shut with a nervous giggle. But it was only Mrs. Bender's husband come to pick her up.

Suddenly I was dog-tired. It had been a long two days of travel. The house was silent after the departure of the Benders. Why not go upstairs, finish unpacking, and curl up with the Good Book? The memory of a sermon of my father's on Ahab and Jezebel added to my curiosity about that pair, and after floundering about in the Old Testament I found their story in the first book of Kings.

"And in the thirty and eighth year of Asa King of Judah began Ahab the son of Omri to reign over Israel: and Ahab the son of Omri reigned over Israel in Samaria twenty and two years . . ." My eyes grew heavy, and it was uncomfortable reading while lying on my side, so I turned over onto my back and held the book up, with disastrous results. "And Ahab the son of Omri did evil in the sight of the Lord above all that were before him. And it came to pass . . ." The sandman was here, but hold it. Here's a fine touch. Snap to. ". . . as if it had been a light thing for him to walk in the sins of Jeroboam the son of . . ." Rather urbane, that. Had one's own father shacked up with a bit of fluff as though it were a light thing? Was the bit of fluff a Jezebel? Had it come to pass that we were all Ahabs and Jezebels? As if it had been a light thing, this rascal "took to wife Jezebel the daughter of Ethbaal King of the Zidonians, and went and served Baal, and worshipped him. And he reared up an altar . . . made a grove . . ."

Here I dozed away, dropping the Bible on my chest. I awoke with a yelp of pain, having broken two ribs. That was what I learned the next day, after going to the doctor's for an X-ray. Probably a first for the Word of the Lord, certainly having no precedent in my own experience except for an acquaintance who'd cracked his sternum dozing off with the Modern Library *Complete Novels of Jane Austen*. Never read omnibus collections in bed, unless you can, literally, "curl up with them."

Deciding the discomfort I was in absolved me from any responsibility to join the others when they returned, I undressed and got into my pajamas. Watching from the window, I saw Stubblefield walking around outside, eating a banana. I think he thought I had gone with the rest. Dusk was gathering, and he drifted out of sight, then back into it, munching contentedly on the banana. When he finished it, he threw the peel up on the roof. At least nobody would slip on it there. Or maybe I would, if sent up to do any more gutter work. When he came into the house, I popped into bed, drew up the single sheet that sufficed in the warm evening, turned my face to the wall, and pretended to be asleep. I could hear him tramp up the stairs.

"You in bed?"

I affected slumbering oblivion, which didn't seem to impress him. Lying on the side other than that on which the injury had occurred seemed to ease the pain. He must have noticed the Bible resting on the table where I had put it, because he said, "What are you reading this for? You getting religion in your old age?"

Regular breathing accompanied by a slight stertorous buzz for authenticity. He began to undress for bed himself, judging from the puttering noises to be heard.

"You bushed from your trip?"

I felt guilty about something. In the pother over the tattered newspaper into which I had walked on arrival, I had neglected to ask him how he was. I had actually revolved a number of variants which would make it impossible for him to give the timeworn reply, "Extant," good enough for two or three times, but now deserving retirement — except for use on people who had never heard it. I had rehearsed "Hello, Stubblefield, how are things?" and "How's tricks," or even *"Wie geht's?"* any one of which would foil him. But now I remembered that gravel had been discovered in his urinary tract, and my heart softened. We are not cruel. We should not deprive an old man of a favored ritual, however threadbare. Now to do the right thing, I even "woke up," rolling onto my back, with some return of pain, and mumbling as though roused from sleep, or if not that, from the penumbral borderline between sleep and waking.

"How are you, Stubby?"

He gave his philosophical, nitchevo shrug. "Extant."

"How about what you wrote me about? I've been worried."

He had overended his pants, clamping the cuffs under his chin, preparatory to sliding the legs over the bar of a hanger. He let them drop into place, and said, "The gravel in the old plumbing? That seems to have cleared up. Drinking lots of cranberry juice, like the doctor says. Supposed to de-alkalize things, keep them acid."

"Thank God."

That reminded me of the morrow's labors, and the question whether I would be able to perform them in this condition. A glance at the lawn as my taxi pulled in had confirmed that its edges were indeed half gravel, and that raking it back out onto the drive would be tedious as reading the Old Testament from start to finish. Why didn't they have the driveway paved? Because gravel was more picturesque.

While Extant was in the bathroom down the hall bathing and brushing his teeth, I heard the others returning downstairs, Bubbles's voice dominant above the gay hubbub in which they entered. She was telling a story about a local grocer with whom she'd been feuding. "He always watches like a hawk me putting cherries in a bag. Yesterday again I was picking out the dark maroon ones one by one, and he came over and said that wasn't fair. He was absy livid. *He* had to buy them by the box, take the dark luscious ones with the pink sour ones, and a customer had to do the same. I had to scoop them up by the handful and dump them in the bag. If everybody picked them out one at a time he'd be left with a lot of pink sour ones at the bottom of a box he'd have to throw out because nobody wanted them. *Or* take them home and eat them himself. That's the way he is. Absy no *joie de vivre*."

Again the dichotomous anguish of love for a dingbat racked me, the red-hots for someone you couldn't expect to have without "doing right by her," and yet marriage to whom seemed a foolproof formula for calamity. Something like hooking up with one of Stubblefield's innumerable flunkensteins. She was a sweet summer joy even in her dingaling chatter — perhaps never more so — which only heightened your fits of wincing enchantment. So now she was taking high-school French — but no *joie de vivre* because you balk at taking a licking on cherry crates raided by choosy customers? What was this? Bona fide dingbat stuff, or talking in the non sequiturs your father said was part of a woman's prerogative, and, in the end, charm? How did he ride it with the bit of fluff? I gnashed my teeth in desire while at the same time cocking an ear for more authentic dingaling to throw cold water on my passions and put me out of my misery. Must I spend the summer like a worm writhing ecstatically on the hook? Some talk about a possible trip to England with her father. I wrung my pillow on "Westminister Abbey," and on "irregardless" stuffed a corner of it into my mouth to muffle a moan. Let's have more ardor dampeners, come on. And where was Miss Doubloon when you needed her? Why wasn't she correcting others' grammar as she did mine? So thoroughly was I polarized that I told myself I seemed to remember some dictionary had recently approved "irregardless."

"Have I ever told you about a woman I had something going with when I was married to my second wife?" Stubblefield asked, climbing into bed beside me. "Something on the side?"

"No," I said, turning on my own side so as to face the wall again. "I don't believe you have." I was soon pleasantly drowsy once more, following with progressively less comprehension the bends in this narrative. I was about to drop off when I sensed a turn in it giving every evidence that we were coming up the homestretch. Now more than ever I could have used a flak vest for his sly nudges. I felt either his knees or his feet planted firmly in my hindgut, poised for the kicker.

"I saw her again years later, long after our little caper was over and done, and her tale of woe was soon told. She had been disappointed in love."

I knew I was again to respond as straight man, thus setting things up for the zinger. That was paramount to his style as a raconteur, and arguably one of my chief duties as personal secretary. It may, indeed, have been one of his reasons for asking me back — why he liked me. You're a fool, I thought to myself, but what the hell. My cooperation even gave the climax something of the antiphonal flavor of vaudeville patter.

"Oh, she was disappointed in love?" I said.

"Yeah."

"How so?"

"She got married."

The impact of the shove that sent me against the wall may have proved precisely the reverse of what would have been expected in my injured state, in that it in some way "set" the broken ribs. I found all that out the next day when an X-ray revealed the bones to be not only broken but set, and beginning to knit, as your hair, of course, resumes growing even as you walk out of the barbershop. The trip to the orthopedist was actually roundabout, via another doctor. In carrying the Bible back downstairs the next morning, I dropped it on my foot, breaking a toe. Slight a matter as that is, it hurt more than the other, since I had to walk on it. Stubblefield took me to a podiatrist, remarking that the word sounded like a name for some kind of pervert. "Maybe you have to have a foot fetish to be one," he said. The only splint for a toe, in case you've never sustained the injury, is the one next to it, and mine was lashed with surgical tape to the great toe. And so out I hobbled after satisfying the doctor's curiosity by telling him I had dropped a huge ledger on my foot, and that I had hurt my ribs in some gymnastic exercises. His tender probings there proving painful, he urged me to see an orthopedist, which I did. The orthopedist's X-rays having shown the breaks, my entire chest was tightly taped up, and off I went again, this time clutching a prescription for a painkiller.

"Take the day off," Extant said as we pulled into his yard.

Well, I couldn't do that, it being already half past three. Besides, I wanted to see how, or whether, I could function in my crippled condition, a determination in which there were no doubt sadomasochistic elements. It went poorly. The upper injury being on my right side, I had to favor that arm and environs, which meant I had to rake with my left, and that alone, limping into the bargain.

"I'm afraid you'll have to get yourself another secretary," I told Stubblefield finally.

"Come in and have some iced tea. I've got Constant Comment. And tomorrow we'll go over some paperwork."

My injuries were the subject of brisk discussion at dinner, or rather their means and origin were, for with family I had come clean, not fibbing as with the sawbones. Could they, too, not have been the work of the poltergeist? Because that lot are defined as noisy and often mischievous spirits who might very well put the Bible to prankish use.

While Stubblefield and I slept soundly through the night, Bubbles and Maggie testified to mysterious noises in the dead of it, footsteps on the stairs, knobs rattled, and in the morning there were the fragments of another teacup lying on a table under a cabinet shelf from which it had fallen, or been nudged. Bubbles had crept down to join Maggie, on hearing her abroad, and they had both seen a "milky luminescence" floating down the stairway and out through the front door. Stubblefield said he had seen something like it once before, stealing down in a nightie that might well have got him mistaken for it, but that was the descriptive term on which all agreed, after Maggie had supplied the noun. It was a milky luminescence. Phosphorescence was too strong a word, and fluorescence smacked too much of contemporary manufacture. Bubbles had ventured down with her camera, but failed to get a picture of it.

Speculations about the supernatural, unexplained psychic phenomena, and the like occupied us far into the next evening, and Maggie — as you will have noticed I now call her — Maggie, who said she had no firm convictions either way but preferred to keep an open mind, trotted out a book dealing with alleged ghosts in English country houses, written and illustrated by a photographer who had sat up through many a witching hour with a camera cocked and ready. There were supposedly authentic pictures of three such revenants, all for some reason floating down a flight of curved stairs at the foot of which stood a grandfather's clock, and all manifestations certainly describable as milky luminescences.

The next night about two A.M. I was awakened by an increase of the pain in which I had fallen asleep, or so I imagined. There was also the suggestion of having been startled awake. I sat bolt upright, like a character in a work of cheap fiction. Bubbles was standing beside the bed, having shaken me by the shoulder. I had been sleeping on the outside, Stubblefield having pleaded feeling even a little less extant than usual and, retiring first, climbed into the wall position, reviving fears that I might be "emphasized" onto the floor at the height of a bedtime story. But there was none this time. Bubbles was a dim silhouette against a moonlit window, in a nightgown over which she had hastily thrown a dressing wrap.

"Get up," she whispered.

"Not another milky luminescence?"

"Shh." She stood a moment, finger at lip, then asked, "Do your hear something?"

I strained to listen, but there was nothing except Stubblefield's breathing, itself extraordinary, with normal respiratory sounds intermingled with noises like ailing hydraulic machinery or Greeks in rut.

"Downstairs," she whispered, pointing.

A floorboard snapped somewhere in the time-honored nocturnal fashion of house bones, and then there was the rustle of a breeze in the maple trees outside the open window, whose lace curtains themselves fluttered rather like ectoplasm into the room. But otherwise there was nothing.

"Come on," she whispered, and I tiptoed out after her in my pajamas. She was carrying her camera. At the head of the hallway stairs she paused and with a nervous laugh gestured for me to lead the way.

"This is all foolishness," I whispered, but followed orders gladly for reasons that can be imagined. Being ghostily afloat with this delicious girl at this hour in a dark house was more exciting than anything our quest might turn up. One of the carpeted stairs snapped like a small firecracker under my bare foot, but other than that we gained the lower floor without incident. We stole on into the dark parlor and, with the aid of familiarity and some moonlight, made our way to a sofa. There we sat and waited for a manifestation.

It was not long in coming. This girl was tempting at any

time, but in a low-cut nightgown of a silken fabric so sheer it was like, well, like woven water, under a wrap fallen open, her hair in a golden cataract to her shoulders, and smelling like a garden, she was irresistible. Any restraint on which I had resolved hadn't, so to speak, a ghost of a chance. I reached for her hand, which readily returned the pressure of my own, and which was relinquished only so I could slip an arm around her shoulder. The camera was forgotten on a sofa cushion as we embraced and kissed. Panting long-pent-up endearments in one another's ear, we stretched out full-length on the sofa, my boiling loins pinning her against its back. I ran a hand along her thigh, then down again so as to repeat the caress under the nightgown. Skin of ripe fruit. Peeled willow wand. Flower of a mouth, hummingbird sucking its nectar. My stem sprang from the gap in my pajamas and of its own accord sought her chalice as she slid under me and my knee pried her thighs apart.

"Oh, my God, Tony," she moaned. "I don't want to and I do. What'll we do? You know how it is."

"I know. You're so lovely. Talk about peaches and cream . . ."

"I don't suppose I'd be your first?"

"You're ravishing."

"I'd be yours."

In a blind daze I both desisted and pursued, easing my importunities by withdrawing my knee but at the same time slipping my hand all the way up her body till it found a breast. Cupping it in a howling palm, I said, "Some things are too damn much to ask, but if you want . . ." I strangled on my own words, wondering myself what the rest would be. "I mean we'll play it your . . ."

It was then that the milky luminescence appeared. I

don't know which of us saw it first. Perhaps Bubbles, because she was half facing the room, and the diaphanous something floated into the parlor from the front vestibule into which the flight of stairs led. But when it cleared its throat, we both sat up, scrambling to set our clothes to rights.

"Well," Miss Doubloon said, tucking in the lapels of the dressing gown covering her own white nightie. "This is a pretty sight."

We two sat in guilty silence.

"I think you'd better leave, Bubbles. Would you, please?"

"The house? For good? You mean pack and all? Oh, Maggie!"

"Of course not, dear. What do you think I am, the wicked witch of the Middle West?"

"Heh heh heh," I said, laughing dutifully at what I took to be a joke, with no appreciable appeasement of the tension. Too, I remained busy packing away my still angry member, an added cautionary note to anyone who thinks it a light matter to be taken *flagrante delicto*. It has little to recommend it.

"I just mean go back to bed, darling."

Bubbles stood a moment after retrieving her camera, but looking at the floor. "Nothing really happened, Maggie. I mean there wasn't any — you know," she said, and hurried from the room and back upstairs.

Electing not to turn on any lights, Miss Doubloon remained a spectral quantity as she paced the room, crossing and recrossing before the sofa on which, in the circumstances, it was best that I stay sitting for the time being.

"Well, Anthony, this seems to be your métier."

"Yes'm."

It was like old times. There was a gruelling sense of

déjà vu about the whole scene, as though it was all unfolding in a classroom in Ulalume.

"I'm surprised."

"No, Miss Doubloon, I'm surprised. *You're* amazed."

"I see you've had good teachers."

"Yeh heh heh. The best. Yeh heh heh."

"Disappointed is really the word I should use. Sadly, sadly disappointed. Not only that you would take advantage of an innocent girl like Bubbles, but that you would in doing so abuse our hospitality."

"That I've done, that I've done." What, again the Irish bit, like with Bubbles in the park? Where did these things subliminally spring from? What unknowable crevices in the dim grottoes of the psyche and so forth and so on.

"I'm no bluenose, as no one should know better than you, and I'm not playing the chaperone here, like some housemother. It's not that. Well, partly of course, to the extent that Bubbles is a kind of babe in the woods, vulnerable. I know I'm not one to talk, considering my terrible slip with you, for which God knows I've paid."

"Please. You don't owe God or man anything. The mother you've become."

"But all that aside, there's another factor now. You've probably guessed what it is."

Here she sat down beside me and drew in and let out a couple of long breaths, as though she were doing some kind of respiratory exercise. In fact she was plucking up her courage.

"I won't hide anything from you. Hank and I have quite fallen for each other, and I think we'll get married."

"Oh, great! Congratulations!"

"Thank you. But," she hurried on, "there are complications. And yet not really. Where will we live? Well, I'd be just as glad to move to Idaho and leave aaaall this behind as he would to pull up stakes and settle here, in what he calls the more sophisticated eastern bustle. He's financially independent, or certainly will be after he sells his land for the prices that fetches there nowadays. As for Ahab, Hank's content to ask no questions. As a child of a cancelled relationship, it's no more or less than a child from a previous marriage. Whatever you may think of him, he's so sweet, such a brick at bottom, that he even confessed to having got a young woman in trouble who he knows for a fact had the baby and put it out for adoption, after totally disappearing from his life. So we're even Steven there, if it comes to balancing the moral ledger. That's life — we're all 'torn' about something at one time or another, maybe forever. You're torn about Ahab, but that you'll have to live with. Maybe never seeing him again. It shouldn't be any worse than if you'd got a girl in trouble and the baby was put out for adoption. Lost, forever, in the anonymous human swarm. That's life. Doors close behind us and others open up before us. One slams in our face, we turn around and look for another. Night falls here, day breaks there. Here a shutter is drawn forever, while vistas open somewhere else. I knew the minute you got here I shouldn't have let you come — again! But now I think it's best that you have. This is the storm that alone could clear so foul a sky. From?"

"Shakespeare."

"Right. But what an incredible tangled skein is life. If you hadn't been an underachiever you wouldn't now be sitting here with me, having this obligatory scene. You remember what we learned about every drama having that. The scene to which everything preceding inevitably leads. But it's only *our* obligatory scene. You'll have more with

other people, about other things. Maybe with Bubbles."
She took on a sterner tone as she turned to me and asked,
"What about her?"

"I don't know. We're not an item, if that's what you
mean."

"You damn well looked like one tonight. But what I
meant to say was, when I marry Hank Breedlove, she'll be
my daughter. That's why my breaking in wasn't doing a
Mrs. Clicko. It was the act of a mother-elect. You understand that."

"Of course I do. You don't want a grandchild in the
package."

She looked at me again, startled by what would have
been crass, save for the purpose it served in dispelling any
suspicions not put to rest by Bubbles's assurance that
nothing had "happened."

"You don't have to worry on that score," I pressed, like
a cobbler hammering a nail already well driven in.

"Promise me one thing about Bubbles."

"Ask away."

"That you won't seduce her frivolously. She's not a light
o' love. *Mean* it."

"I promise. I almost meant it tonight."

I rose and waited inquiringly, like a pupil asking by
implication whether he hadn't been kept after school long
enough. She said nothing, lowering her eyes and gazing
into hands folded upside down, like a child playing "Here's
the church, here's the steeple, open the door and see all the
people."

I paced across the front of the sofa myself now, a few
steps and back again.

"But it is amazing, the complicated tapestry of life. How
we are woven in and out of each other's, watching always

for the pattern to emerge, if it ever does. I feel as though I'm fifty years old now and have packed in enough experience to be talking this way. Because I required tutoring, you needed a sitter for the result, whose father you're now going to marry and move to Idaho, leaving the girl behind for you to worry about, here or some college town she lands in. Sometimes these cogitations still amaze the troubled midnight and the noon's repose."

"I know you expect me to ask what that's from."

"Poem of Eliot's, 'La Figlia Che Piange.'"

"What does that mean?"

"'The Girl Who Cried,' I think. Something like that. Well, good night again." She stayed me with a gesture.

"But you won't make Bubbles cry?"

"Never."

I went back upstairs, hearing behind me, I thought, a soft sound of sobbing, like that a phantom might make in a dark house, deep in the dead of night.

12

I solved the ghost problem myself, quite unintentionally, thanks to close listening to Stubblefield's rambles, an equivalent of the close reading scholars give the texts of authors they are editing. This was no more a crystallized curiosity about his womanizing than a matter of keeping a sleuth's ear cocked for inconsistencies such as often trip up the braggadocio, though I had become a student of his shenanigans. I had little doubt that the conversations he reported were doctored in his favor, particularly when it came to related repartee. "I know he died and left you, my dear. How *much* did he leave you." There's always a limit to how much of that can be taken without a grain of salt, or even with it.

We were sitting side by side in the old Buick, which he was driving to a garage to have a slow leak in the left rear checked. Plans to overhaul her had been abandoned, thank God, dispelling a waking nightmare of mine that after a diagnostic dismantlement I would help put her together again with six or seven parts left over. Instead, Stubblefield was toying with a plan to drive her to a convocation of motorists foregathering for the purpose of destroying their lemons — strictly definable as cars that cannot be repaired. The Buick, which took five minutes to start and then made off with a gargantuan belch, certainly fit into that category. The ignition was perverse to the point of malevolence, the headlights were cross-eyed, sending intersecting beams into opposite ditches, and it ran as if lubricated with peanut butter, Stubblefield's chronic description of her sluggish performance. "I may just enter this clunker in the lemonstration," he said as we pulled out of the driveway.

"The what?" I asked, not sure I had heard right.

"Lemonstration. That's what they call them."

As God is my judge, they do. You may not believe it either, unless by chance you happened to catch a coverage of an actual such event on the Six o'clock News, some years later. That was held in Connecticut somewhere. Definitively fed-up motorists from miles around drove their cars into an open field and set upon them with axes, sledgehammers, knives, rocks, anything they could lay their hands on with which to slash tires, shatter the windows, shred the upholstery, and demolish the engines in a kind of bacchanalian ecstasy well worth, presumably, what they would have got in salvage money from a junkyard. In the end, Stubblefield didn't enter his heap in this upcoming lemonstration, opting instead for the hundred dollars trade-in value she still had, but he did attend the event, the high point of which was the arrival of a man in a Dodge whose alternator had conked out on the way, necessitating his being towed to the scene, to the cheers of hundreds, the hero of the day.

"A car can be like an exasperating wife," Stubblefield said, segueing into his favorite theme. "This one reminds me of my third. All she did was eat. I don't know which is worse, that or drinking. I kept after her to cut down, which of course put me in the position of nag, reversing what is the God-ordained pattern. 'You're getting fat as the Sunday paper,' I said. 'You're going to need two chairs to sit on pretty soon, like that woman we saw in the restaurant that time. You —' "

"Hold it."

A light had dawned.

"What do you mean?"

"Back up a bit. You say you told her she was getting fat as the Sunday paper."

"It's a gift people say I have for picturesque similes. I told her over and over. She'd put on four or five more pounds and I'd say, 'Well, we're expanding the rotogravure section I see,' or 'They've added a magazine supplement.' It would drive her crazy, but that was the purpose. To needle her into some realization of what she —"

"Then that's it! What's happening to your *Kalamazoo Gazette*. Three weeks running now it's been torn to shreds on your front porch. She's the ghost who's doing it. It's the only possible explanation."

"I'm a sonofabitch if you may not be — she used to do that with *our* paper, when she got mad at me. The way she'd break up the dishes. But hold it. She's still alive. That shoots your theory."

That gave me pause, but not for long. "Not necessarily," I said after a moment's thought. "Why couldn't a house be haunted by a living person as well as dead? There'd be a more animate motivation — harassing an ex-husband in poltergeist form."

Stubblefield stopped at the roadside, putting the car in neutral but not taking the risk of shutting off the engine.

"It's certainly Thelma's hallmark. She threw absolute

fits in the lawyer's office over the terms of the settlement, especially the alimony."

"How much do you pay her, if the question isn't too indelicate?"

"Nothing now. I just got sick of it last year and stopped. She's living with some guy, as I know for a fact, so let him support her."

I spread my hands. "Well, then, there you are. It's her revenge."

He shook his head dubiously. "I don't know. I mean there aren't *that* many things in heaven and earth, Horatio. Are there?"

"There's only one way to find out. Psychic phenomena take peculiar turns. Societies for researching them, particularly the British, find most of them are either hoaxes or have rational explanations, but there's a stubborn handful that don't. This one would have a peculiar twist all its own, granted. I'll tell you what we'll do. We'll resume sending those checks and see what happens. If the manifestations *stop*, we will have validated them as extrasensory occurrences, while getting a succubus off your back."

"I like these 'we's' when it's me who has to do the coughing up."

"It's a small price to pay for what we can then give the world. A house haunted by the spirit of someone still alive. A first if there ever was one, and our names forever linked with it. Let the Society for Psychical Research put *that* in its pipe and smoke it."

Stubblefield (who might soon have had the law on him in any case) ponied up the alimony he had been withholding, and lo and behold, the visitations stopped. In a sense, to our regret, as we all in our heart of hearts hanker after evidences of a supernatural. We all like to see the apple cart of rigid rationalism overturned, all like to see signs of "something beyond" the confines of this mortal coil.

The problem of cooling the hots for Bubbles Breedlove was more stubborn, what with Daddy Hank adding his patrol to Maggie's — for he didn't go back to Potlatch and he didn't go back to Potlatch. I had waking nightmares of rolling out of a horizontal embrace to find *him* standing over us, thumb in belt, drawling in his best John Wayne, "Well, I reckon I was wrong in. Putting it past yuh, mister. We still kinda adhere to thuh. Double standard in these parts in thuh. Sense that the young lady is a chosen vessel whose purity is a. Gift to give, not some treasure to be stolen. So I'll thank yuh to kinda climb back into your britches so's we can all take a. Stroll on down to thuh. Parson if yuh get my drift."

The problem of banking my fires for Bubbles was abruptly suspended when my mother suddenly underwent emergency surgery for a ruptured appendix, and I hurried home to be at her side. There were no complications, except those posed by the coincidental return of my father, whom she had also in her apprehension telephoned. So there he was, dressed to the nines, and beginning to *look* like a dog after nearly two years of voice-overs for Kennel King. He supplied a kind of Joycean interior monologue for a dapper poodle named Alphonse, who was snobbishly disdainful of the leading brands except Kennel King, mouthing scorn for all dry and canned substitutes, instantly detectable as such and dismissed with the most withering mots, perking up only when the real thing was put under his nose. My father's golden diction had become famous, and he quite rich in what can apparently be a fabulously lucrative occupation. He was also increasingly the man about town — nearly as debonair as Alphonse himself.

"You're going to be all right, my dear," he assured my mother as he leaned negligently against the wall of her hospital room, looking quite nifty in one of the Mark Twain white suits of which certain fashion leaders had effected a revival that year. The Curator, standing at the foot of the bed in his gray worsted and two-tone shoes, looked a proper cornball by comparison. It was then Mother asked the question the answer to which we were all dying to hear.

"You say your New Rochelle house has ten rooms. Are you . . ." She lowered her eyes to the bedsheets. "Are you all alone in it, or — or what?"

"Oh, one has guests. A perpetual round of weekenders."

As long as Dad had a woman on the scene, the question of a return match was more or less academic, since he would be that much less a candidate for reacquisition by Dearest. Even if his faith were restored in the disputation, he might still not want to give up, say, the bit of fluff. That would make him unopen to repossession, while the Curator's restoration to infidelity would have made him thoroughly incompatible as a helpmeet. Now the subtly extracted realization that the bit of fluff had gone, with no visible successor even on the horizon, changed all that. Dearest wanted me to reopen the question of a return bout with all haste. Now was the time, with both men here.

I put it to my father over lunch at a local restaurant, waiting for the right opening while he sipped a Scotch-and-soda and regaled me with stories of multitudinous retakes of Kennel King commercials. Evidently voice-overs could be gruelling, a fact little known to the public at large. At last I simply blurted out my proposition. He laughed and said, "Why not? It might be amusing." And the thing was done.

Except not for nine months, which was the length of time before a gap in his shooting schedules permitted. For he did voice-overs for more than Kennel King. There was Marveloaf, which built bodies fifteen ways, three more than Wonder Bread; Lotus Soap; and Slumber Eez, a mattress coming in twenty firmnesses. Too, there was the Curator's own busy schedule, which in addition to his practice included barnstorming appearances at evangelical rallies everywhere in a Midwest afire with religious revival. So the two had to, as theatre and film folk say of stars sought for the same production, "match availabilities." But at last the following summer the great rematch came off, and there were again people from miles around pouring into Central High's auditorium, to hear antagonists each of whom had in the interval achieved a certain renown in his own right, one flashy, the other of the meat-and-potatoes variety.

There would be little point in a detailed account, since it was a replay of the first debate with the principals simply switching roles, though enacting them with increased fervor. It seemed at times that each was mouthing the other's stuff, as remembered; at others, there were some arresting variations, offered as personal insights when not the reflections of cited authorities. Pop hammered away at the unreliability of Scripture as determinedly as the Curator had the first time, such as discrepancies in the Gospels over which even Martin Luther had thrown up his hands; the sheer idiocy of believing Noah could have herded into an ark that size two each of 38,000 separate species estimated to have been in existence at that time, and so on. The Curator, no tub-thumping fool, had learned to go with modern theologians like Barth and Tillich, for whom such things mattered little — and it wasn't God's fault if the Incarnation he had wrought had been garbled in the telling by fallible mortals for whose benefit it had been ordained. Of course the air was thick with quotations as the big guns were hauled into position. Pop rolled out a roster of names far weightier and more numerous than the Curator had in round one. Montaigne, Schopenhauer, suave Santayana, the blunter André Breton ("Everything that is doddering, squint-eyed, infamous, sullying, and grotesque is contained for me in the single word: God"). There was good old Mencken, fully as gamy. "Worship, as carried on by Christians, seems to me debasing rather than ennobling. It involves groveling before a Being, who, if He really exists, deserves to be denounced instead of respected." One of Pop's own more telling thrusts went like this. "The idea of a Supreme Being who creates a world in which one creature is designed to eat another in order to subsist, and then passes a law saying 'Thou shalt not kill,' is so monstrously, immeasurably, bottomlessly absurd that I am at a loss to understand how mankind has entertained or given it house room all this long." A prolonged burst of applause for this one indicated how many village atheists there really are around.

The Curator's supporters responded in kind when he countered as effectively with Pascal, C. S. Lewis, Chesterton, Graham Greene, Mauriac, Eliot, and Malcolm Muggeridge, who articulated for him what was perhaps his most telling point, the eternal solidity of Belief itself. "The Church is the miracle, not Christ." So that even if Christ had never existed, the Christianity meaning all that much to millions upon millions, from the martyrs burned at the stake to the John Does in Squeedunk, was itself a marvel not to be dismissed by skeptics and scoffers chattering away about the existence or nonexistence of a "God." He deftly enforced this with Lewis's summation of the Christ who did live. He was either the son of God or the biggest fraud who ever walked the earth. It is pointless to seek refuge in some other alternative, for he has left us none.

There was no format this time, and no judges. The two just stood on the platform and boxed, like two men arguing at a party whom all the other guests gather round to listen to, mixing it up more heatedly by the minute as the evening wore on, and questions from the audience progressively fired them both. They wound up in shirt-sleeves, like Darrow and Bryan in Tennessee, mopping their brows as they shook hands at last.

There was coffee for a few dozen friends at the Curator's house, with Mother of course dying to know whether history had repeated itself with a double knockout. Pop was seen, cup and saucer in hand, looking at the floor and nodding as he listened to some afterthought the Curator was emphasizing.

"Yes, true, there's a lot in what you say," he agreed finally.

"And you made some telling points yourself, Matt. I can't deny that. One really does have to keep reexamining his position."

"I certainly have mine, Humphrey."

"And I mine."

That was it in a nutshell. History had repeated itself — up to a point. Each had brought the other halfway back to his original position, by violently winnowing out the pros and cons of respective convictions. The Curator had been reminded of truths he had forgotten in a certain overeagerness to be converted and thus find an anchor hitherto missing in his life. Pop was convinced afresh of the practical human value of the Church he had himself once served. The upshot was that they both ultimately embraced and came to espouse what might be called Christian atheism. Or turn it around and call them atheistic Christians, adherents of a faith and a religious discipline all the more necessary to a species sprung mysteriously into being in a universe devoid of any provable governance, or any evidence of meaning or purpose properly so called. Let, then, the Church serve in a Void: it was all the more essential for that. Voltaire was right. If there were no God, it would be necessary to invent one. And invent Him mankind jolly well had, to see him through this vale of tears.

So then. We shall no longer like college sophomores in a dormitory bull session labor the importance of illusions to human endurance, shall we? We shall simply take it for granted, and howl and simper and snivel and roar no more. There is a point beyond which the poor dumb beast simply cannot be pushed, without some sustaining myth. Belief without an intellectual foundation is better than none at all. Aren't you "saved" if you think you are, considering that, gone, you'll never know the difference anyway? Think of the millions now dreamless dust, whose passage from life to death myth has eased, like mountain travellers traversing a bridge of snow and ice safely spanning an abyss of whose existence they were blessedly unaware.

None of this meant much to poor Dearest, who could neither follow the subtleties of compromise nor see any reason to shed one newborn existentialist for another equally unsuitable, on that ground, as a helpmeet for her. She might as well schlep along with Humphrey Mallard, both retaining their connection with the church for whatever personal motivation, while Pop went back east, where he continued to rake in pots as a voice-over, contributing handsomely and steadily to a denomination of Christian atheists which he helped found.

13

ALL through my college years, at Northwestern, I kept in fluctuating touch with Bubbles Breedlove, now by mail, now with another panting trip to Kalamazoo, where hot youth found its passions again balked by a *cordon sanitaire* of chaperones, not the least of whom was the hawkeyed aunt with whom Bubbles continued to lodge throughout her own college days there. Probably even more restrictive than anything was the moral force of my promise to Maggie the night of the foiled seduction, that I would not deflower her stepdaughter-elect unless my heart was in it: to wit, object matrimony.

You can imagine the sheepish embarrassment I felt at being a celibate onlooker at the saturnalia I had supposedly set in motion, a chagrin that reached humiliation level every time I ran into Spuds Wentworth. His tales of sexual revelry grew ever more flamboyant. One concerned an extravaganza with a girl known as Twinkie, his then main squeeze, a feat of virtuosity in which the simultaneous gratification of all the senses was sought, and achieved. Perfectly synchronized orgasms were themselves timed with the climax of Tchaikowsky's 1812 Overture, set going on a hi-fi as they climbed between the sheets, while chocolate cherry cordials exploded in their mouths, strobe lights wildly vivisected the walls, and the odors of gardenias and carnations were wafted across the bed by an electric fan. The tactile sense was of course accounted for by the embrace itself, making the amalgamation complete.

"That'd be a hard act to top," I said to Bubbles, in relating it over the long-distance phone.

"J'agree. Unless you did it on a trampoline."

The spring vacation of my last year was approaching, and I spoke of possibly renting a car for a spin out Kalamazoo way.

"J'approve," she responded in the pidgin French she had invented for herself as a social enhancement. It was beginning to get on my nerves, but then hardcore chastity was fraying them anyway, together with this lousy sense of inverted shame, and our friends seemed to think it charming. Perhaps it was, at any rate in small doses, and my irritability was indeed a symptom of repression, one, to complicate matters further, relating to a young woman over whom I had been blowing hot and cold from the beginning. We were not really compatible. I decided to break it off. That's what I would go to Kalamazoo for. Doing so by letter seemed a little cowardly.

Dinner at a favorite French restaurant there found me drawing heavily on a second bottle of Chablis in the attempt both to loosen and to steel myself for the ordeal. There would be the gasp of surprise, the hurt look. Possibly tears. But better these, and a few months of heartbreak, than years of married abrasion. I finished off the last of a last glass of wine. I cleared my throat, scratching an ankle through a sock. Bubbles had been silent for some time, thoughtfully turning her wineglass by its stem. At last she spoke.

"Tony, I think maybe we should call it quits."

"*What?*" I gaped at her in stunned amazement.

"Split up."

"Well! This certainly comes out of left field. A bolt from the blue if I ever heard one. Give a guy the gate just like that?" I snapped my fingers to indicate puzzling peremptoriness. "What brings this on all of a sudden?"

"It's not really all of a sudden. I've been thinking about it for some time. Often when you've been just like tonight. Silent spells. The faraway look. Then the way you talk when *I'm* that way. 'When are you going to get back from Pittsburgh?' Or the one that gravels me even more. 'I see you're still out to lunch.' Those kind of jazzy expressions that are supposed to be like mod, but really get on the nerves. Très corny."

"I'm sorry. I'll retire them from my repertory. It's good we're bringing all this out in the open. Long overdue. Clears the air." Sick with an old desire, I wanted her then and there, let the army of unalterable law — Maggie, Breedlove-cum-Wayne, the harpy of an aunt, the frog proprietor's wife taking all this in from the bar — let them all line up and watch while I gobbled her like a ripe peach, working methodically, steadily downward, then upward, then downward again to the spiced loins, slavering, lupine. "We have a lot in common," I observed.

"I've never heard them anywhere else, those expressions about Pittsburgh and out to lunch."

"I got them from Spuds Wentworth."

"The one who synchronizes all the senses?"

"The same."

"Look, can we have a brandy or something, to get through this?"

"J'expect. Waiter. Look, Bubbles, my dear." I leaned toward her, an elbow slipping off the edge of the table as I tried to settle my arms along it. She giggled, perhaps a good sign. I didn't really need that brandy, but I ordered two anyway. "Look," I resumed when the waiter had gone, "do you know what I think? I think we're getting on each other's nerves because we stir each other up and then — poof. Lent. Prohibition. It's only half a semester to graduation for both of us. I'm sure I can get enough coming in — my father's certain I can break into voice-overs, which are quite lucrative — for us to get married."

"Oh, let's not spoil a good dinner with a reconciliation scene. We've hardly split up. We'll get to be like two old people who can communicate, and nothing's boringer than that." Here she giggled and hiccuped both, and then began to laugh at great length, with a helpless silliness for which we no doubt had the wine to thank. The spectacle she made was of a kind often seen in a movie, when the heroine laughs at what she's saying, then more heartily still at the fact that she's laughing. She shook her lowered head, as though deploring herself and the turn she was giving the conversation.

"You're a ripe mango, a meadowful of clover," I said thickly.

Whatever she replied was strangled in mirth. She put a hand to her brow, now shaking her head as though begging me to desist.

"I'm not going to give you up without a fight, Bubbles."

That did it. She took herself off to the ladies' room in helpless hysterics, as at a line with which a fatheaded

212

home-town character, the square next door with a steady job at the bank, had with a stroke demolished the Lubitsch touch she had at least for the moment imparted to the scene. Frozen-faced, chin in hand, I watched the door reading "Mesdames" flap shut behind her. "Monsieur," said the waiter, bowing as he set the brandies down. The proprietess ended her vigil at the bar when I turned with an intimidating stare.

Naturalists tell us that a mole can turn around in a tunnel dug only to accommodate its width. Or maybe it's a woodchuck, or hedgehog, or all three. No matter. The point is the same — a reversal theoretically impossible. It would be like a man executing a complete about-face inside his own suit of clothes, and that on all fours. Physically out of the question, but apt enough as a metaphor for our behavior in matters of the heart. Here there is an instinctive dislike of being issued one's walking papers. One would infinitely rather do the issuing onself.

The backlash plunged me into a state of glum distraction settling like a fog over Kalamazoo, of which Maggie was quick to take acute note, ever watchful as she remained of how things fared with her young charges. Driving aimlessly around town in my rented Pinto a couple of days after being given the gate, I heard an insistent honking from a car drawn abreast of me on my left, and there was Maggie waving me over to the curb. After I had drawn obediently to a stop, she pulled in behind me, came over, and sprang in beside me.

"I hardly recognized that long face," she said, clapping the door shut. "Especially under that headpiece. Did you lose an election bet or something?"

Outsize pie caps were a fad of the hour, and this one was moreover cut into divergent "slices," each of a different fabric and pattern, checks, stripes, herringbones and the like sewn together in striking juxtaposition. I removed and chucked it over my shoulder into the back seat, with a mumbled explanation that the garment was not to be taken more seriously by neutral observers than it was by the wearer himself, and the reminder that she of all people should know that we had entered an era of iconoclastically assertive garb, at once nonchalant and tendentious.

"Tendentious," Maggie mused. "You once told me what that meant, back in schooldays. God knows how many chief products were neglected to learn it. Now I've forgotten. I shouldn't, since it keeps cropping up in book reviews. I get it mixed up with 'tenebrous.' That means dark and gloomy — the way you look now, out from under the pie cap. Or not really dark, no. More like the knight palely loitering, in 'La Belle Dame Sans Merci.' Remember when we read that in class? But what does tendentious mean again?"

"To hell with it. We're both adults now."

"Speak for yourself. I'm a crazy mixed-up kid, who teases others till she gets her way. What does it mean?"

"Written or said to promote some cause; not impartial; biased," I said, visualizing the dictionary semicolons as I looked sullenly out my window. I disliked this encounter, easily enough divined as having some kind of tendentious side of its own. That didn't take long to emerge.

"Tony, I want you to do me a favor."

"What?"

Maggie was wearing a light spring coat (of large checks hardly less resonant than my pie-cap slices if it came to that), an end of which seemed to have got caught in the door when she slammed it. She opened it long enough to free the coat, and herself for a more direct communication, which consisted in drawing her knees up and curling around on the seat to face me — who remained resolutely in profile.

"It's about Bubbles. She's doing fairly well in the rest of her studies, but her English seems a bit rocky. A course in the seventeenth century. Dr. Chevrolet is a tough old bastard. I had him myself a hundred years ago. The thing in a nutshell is, she could do with some tutoring to help pull her through, and who'd be better for that than you? Just the ticket. We'd both hate to see her wind up with an Incomplete, and summer makeup work hanging over her before she got that old sheepskin, wouldn't we? What do you say?"

What was this, some kind of game? Had Maggie's ambivalence about the romance, all along nearly as great as my own, suddenly turned to partisanship now that the rejected suitor's true feelings had been forced to the surface from their murky bottom? Maybe her emotion for me had strengthened enough for her to want to see me incorporated into this already very skewed family, especially since time had shown our Dickensian "secret" could be securely kept. Strengthened sufficiently for her to use any crafty device as a matchmaker — or match-patcher — for throwing Bubbles and me together again. Or maybe there were no ulterior motives at all — she just wanted to see the girl successfully graduated from her own alma mater.

In any case, the whole thing struck me as academic from more points of view than one.

"I'm only staying till Saturday. This is Tuesday."

"You can get a lot done in three days."

"I'm not all that up on seventeenth-century England. Except for my term paper on Sir Thomas Browne."

"Coach her on that! She hasn't picked the subject for her own paper. We'll suggest that to her, and let her use your own as a source of, well, kind of source material. No more, of course."

"I don't have it with me, obviously."

"Oh. . . . Tell you what. Think about it, and meanwhile plan to stay till Sunday. Hank and I are giving a cocktail party Saturday and we'd like you to come. Just on your, you know, own. One of those big bashes you wouldn't be caught dead at. I know you hate huddled masses, however upper-bourgeois. It's at five o'clock. Won't take no for an answer. See you." And out she sprang and bounded back to her own car.

The party was as billed, one of those jams to which wild horses can't drag me. The din of voices, audible from the street where I parked my car after the drive from my motel, beat like a storm surf when I walked through the open door. Why no one ever sits down at a cocktail party remains one of the social mysteries. Not a stick of furniture was occupied by any of the perhaps forty people there. The great sofa on which I had come within a hair of possessing Bubbles was empty. I longed to stretch out full-length on it and smoke half a pack of cigarettes and nurse a quart or two of beer in blissful solitude. Instead, I was snatched by Maggie and towed across the room to meet Dr. Chevrolet. "Butter the old dragon up," she whispered to me. How that would get Bubbles a passing grade and a diploma I couldn't imagine.

I found Chevrolet hardly a dragon. More one of those academic capons whom a lifetime of unchallenged pontificating in the classroom has left with the conviction that they are also arresting outside it. The term "interesting bore" springs helpfully to mind. He must have been well into his sixties, fleshy and ruddy, with a hooked nose on which you wanted to plant a pince-nez to complete a general sense of stereotype. In fact, years later you might remember him as wearing them, possibly with a black band. Here as with Stubblefield I found myself the victim of prepared material. I expected to have my ear chewed off.

"Maggie says you're terribly interested in the seventeenth century," he said. Women know no shame in politicking for their own. Mumbling something inane about finding lots of merit in the period, I lit a cigarette from the stub of another, and got set to listen.

"I remember once discussing it with Thornton Wilder over lunch at the Algonquin," Chevrolet said. "Tetty and I stop there when we're in New York, and we do coincide with Thornton now and again. At the time in question, Billy Wilder and Alec Wilder were also registered there, so that was the day a bellman paging Mr. Wilder hit the jackpot. Mmmbahaha. Thornton has read omnivorously in practically any period you can mention, so he's familiar with the lesser figures as well as the major. At one point he said something quite trenchant. He said — behind his hand, for some reason, as though playwrights aplenty might be listening in the vicinity, as well they should — are you a writer by any chance?"

"No-o."

"Thornton said, 'We need a new trash, let alone a new literature.' He went on to develop the point that in great eras, like the Elizabethan, the trash was good too. One of those — epiphanies, you know."

I shifted my position slightly from time to time, describing in all about a forty-five-degree arc, so as to take in as much of the room as furtively as possible in my lookout for Bubbles. At length, and causing Chevrolet to pivot likewise in consequence, I caught sight of her. Half sitting and half leaning against the bulkily upholstered arm of "our" sofa, she was chattering blithely with two or three young men roughly our own age. Having achieved my goal of getting her squarely in my field of vision, I could give fuller attention to Chevrolet.

I had by this time discerned another similarity between his conversational method and that of Stubblefield. They both had ways of telegraphing that a corker was imminent. Chevrolet set you up with an arch expression that consisted in working his pursed mouth, as though sucking on the mot a moment before discharging it, like a lozenge to be savored. There was a pregnant pause in which he also cleared his throat in a preparatory fashion, with a rattling noise like that of a clock before it strikes. Then the sockeroo.

"Thornton's avocation, as you may well know, his obsession, is *Finnegans Wake*. 'Some people play golf. I read *Finnegans Wake*,' he was to tell a reporter that very afternoon. He sits friends down and reads aloud to them, with commentary. Captive audiences."

"So I've heard."

" 'I have my Joyce with me, it's upstairs in my room,' he said, 'but I'm sorry I must run and haven't time to read to you.' So Tetty and I missed that" — he fixed me with a twinkling eye, along with all the mouth twitching and throat clearing — "by the skin of our teeth."

"Mmmbahaha. That's rich. I must tell Maggie that, and

Miss Breedlove. By the skin of our oh, that's rich." How's this for a grease job? And what conceivable good will it do?

A white-jacketed waiter came by with a tray on which were cups of punch, from which I plucked my first and Chevrolet his second, setting his empty cup down on it after a last swig. Hank Breedlove joined the group of which Bubbles remained the laughing center. I fancied he looked my way, which made me smartly return my attention to Chevrolet.

"One goes to the Algonquin so conscious of the ghosts as well as the guests that one instinctively keeps one's ear cocked for some of the witty remarks of which one has heard so much," he went on. "I, too, strain to overhear conversations at adjacent tables, but in all the years I've stopped at that fabled hostelry, I've only heard one thing I can honestly say I wish I'd said."

"What was that?" I dutifully put in as straight man.

"A man at the next table said to his woman companion, 'My last book sold a hundred and eighty-seven thousand copies.'" Sparkle, twitch, ahem. "I wish I'd said that."

"Mmmbah. Maggie tells me you publish regularly, and not because you'll perish otherwise. Things quite respected in academic circles."

He shrugged, with a gesture sufficing as the pantomimic version of "Pshaw," by no means to be taken seriously. "I've written a few monographs on the authors I teach. I may join the twentieth century and turn out a little something on Thornton. I say, fellow, you're a chain smoker. Bad habit to get into."

"Don't I know it."

"I no less. Used to be a three-pack-a-day man. That was when I was young, like you. Know what cured me?

No conscious effort at all, cold turkey or otherwise. On my first sabbatical I, ah, you might say, ahem, defected to the West. Banged about Arizona, New Mexico, Wyoming, and I found the oddest thing. Deep drafts of that absolutely inebriating air, under those dazzling blue and gold skies, were all the stimulation I needed. Still spend our summer vacations there, Tetty and I. So my advice is" — here he positively beamed with anticipation, while flashing all the usual signals — "if you want to kick cigarettes, come to Marlboro Country."

Three zingers in practically as many minutes. You want a new trash, you got it. Would have done credit to a Bob Hope Special.

It was at that moment I was dealt a sudden blow: that of learning how Bubbles had got her nickname. My first curiosity had vanished with the assumption that her natural effervescence of spirit had earned it. Later, I had given it no thought, being accustomed to it. Now an especially loud burst of laughter from her jolly circle drew my attention. She was *blowing* bubbles. And this on her own, without benefit of pipe or one of those novelty-shop hoops that come with a jar of suds. The creature could do it on her own, on demand, and limitlessly, as was obvious from the stream of tiny opalescences floating from her lips and over the heads of her onlookers, some of whom reached out to catch them. The crowd clustered about her grew. Some made a try at the trick, unsuccessfully, wiping their chins in defeat. The bubbles were manufactured by some process of which she alone knew the secret, being expelled through pursed lips from a tongue apparently folded double lengthwise.

I was appalled. Then after my first shock, I felt a profound sense of relief. Relief at knowing the social worst about a girl the loss of whom there was now no reason to regret. It was clearly best to have broken off an affair that might otherwise have led to a marriage racked with incompatibilities possibly worse than divergent opinions about blowing bubbles as a means of becoming the life of the party. What such a girl needed was a husband who clowned around with lampshades on his head. I had had my doubts before about the wisdom of this union. A last straw had made them stark certainties. I was finally disenthralled, thank God, and, as such, free. Free! I was off the hook. I could go over and join the rowdy group with no regrets, laughing with the rest.

I saw that Dr. Chevrolet had finished off his punch and set his cup down on a nearby table, preparatory to moving toward the front door.

"Leaving already?" I asked.

"No, no, only going to the bathroom. My club is just across the street."

Nevertheless, I was sorry to learn in early June that Bubbles — Kim — had not graduated. Chevrolet had given her an Incomplete. Summer makeup work would be necessary if she wanted to get her diploma. Maggie phoned long distance and asked whether now I would come out and tutor the poor girl through. She quite understood there hadn't been enough time on my spring-vacation visit, but would I be a pal and take a few weeks off?

"Of course we'll pay you."

"Oh, for God's sake, Maggie. Yes, I guess I can do it."

"And bring your paper on Thomas Browne. I suggested

him as a subject for her own essay and Chevrolet went for it, but she just never got it finished. Bogged down in it. You're a brick."

Was I? You'll have to judge for yourself, having already surmised that getting away from "home" was again a welcome prospect.

Maggie and Breedlove, his potato domains sold at a no doubt princely profit, had married, and were living in the old house pending what seemed early removal into that of the aunt, failing rapidly in a nearby nursing home. Her will had arranged for its passage to Breedlove, then ultimately to Kim, as I now called my ex-girlfriend, stoutly refusing to give do-it-yourself bubbles house room as valid social enhancement, let alone basis for a nickname. Standards must be hewed to, criteria sustained, though one often felt oneself growing round-shouldered as an overburdened telamon upholding the crumbling entablature of Taste. Maggie was interested to learn that a telamon is the male counterpart of a caryatid, as are you, but Hank Breedlove couldn't have cared less. He probably thinks a caryatid is some kind of insect whose metallic chirring signals the end of summer, with thoughts of youth reverting to college, lights along the Quad, and limburger set by wits on dormitory radiators once again turned on. All that was over for me now, of course, except as fading artifacts in the archives of nostalgia.

I was to occupy my old bedroom alone, Stubblefield being in dry dock for some minor surgery like the removal of a cyst, but guaranteeing me, as bedside visitor, fresh installments of his sexual saga, now rivalling even Holy Writ for discrepancies. The aunt's house having an interim rental tenant, Kim was again staying in her old room, again a part-time nanny to Ahab. He was visiting a chum overnight when I arrived, and with the Breedloves heading for a movie, Kim and I had the house to ourselves for the first evening of the lessons.

"She has all her papers and books and things in her room, so you might as well start up there," Maggie said, looking at the floor as she got into her coat.

As I passed her in the hall, lugging my briefcase, I sensed a familiar scene in the making. She stood by the bottom step, one hand on a newel post, watching my ascent. The tableau struck a familiar chord in my memory. I turned halfway up the first flight of stairs and looked down.

"Do you want me to keep the door open, Mrs. Clicko?"

"Suit yourself. We don't stand on ceremony here. Just our sacred honor."

"Pretty scary."

"What the heyell is this?" Hank Breedlove said, donning his five-gallon hat. "Who is Mrs. Clicko?"

"Just a friend, to whom we owe so much," Maggie said. "We'll probably stop for a hamburger and a beer after the show, Tony, so we won't be home much before ten-thirty or eleven. That should get you a lot done."

"I'm sure," I said. "Have fun."

The pupil was propped up in bed taking notes from a book open in her lap. She was dressed in blue jeans and a red silk blouse. A half-eaten apple stood on a table beside her. She swallowed what she had just gnawed off it, and grinned as I entered through the open door.

"Hello, stranger."

"Hello, beautiful. You haven't changed a bit in all these weeks." I set my briefcase on a cluttered desk and took the more comfortable of two chairs. "How shall we go about this? Shall we lie down and talk the whole thing over like two civilized people? Or shall I lecture?"

"Lecture, but in a nice way, and walk the floor while you do it, playing catch with a piece of chalk. That's what Chevy does. Give the whole thing a more authentic flavor."

I laughed at the thought of anyone pacing in a room the size of a prison cell, and as jammed with furniture as this one. The double bed took up a third of it. I sat down and started by reading aloud my own paper on Sir Thomas Browne, fished from the briefcase. Kim had some white wine, which we took turns swigging straight from the bottle, like hoboes, passing it back and forth between us. I read my essay with feeling, even expression, as befit respect for the material, supplementing it with interpolated comments, additions, explanations, and the like. Of all the pregnant pauses which I could successfully engineer, none was so profound as the hush that fell when I had finished. Kim had sagged steadily downward on the two pillows against which I had found her erectly propped on arrival; the empty wine bottle lay on the bed, the neck loosely held in one hand. The apple had grown yellow with neglect. Turning her head toward the window, she said, "You're one smart sonofabitch."

"The thing about Browne," I said, quickly rising and coming over to heal any breach in the spell I had woven such as might have been dealt by her remark, "what makes him appeal to the modern mind, over all those centuries, is his combination of faith and skepticism. Doubt is almost a *leaven in his belief*. Have you read *Religio Medici*?"

"I certainly hope so."

"You find that . . . ambivalence beautifully expressed

in it. I have it in my briefcase there. You should touch on it even more than I have in my term paper. It's his most important work, as it was his most popular, a burning, intimate examination of his deepest beliefs. It contains my own personal choice for the title of Most Beautiful Sentence in the English Language. I think that every time I say it to myself." Feeling I had become a mite too professorial, standing there lecturing, I sat down on the bed. "It goes: 'Though my grave be England, my dying place was Paradise, and Eve miscarried of me before she had conceived of Cain.'"

"Poor Tony," she said, letting go her half grip on the bottle to take my hand.

"Doesn't that send the chills up your spine? My God, what an epic line. The very galaxies part to make way for it. It's the most consummate expression of determinism — you might say this in your paper, we'll find the passage in *Religio* in a minute — of determinism imaginable. More telling, in its way, than a similar line from the Rubáiyát: 'The first morning of Creation wrote what the last dawn of reckoning shall read.' But determinism — that's different from fatalism," I said, finger aloft in the air. "It is equidistant from both — now the mice are really playing, with the cat away."

"What do you mean?"

"Your mother would soon remind me that 'equidistant from both' is redundant. But hell, she's safe in a movie. Where was I? Movies. Oh, yes. Determinism is equidistant from both Doris Day sitting at the piano singing 'Que sera, sera,' in that Hitchcock picture —"

"*The Man Who Knew Too Much.*"

"Yes. From that, and from your Dutch Reformed Calvinist dragging across the darkling polder that sack of rocks, predestination. I'm a determinist." And I related the story of how my mother and I had nearly lost our lives because my father's discovery of a translation error in the King James Bible made him euphorically oblivious of the storm into which he let us venture.

"Poor baby." She reached out to give her other hand in offering. "I'll bet you're glad you're here."

"That I am, that I am."

"Those scholars."

Feeling this had gone quite far enough, I lay down on the bed, rolling gently over onto my back with a sigh sufficing to express for both of us a fatigue at the mental strain we had been undergoing. There is a tide in the affairs of men which, taken at the flood, sometimes saves nine. I suddenly saw Kim Breedlove in a new perspective, namely as one who might well combine the elements of wife and bit of fluff all rolled into one, thus sparing a man the rumored wear and tear of a bit on the side. Not the most edifying of concepts, but there it irresistibly was, like this sweet-smelling girl herself. She smelled like a small room in which persimmons have been recently eaten, a pleasantly pungent aroma mingled with an addling collaboration of cologne. I wondered if my thought about a woman combining both sacred and profane love, so that a husband could cheat on the one *her* with the other *her*, had ever been previously entertained in all the immemorial annals of shenanigans. Perhaps not. But here she irresistibly was, as was the passion unmistakably kindling us. We had denied ourselves, and each other, often and long enough. Honor was to be satisfied in my case by releasing from the long chagrin of chastity one who had struck the shackles from others; in Kim's, by the commitment my ravishing her would carry with it. Had I not solemnly promised her mother-elect — now mother — that I would do her no wrong? In the heat of passion, as we tore the clothes from each other's body, the wine bottle rolling to the floor, even the homemade bubbles seemed unimportant. Think how long it had taken me to learn of this talent — proof enough of how little store she set by it herself. It might be kept satisfactorily within limits, with no lasting social detriment. A few words discreetly murmured at the right time, to one who had come to realize herself that she needed toning down. . . . Perhaps the simple daily example of a finer-grained spouse would make even those unnecessary. . . .

"Blow us some bubbles, darling," I even whispered in her ear when we had become one flesh at last, to laugh the whole thing out of court, to remove any implication of tarnish on this ecstatic union, admitting no impediments to the marriage of true minds, and laughingly she did, the spindrift wafting across what must now be deemed as good as the bridal bed, or, more fancifully still, our nuptial bark, on which we drifted together, as on gently plashing waves, to, or from, the Enchanted Isles.

14

*T*HE love-bed fancy of my girl as two people, sufficiently divergent in her facets to double as helpmate and plaything, which you probably remember as the rationalization of a trapped swain doing a snow job on himself, has proved surprisingly durable throughout these early years of marriage. As an amateur psycho-sociologist with as much right to coin jargon as the next man, I call it "aspecting." In this case, creatively sorting out elements in my marital union in such a way that it becomes both sacred and profane. You are untrue to a woman with the woman herself — actually an extreme application of G. K. Chesterton's point that a woman is so variable a creature to begin with that any monogamously attached man can regard himself as living in a harem. Thus (a protean figure myself) every morning I kiss a wife goodbye, and each evening hurry home to a bit of fluff. Not even learning that I was to become a father has disrupted the game. I heard the news when I popped in one midday, as was also my wont when my schedule permitted, for a quick dalliance with still a third piece — the "bit on the side" with whom I was cheating on both wife and mistress. Pretending I had the bit on the side in a jam was an extra kick in the adventure. What a mess! What a shambles I had made of my life just for an ankle down the old primrose path!

"Oh, my God, Bubbles," I said, burying my face in my hands. "What'll we do?"

"Run upstairs and put the ears on the kid."

Such was done, as yet again I sank into those great beautiful slippery loins as into Sin itself.

She seemed to divine my game and freely fall in with it, without a word of conscious collaboration, waving goodbye from the breakfast table in curlers and an old wrapper (a housewife with an A.B. and a struggling trade in child photography) and greeting me come nightfall in silk pajamas, freshly bathed and scented (the *saftig* dish who just squeaked through with a C-minus makeup for an English Incomplete, on a term paper probably largely cribbed from her steady).

At least the marriage is more enjoyable than the wedding was. My father having unfrocked himself, and the Breedlove clan being vaguely Episcopalian, a Kalamazoo minister of that faith was engaged to tie the knot.

I was out of the sacristy and halfway to the altar where I was to claim my bride when it struck me all of a heap that I was chewing gum. I could see Maggie sitting in the front pew with Hank Breedlove, thinking to herself, "He's chewing gum. He chews gum during his own wedding ceremony." I had been well on the march when the term "claim my bride" had popped into my mind, already half sinking the occasion in absurdity, and now this. What I had done was inadvertently retain the pellet of Spearmint — two sticks, actually — that I had been nervously worrying about in my teeth throughout preparations for the ceremony, fully intending to dispose of it before heading toward the chancel, but forgetting to do so. In the confusion it had completely slipped my mind. An Episcopal church would naturally be wanting in sandpots or the like in which to drop any such debris, certainly on this leg of the nuptial route — the Last Mile, as it was called by the plainsman who was now within five, maybe six minutes of becoming my father-in-law. Too late to dispose of the quid now.

I tried to swallow it, but it refused to go down. It was like trying to swallow a pill without water. I gulped again — to no avail. The offending cud remained perversely stuck on the back of my tongue, even threatening, with my mouth getting progressively drier, to gag me by lodging against the uvula. Isn't that little thingy hanging down in back there, through sun and storm and changes of empire, called a uvula? Perhaps if I faked a cough I could unobtrusively raise a hand long enough to pop the gum into my fist, as the wellborn are said to do with a fruit pip or an olive pit to be disposed of in polite company. What would I do with it then? I remembered how as children we would paste it to our wrist or behind an ear, for later re-use, and there was that old song I'd heard Stubblefield sing, "Does the Spearmint lose its flavor on the bedpost overnight? If you put it on the left side will you find it on the right?" What must the congregation think of this strained gulping on the groom's part? That he was choking up with emotion — that would be the happiest construction to put on it. In any case, there seemed nothing for it now but to enact the exchange of vows with the gum secreted in a corner of one cheek, or under my tongue.

Then suddenly there was the bride coming down the aisle, providing the solution. With all eyes turned to take in the vision, I slipped the cud into my hand and popped it into a coat pocket. The minister noted the too-abrupt move, and his eyebrows went up in a quizzical expression. He didn't like me. I had peeved him during yesterday's rehearsal by referring to the stylized tread affected by wedding parties, each step broken by a momentary pause of one foot beside the other, as the Episcopalian drag. He would have his revenge. In a few minutes, he would pronounce me that most ridiculous of all things, a husband. I spent some of them wondering what he would think if he knew the pedigree he would seal with his blessing in so doing. You would be hard put to it to record it in any family Bible. An offspring of my own is my father-in-law's stepson and my wife's stepbrother. I am to live in a kind of incestuous relationship with my son's stepsister, as I already have in a sort of warmup sense with my now and future mother-in-law — who at the time of the nuptials is again great with child, who will turn out to be another boy, giving my semilegitimate son and my wife both an additional stepbrother, Tom, who, however, will call my wife and me Uncle and Aunt. The question of where my future children will fit into this is one that boggles the mind, but it should all pretty much satisfy the current taste for sick fiction, or, put in stage terms, what is known as "twisted" theatre. I mean, what more could you ask of a chap in the way of delivering you on a silver platter the raw materials for a classic Greek house mess? I feel a kind of dark stature here, augmented with a secret Mephistophelian satisfaction in knowing that an orthodox clergyman has given the church's blessing to it all.

Waiting for my bride, there, I secretly devised a little counterplay, something on the order, in fact, of a profanation — my farewell gesture as antichrist. In retaliation for being pronounced a husband, that most ludicrous of creatures, and being given then the proverbial permission to kiss the bride, I would get in a spot of the French work that had had her swooning from the first, often coming up for air in a parked car with an appreciative "Whew," followed by some remark such as "Regular anteater." Yes, I would do that part of the ceremony tongue-in-cheek — the bride's cheek. It would survive as "our" joke, how I had prolonged the seal-of-good-housekeeping peck suitable to the house of worship with a little of the old hydraulic stuff, heads rocking in wet, labial bliss, my mouth corkscrewing away at hers, maybe a hand slipping along her flank, until the minister coughed reproachfully, then yet again, and the congregation exchanged glances and then murmurs of disapproval swelling in volume till they rose to their feet as one, shaking their fists and crying, "Outrage! Blasphemy!"

"Do you, Anthony, take this —"

"I do."

"And do you, Kimberly —"

What? What the hell was with this Kimberly? Then the Kim he'd known her as was short for some damn family name they'd stuck her with? He was to be married to somebody named Kimberly, as though she were a mining corporation or a gypsum plant? What was this? Why had he not been told of this before? What a time to spring a lulu like that on a chap.

"I now pronounce you man and wife. You may kiss the bride."

He touched his lips tenderly to hers, for just a moment, before chastely withdrawing.

Thou hast conquered, O Galilean!

Christian atheism seems to me the most tolerable accommodation of faith and reason to each other for our

232

time, providing a discipline of belief and necessary ethical imperatives on the one hand, and intellectual realism on the other. Its maiden congregation, which as I have said my father helped found, is located in a Connecticut suburb, and is served by an everchanging succession of pickup preachers, among them my father, and, in a pinch, me. The comfortable living I now likewise make in voice-overs of course requires my living in New York or within commuting range, and we've settled in a town in Fairfield County that seems as good as any, certainly better than the dispiriting loft in the Wall Street section we rented on first coming east. Whenever my schedule permits, I like to go on little fund-raising sallies for the new faith, sometimes combining them with house-hunting. The departed aunt has left Kim enough to make a switch from rental to ownership a practical possibility. Of course I have my income as a eulogist for peanut butter, storage batteries, and designer jeans, as well as my stock in T-shirts Unlimited, now enlarged with a booming new line, tote bags. Liking contacts with people on the grass-roots level, I am often to be seen shaking a slotted collection can as I pace before supermarket entrances, or stroll up city streets between sandwich boards proclaiming the new faith, or canvassing door-to-door, offering an explanatory spiel to anyone who will listen. It beats playacting as the antichrist, a really ill-fitting persona as much a form of amusement as anything else, though both guises have been firmly founded on unbelief. My new mystique is the more constructive in that I am both cursing the darkness and lighting a candle.

I have never for the life of me seen any reason why we must choose, as the old saw seems to imply. Why not a little of both? I have often done them simultaneously, or tried to, occasionally burning my fingers, thereby subtracting very little from the gloom under imprecation, but even so. Such is life, what? I was once bitten by a watchdog to whose, I must say rather slatternly, mistress I was trying to explain the nature and purpose of Christian atheism. "We're a new young denomination, a thing, we think, of the future, founded only partly as a sardonic mockery of all the thousandfold faiths that have untenably preceded it, and of the human gullibility on which they have relied, but mainly intended as a pluckily human commitment to the rock-bottom, undeluded maximum belief palatable to an intellect worthy of the name —" I was saying when this Doberman, a gumboil lot by any standard, charged onto the front porch where I was expatiating and sank his teeth into my fundament, as though I were a hobo asking for a handout and a bit of whose trouser-seat must wind up in his jaws, in conformity to comic-strip cliché. The woman recovered and held him by the collar with one hand as with the other she secured her bathrobe lapels about a pair of jugs on which I certainly had no designs, and would have had none were this hell itself and things tough all over.

"Yes, go on," the woman said, batting her eyelashes. I continued with my presentation, a kind of basic set piece explaining how the flaunted irony of our cause, a beautifully convoluted nuance really, fell just short of what it would have been if Christ, on top of not being the son of God to begin with, had not even existed. Then what a snook we might have cocked at an empty universe apparently devoid of any celestial supervision as it rolled on toward its inevitable pile-up on the galactic junkheap. As it was, we must make do with the indisputable historicity of Jesus.

I would be his Paul, I thought, as I hobbled off a dollar richer for the cause, an apostolic co-founder suffering, if not shipwreck, hunger, and imprisonment, then at least injury and possible rabies from dogs that had cut their eye-teeth on local mailmen, to say nothing of the impatience of philistine husbands eager to get back to their television sets, or short shrift from women slamming the door in my face to safeguard nubile daughters from probable lunatics. Many kept their doors on chains, leaving me four or five inches through which to discourse on the new persuasion no evolutionary hypothesis could unsettle, one that, being firmly grounded on *Nada*, would last till ants alone inhabited a clinker from which we ourselves had vanished.

I was dilating on these stern but adult truths when, so help me, another dog put as much as he could of his snout through such a gap and began to bark furiously at me. I had the notion that he thought he could smell nihilism on me, as the Stubblefields' Airedale had Weltschmerz and existential dread, but I continued unfazed above the racket that he made. I explained to the man trying to quiet him that our sect was not nihilism, but a doughty, if last-ditch, resistance *to* it.

"That's just it. We strew with flowers —"

"Quiet, Max," the man said, slapping the mutt on the nose.

"We strew with —"

"Down!"

"We strew —"

"I said quiet!"

"We strew with flowers the precipice on which we live our summer hour, spreading if possible a picnic there," I rattled off as fast as I could in the momentarily effected lull in the pup's yapping. "We live as *though* life had meaning, and lo — it does! We live as *though* we are Christian soldiers following in our Captain's command,

235

and lo — we are! Our best writers have told us this life is a flimflam, even some of the Old Testament prophets, but to the extent that we're wise to the scam, it isn't. Hemingway called life a dirty trick, Mark Twain a swindle, Fitzgerald a fraud, Shakespeare a tale told by an idiot, and on and on, but knowing all that, we nonetheless put it by as ungermane."

"As — shut up, Max! As what?"

"Ungermane."

"Well, I don't like to get into ethnic things. Slurs and what not. My people came from Northern Silesia myself and—"

"No, no, not in that sense, the Teutonic. Good heavens, no. There's good and bad in all races. One of my own grandfathers came from Düsseldorf," I said, fabricating an ancestor to keep his interest if not recover his favor. "The point I'm trying to make is that it takes more faith to live life without belief than in the cozy self-delusions of what has traditionally been called faith. That is our doctrineless doctrine, our creedless creed. Give what you can."

"Well . . ." The man dug into his pants pocket and came up with six bits — a quarter and a half-dollar — which he pondered in his palm a moment before dropping the fifty-cent piece into the can I extended through the gap, well above Max's leaping nips. I thanked him and made off, shaking the can like a tambourine as I thought of Chesterton's reference to Salvation Army–type volunteers as "corybantic Christians."

I rattled it to keep my spirits up, even executing a step or two as I approached the next house, where a fat woman answered the door and cheerfully seized the offensive with a sales pitch of her own for some artificial flowers she made as a shut-in with arthritis. "Look at these fingers, that do this." I bought a posy of silk daisies for a dollar, refreshed by the setback rather than otherwise, the dollar being fairly deductible as a business hazard sustained by the First Church of Christian Atheists.

I collected several hundred dollars over the next few years. People seemed unready to open their hearts, much less their purse strings, for a denomination purporting to wring a few last remaining drops from the withering orange of illusion, even when I boasted for it a bone fide saint, Saint Bertrand — deeming it wisest not to reveal that his last name was Russell, the great all-time infidel humanitarian of the twentieth century, claimable as a Christian atheist despite his pains to explain why he wasn't a Christian, and even though both my father and the Curator had cited him in the unbelieving phases of their debates. He went down much better in speeches I delivered for the cause in such places as Harvard and Yale.

At Harvard particularly, some intense interest had been generated among a few who had every confidence we were the vanguard of a movement destined to swell to God knew — oops — to no one knew how many members. Only about thirty people, mostly graduate students of comparative religion, turned out for my lecture, but they gave me not one, but two, standing ovations, sitting down again midway the first in order that they might rise and honor me with a second, a burst of enthusiasm gratifying indeed. There was a cold-cut luncheon in my honor, after which some of us grew deathly sick from, it would appear, roast beef tainted with salmonella, so that I nearly called for a priest, but before any symptoms manifested themselves my hand had been wrung in prolonged farewells, and promises exacted that I would continue to stump for Christian atheism, though in my breast of breasts I doubted that invitations to speak would be many, or audiences large. New Rochelle, the Hamptons, Aspen, the like of that, maybe. But as for Little Rock, Muncie, even Kalamazoo, forget it. Still, who knew? People want Something. The harvest is always white and the laborers few. Go ye therefore . . .

It was on the road that my loyalty and possibly ultimate durability as a husband and family man were tested, and proved. For a lecture to a cultural group in Princeton, I was introduced by a woman who had once clearly been a crate of melons, and not so long ago at that. She was still an obstacle course. I was conscious of her sitting behind me on the platform throughout my lecture, and, turning once, pleased to see that she was among those taking notes, spiral pad propped on a shapely knee. I gave the usual exposition of my religous views, shooting the Bible full of aoles and ridiculing prayer, but one does like to work a gag or two into the solemnities whenever possible, and as I neared my conclusion, I was hit by an idea for a sock finish — one I hoped might even meet Wilder's standards for a new trash. See what you think.

"And so, dearly beloved," I said, gathering up my notes, "if there's one thing I'd like to drive home tonight, it's the woman who introduced me."

And so I did, for the three short blocks involved, staying for a drink and then receiving an invitation to dinner the following day. I was stopping over anyway, for some interviews and talks with students on the New Faith. She called for me at my motel early, around four-thirty, so that we might do a spot of sightseeing in her Mercedes. It was spring, and she had on what must have been a new Easter outfit. It consisted of a dusty pink linen suit and a hat like a shot fowl. It was tilted down one side of her face at an intendedly jaunty angle, but recalling rather something plunging to earth in the autumn weather, this image to be linked with that of men crouched in duck blinds or taking aim from rowboats in the pitiless weft of things: predators themselves predestined prey in the immemorial Necessity; kin together not only with the poor feathered thing plummeting earthward in the gray dawn, but with all sentient life locked forever in communal doom. That kind of hat.

There was roast beef and Yorkshire pudding, but the main dish was Mrs. Thralling herself, or could have been, 'or there was no doubt that a bedded sequel was mine for 'he taking. She was a divorcée, quite wealthy in her own right. She openly disliked living alone, but had declined a succession of suitors, the last of whom she described as a bowlegged pantheist from Milwaukee. Food was prepared and served by her only servant, a creaking old woman named Georgia who licked her thumbs after serving the soup. "I know you don't like it piping hot or too cool either, Mrs. Thralling," she said, "but lukewarm. I hope this is just right. It's as luke as I can get it."

"Your ears didn't deceive you," Mrs. Thralling assured me when the woman had vanished into the kitchen. "That's how she talks. I don't know what to do with, or about, the dear old thing. She's a walking example of what you described in your lecture as the human need for Something. She tunes in regularly to a television preacher who says the end of the world is at hand, and listens expectantly for the last trump. You don't believe in any such thing as the last trump."

"The last trump is the king of spades," I answered. "No more or less."

"Shoveled away, covered over, and that's it." My ravishing hostess sighed. "I know you need money for your church, and I do like to give to as many worthy causes as I can, but I'm afraid . . ."

"Afraid what?"

"I believe in God."

"That's all right," I said. "We take all kinds."

"Are you — you know — very married?"

Here I produced the perennial bastion of monogamy, wallet snapshots.

"That's my wife. We've been married five years now. And this is our three-year-old son, David. He takes after his mother."

"And lucky he is."

The ritual was interrupted by the reappearance of old Georgia, come to collect the soup plates. When she had hobbled out again, trailing laments about her declining health, Mrs. Thralling said, "She's a hypochondriac on a very creative scale, as I guess most of them are. Lately she complains about feelings of nausea in her legs. I'd like to have someone to share such a jewel with," and came out with a laugh, followed by a wistful smile, then another sigh. "I guess I'm too chary about undertaking another voyage in the old matrimonial bark. It foundered so badly the last time. There are those as say she's scuttled for good."

Here Georgia tottered back in with the roast beef, which she set down before me. It appeared I was to do the carving, like the man of the house. It was a role into which I heartily plunged, not without some fleeting fantasies about all that might imply under this roof.

"So what do you think about it?" Mrs. Thralling asked when we were once again alone.

"About what?" I asked, falling to with the carving knife and fork.

"The matrimonial bark."

" 'Reason wills not that I cast love by' still seems to come through loud and clear from old Villon. Our sad, mad, glad, bad brother, as Swinburne called him, though I may have the adjectives out of sequence."

"What about the matrimonial bark?"

"I think it's worse than its bite. Would you pass me your plate, my dear?"

For a complete list of books available from Penguin in the United States, write to Dept. DG, Penguin Books, 299 Murray Hill Parkway, East Rutherford, New Jersey 07073.

For a complete list of books available from Penguin in Canada, write to Penguin Books Canada Limited, 2801 John Street, Markham, Ontario L3R 1B4.